DYING FALL

A DCI Charlie Woodend Mystery

A charred body is discovered in an abandoned cotton mill, and the crime scene presents DCI Woodend and his team with many questions, but very few answers. As Woodend attempts to solve a murder with no clues, he must also battle against a police authority blocking him at every turn. And worse is to follow, because Elizabeth Driver, Inspector Bob Rutter's lover, has almost finished the book which could destroy everything he has ever worked for.

DYING FALL

A Chief Inspector Woodend Mystery

Sally Spencer

Severn House Large Print
London & New York

This first large print edition published 2011
in Great Britain and the USA by
SEVERN HOUSE PUBLISHERS LTD of
9-15 High Street, Sutton, Surrey, SM1 1DF.
First world regular print edition published 2008 by
Severn House Publishers Ltd., London and New York.

British Library Cataloguing in Publication Data

Spencer, Sally.
    A dying fall. -- (A Chief Inspector Woodend mystery)
    1. Woodend, Charlie (Fictitious character)--Fiction.
    2. Police--England--Fiction. 3. Detective and mystery
    stories. 4. Large type books.
    I. Title II. Series
    823.9'2-dc22

    ISBN-13: 978-0-7278-7959-2

Severn House Publishers support The Forest Stewardship Council
[FSC], the leading international forest certification organisation. All
our titles that are printed on Greenpeace-approved FSC-certified paper
carry the FSC logo.

MIX
Paper from
responsible sources
FSC® C018575

Printed and bound in Great Britain by the
MPG Books Group, Bodmin, Cornwall.

Prologue

The moment the weak watery sun had finally set in the darkening sky, the temperature began to plummet, and by midnight a freeze had set in which made the ground crack and groan. It was a bad night to be homeless, and Nature – in her cruel, unrelenting winter mood – had not finished yet.

A wind sprang up – the kind of wind which is not content merely to chill those who stand in its path, but instead must hunt and harry its victims, turning corners with apparent ease and rushing forcefully through almost-invisible gaps in walls.

The old tramp, huddled in a corner in the disused cotton mill, felt this wind cutting into his flesh – working its way slowly and stealthily towards his bone – and shivered.

It was on nights like this that men like him died. It was on mornings *following* nights like this that bodies were discovered curled into stiff frozen balls.

The tramp rummaged through the pockets of his dirty, threadbare overcoat. In the left pocket, his arthritic fingers grasped a box of matches and the cigarette ends he had picked up off the street. From his right, he produced the bottle of methylated spirit he had bought earlier in the day.

He sighed. He had something to drink, and something to smoke. What more could any man want?

He unscrewed the bottle, and was on the point of raising it to his lips, when the sudden – and totally unexpected – thought came to his mind that this would be *his* last night on earth – that he would die before dawn broke, and someone would find his frozen body in the morning, just as he had found so many others in the past.

It was then that he heard the stealthy, shuffling sound, and realized that he was not alone.

'Who is it?' he called out in a hoarse, fearful voice.

There was no answer.

'I've got a knife!' he said. 'And I'll use it if I have to.'

Minutes passed in silence.

It had been nothing but a rat, dragging its dropsied belly along the ground, the tramp persuaded himself.

He raised the meths bottle and took a swig. A shudder ran through his body, but he felt no desire to vomit, as he had the first few times he'd forced himself to swallow the noxious liquid.

He heard the shuffling sound again, and knew that it wasn't – couldn't be! – a rat, after all.

And then he saw the dark figure moving towards him.

'Go away!' he said, in a voice which was half-command, half-plea.

But the dark figure kept on coming – could almost touch him now.

The tramp began to struggle to his feet. But he had left it too late – far too late! – and he was still on his knees when he felt the heavy boot smash into his chest.

He fell back into the corner, his head banging against the wall, his spine jarring as it hit the floor.

The dark figure's arms began to rock rhythmically, there was a swooshing noise – and, suddenly, the tramp was soaked in a cold liquid.

But it was not water he was being doused with, the tramp told himself.

Water didn't *feel* like this.

Water didn't *smell* like this.

'Please, no!' he gasped.

His attacker struck a match.

Now, for the first time, the tramp could see his face. And *what* he saw in it filled him with horror – because though the face itself was human, the expression it had contorted itself into was not.

The man's eyes were blazing with hatred and anger. His nose was flared like that of a wild animal moving in for the kill. And the twist of his mouth said – more clearly than words could ever have done – that compassion and mercy were strangers to him.

'Don't...!' the tramp croaked.

But he knew he was wasting his time, because this man was driven by contempt – for his victim, for the world in general, and even for himself.

So his earlier forebodings had been right, he thought with that one small rational part of his brain which had not yet been engulfed in panic. He *would* die that night.

But his death would not be the slow, gradually numbing one brought on by the cold. Instead, it would be swift, and hot and agonizing.

Even the idea of it was enough to drive a man mad.

But there was no time for such madness to develop, because his attacker threw the match at him, and soon every nerve in his body was screaming with agony.

Part One
The End of an Era

One

A dozen corporation buses – each one packed with hunched, coughing smokers in flat caps – trundled along half a dozen arterial roads towards factories in which screeching hooters were already announcing the imminent start of the day's work. In the shops, assistants were busy polishing the windows and counters, as a prelude to opening the doors through which the customers would soon begin to walk. And in the old abandoned cotton mill which formed part of Whitebridge's industrial graveyard, two men stood on the threshold of the former manager's office, looking down with disgust at what lay on the floor.

One of them, Chief Inspector Charlie Woodend, was a big feller who looked like he had been hurriedly – and carelessly – carved out of a piece of very hard rock. He was dressed in his customary hairy sports jacket and cavalry-twill trousers, and had a Capstan Full Strength cigarette tightly held between two nicotine-stained fingers in his right hand. His companion, Inspector Bob Rutter, was younger, slightly smaller – and much more elegant. He was dressed in a smart blue suit, and though he, too, had a cigarette in his hand, it looked more like a prop, and

11

less like a natural appendage, than his boss's did.

Woodend sniffed. The air was thick with the smell of cooked meat – and the source of the smell lay in a charred mound next to the large hole in the wall which had once contained a window.

'Bastard!' Woodend murmured, almost to himself.

Rutter nodded. 'The fire started there,' he said, pointed to a piece of blackened concrete in one corner of the room.

'Aye, there was one hell of a wind last night, an' he'd have been hunkerin' down to get what protection from it he could,' the chief inspector replied.

'We think he jumped to his feet, and tried to make it out of the window,' Rutter continued.

'More than likely.'

'Which was, of course, precisely the *wrong* thing to do. By exposing himself further to the wind, he would only have fuelled the fire. What he *should have* done was roll over and over on the ground.'

'The man must have been a complete bloody moron, mustn't he?' Woodend said.

'I beg your pardon, sir?'

'I said he must have been a complete bloody moron to do exactly the wrong thing.'

'I'm not sure I would go quite that far myself, sir. What I was doing was merely pointing out that...'

'Mind you, it *is* a little hard to think straight when you can feel your flesh meltin' on the bone.'

His boss was angry, Rutter thought. And the source of that anger was that he was taking this case personally. It was something he often did – and it was both his greatest strength *and* his greatest weakness.

'What's our main purpose, Bob?' Woodend asked. 'Why are we in this job at all?'

'To see that justice is served?' Rutter suggested.

'To protect those who are least able to protect themselves,' Woodend said. He paused, to light up a fresh Capstan Full Strength from the still-smouldering stub of the one he'd just been smoking. 'I'll have the swine who did this,' he continued, blowing smoke down his nose. 'I don't care how clever he's been – I'll have him.'

Chief Constable Henry Marlowe looked down at the official request which was lying on his desk, and then up at the big man in the hairy sports coat who was standing in front of it.

'What you're proposing would cost us a fortune in overtime, Chief Inspector,' he said.

'Yes, sir, I imagine it will,' Woodend replied flatly.

'We seem to be talking in different tenses,' Marlowe pointed out. 'I say "would" and you say "will".'

'You say "tom*ar*to" an' I say "tom*ay*to",' Woodend agreed. 'Unfortunately, sir, this bein' a murder inquiry, we simply can't "just call the whole thing off".'

Marlowe frowned. 'I'm not sure I like your attitude, Chief Inspector,' he snapped.

As understatements went, it was the equivalent of saying that Genghis Khan might just possibly, on rare occasions, have been a little bit aggressive.

The truth was that the chief constable *hated* Woodend's attitude – and on numerous occasions he had done his damnedest to get rid of the bloody man.

'You have to consider what the newspapers might say, if you're seen not to be takin' this seriously, sir,' Woodend said innocently.

Henry Marlowe shivered, as he always did at even the *thought* of getting a bad press.

'I'm not saying that we shouldn't *investigate* the incident, Chief Inspector,' he conceded.

'Investigate the *murder*, you mean.'

'But I wonder, given the scale of the investigation you seem to be envisaging, if you're not perhaps attempting to crack a peanut with a sledgehammer. After all, it should be a relatively simple case to solve.'

'Should it, sir?' Woodend asked.

'Of course. Who could have any interest in killing a down-and-out but *another* down-and-out?'

'So you believe that a tramp did it, do you?'

'I should have thought that was obvious.'

'The victim wasn't knifed, an' he wasn't beaten to death,' Woodend pointed out.

'I can *read*, you know,' Marlowe countered. 'I have *seen* the report. I *know* he wasn't stabbed or bludgeoned. He was burned alive.'

'Well, there you are, then,' Woodend said.

'*Where* am I, exactly?'

'For a start, where would a tramp get a can of petrol from?'

'From a garage, of course – like everybody else.'

'So he goes to a garage to ask for it, even though he knows that will lead us straight to him?'

'Lead us straight to him?' Marlowe repeated, mystified.

Woodend sighed. 'The garage owner would be bound to ask himself how a man who couldn't even afford a decent jacket could possibly own a car, wouldn't he? So the transaction would stick in his mind. An' the tramp in question would have to be pretty stupid not to realize that.'

'Tramps are stupid. They would never become tramps in the first place, if they weren't,' Marlowe said dismissively.

Woodend shook his head. Even after all his experience of dealing with Marlowe in the past, he could still be amazed by the chief constable's one-dimensional, black-and-white vision of the world.

'There's a lot of reasons, other than stupidity, that a man might become a tramp,' he said. 'But even allowin' that you're right, sir, an' the killer is as thick as two short planks, he'd still never have used that particular method to murder his victim.'

'I'm afraid you've lost me again,' Marlowe said.

'Tramps come from all kinds of backgrounds, but they nearly all have one thing in common.'

He paused, giving the chief constable the

opportunity to do a little independent thinking, but rather than avail himself of the opportunity, Marlowe said, 'And what might that one thing be?'

'They're alcoholics.'

'So?'

'So if the killer was a tramp, an' he did get his hands on some money, he wouldn't go wastin' it on petrol. The first thing he'd do is buy booze, because nothin' would be as important as that to him. Not hatred! Not revenge! Not anythin'!'

'You may have a point, but I still think...'

'He'd get blind drunk, an' it wouldn't be until he'd sobered up that he'd start thinkin' about killin' again. An' when he *did* think about it, he'd choose a knife or a blunt instrument, because they'd cost him nothin'.'

Marlowe smirked. 'I would not wish to question your expertise on drink-dependency, Chief Inspector, since from what I have observed of your own habits, you seem to have a great deal of personal experience,' he said. 'However, I am responsible for overseeing a great deal more than one simple little murder. Traffic has to be regulated, football matches have to be policed ... I could go on, but I see no need to. The simple truth is that there are a thousand tasks which must be accomplished within my budget, and I am reluctant to commit as many resources as you seem to be demanding to your investigation.'

'The press...' Woodend began.

'You have already used that particular threat once today,' Marlowe pointed out. 'For a moment, I freely admit, you unbalanced me, but thinking about it, I can't really see why the newspapers should be the least bit interested in this sordid little killing.'

'Maybe the newspapers in general *wouldn't* be interested,' Woodend conceded. 'But I'm a little concerned – lookin' at it from your point of view, as the man in charge of this police force – that Elizabeth Driver *would.*'

The remark hit home, just as Woodend had known it would.

Elizabeth Driver, a tabloid journalist with the moral compunctions of an earthworm, had been a thorn in Woodend's side since his days in Scotland Yard, but recently – since she had embarked on a so-called *secret* affair with Bob Rutter – the chief constable had been her main target. In fact, it was only due to one of her articles in support of Woodend that Marlowe had back-pedalled on his intention to get rid of his least-favourite chief inspector. Woodend still worried about *why* she had done it – nasty motives being the only ones she had – but he saw no reason not to turn it to his advantage now.

Marlowe had started to sweat. 'You think she might take an interest in this case?' he asked.

'I wouldn't know, sir,' Woodend said. 'But it's always better to be safe than sorry.'

Marlowe nodded resignedly. 'Very well, Chief Inspector, I will give you free rein for your investigation for the moment. But I will expect – no, I will *demand* – a very rapid result on this case.'

Demand what you like, Woodend thought. It won't influence the way I investigate the case one way or the other.

But aloud, all he said was, 'I'll do what I can, sir.'

He was almost at the door when Marlowe said harshly, 'One day, you will dig yourself so deeply into a hole that you'll not be able to get out again, you know. And when that happens, I'll be right at the side of that hole, filling it in.'

Woodend turned and smiled at him. 'We all have our little hopes an' dreams, sir,' he said. 'It's what keeps us goin'.'

Two

Pogo, sitting in the bedroom of the decayed terraced house where he usually stayed when he was passing through Whitebridge, had been watching the woman ever since she had parked her car – a flashy red MGA – at the corner of the street.

He was intrigued by the fact that she hadn't locked her vehicle, which argued either confidence or stupidity, and for the moment he had not decided which of the two it was.

The woman had headed straight for the house closest to her car. The place was empty and boarded up, but then *all* the houses in this street, being ex-mill-workers' cottages, were empty and boarded up. She had first tried the front door, then, when it wouldn't open, had walked over to the window and tested the boarding to see if it was really as fixed as it appeared to be. Satisfied it was, she had moved along to the next house, and repeated the procedure. Within a few minutes, she had checked half the other side of the street, in the same slow, methodical way.

Pogo didn't ask himself *why* she was doing it. He had long ago stopped asking himself why people in the 'normal' world did things. They had their rules, and he had his, and the two

19

rarely crossed.

But though he did not wonder about her motives, he did find himself wondering about *her*.

She was somewhere around twenty-nine or thirty, he guessed. She was wearing a red sweater which hugged her rounded breasts and a black-and-white check skirt which was short enough to reveal a pair of very good legs. Her nose was a little larger than those normally issued locally, but it was still an attractive one, and it reminded him of a Ukrainian girl he had known in Berlin, shortly after the War. The woman's hair was blonde and wavy, and looked like it might feel silky to the touch. Pogo did not 'fancy' her – it was years since he had felt emotional desire for a woman, and doubted that, even if he ever did again, his equipment would be up to the job – but looking at her still left him with a slight tinge of regret that he had fallen through a crack in society's floor and now floated in the sewer of its – and his own – disgust.

As the woman moved further up the street, she went out of his range of vision, and with nothing left to watch, he decided he might as well close his eyes for a moment.

He was awoken from his unintended sleep by a crashing sound. He was not instantly alert, as he would have been in the old days, but within a few seconds he was ready for whatever piece of shit fate had decided to throw at him now, and as he rose – a little creakily – to his feet, he was already reaching into his pocket for his knife.

There was the sound of footsteps downstairs –

the clicking of a woman's high heels – and then the sound got closer and he realized that she was climbing the stairs. He slipped the knife back in his pocket – even in the state he was in, he didn't need a weapon to handle a woman! – and patiently awaited her inevitable arrival.

He did not have to wait long. Just a few seconds passed before she pushed open the door and saw him. He was expecting her to be scared – the sight that he caught of himself, on the rare occasions he glanced at his reflection in a shop window, was enough to scare any woman – but if she felt any fear, she didn't show it. Instead, she reached into her pocket, produced a small leather-bound document, and held it out for him to see.

'Detective Sergeant Monika Paniatowski,' she announced.

At the sound of a rank, Pogo found himself stiffening. 'What can I do for you, Sergeant?' he asked.

'If you don't mind, sir, we'd like you to come down to police headquarters for a while,' Paniatowski said.

'What is it I'm supposed to have done?' Pogo demanded.

'Nothing at all, sir. We'd just like you to help us with our inquiries.'

'And what could I possibly know that might be of any use to you?'

'You may not have heard about it yet, but a tramp was murdered last night,' Paniatowski explained.

'Didn't know the man,' Pogo shot back at her.

21

'How can you be so sure of that, before I've given you any of the details?' Paniatowski wondered.

'Don't know *any* tramps,' Pogo told her. 'Why would I?'

'Well, because you're a...' Paniatowski began.

'I'm a what? A tramp myself?'

'Well, yes.'

'I'll have you know, madam, that I am in fact a highly respected City stockbroker, midway through what is turning out to be a very unconventional adventure holiday,' Pogo said sternly.

Paniatowski grinned. 'You're pulling my chain,' she said.

'Well, obviously,' Pogo agreed, grinning back.

'We really would like you to come down to the station,' Paniatowski told him. 'It's a very serious case we have on our hands.'

'The murder of a tramp!' Pogo said dismissively.

'A tramp who was drenched in petrol and then set on fire,' Paniatowski told him.

Pogo rocked on his heels and said, 'Jesus!'

'So you'll come voluntarily?' Paniatowski asked.

'Meaning if I won't, I'll be coming *involuntarily*?' Pogo asked.

'It should be easy enough to find an excuse to pull you,' Paniatowski said, matter-of-factly. Then she grinned again, and added, 'After all, you know what bastards the police are.'

Pogo nodded. 'I'll have to collect my stuff together first.'

'Fair enough.'

His 'stuff' consisted of a sleeping bag, a small knapsack, a tin plate, a mug, a knife, fork and spoon, a Primus stove and small metal pan and a cigarette-rolling machine.

Most tramps probably had some, or all, of those things, Paniatowski thought. But she doubted that most tramps would have arranged them in the way that this one had. The articles were laid out in two straight lines, the first line being roughly a foot from the second.

Or was there anything *roughly* about it? Paniatowski found herself wondering, and decided that if she'd had to make a bet on the distance between the lines, she'd have to put her money on them being *exactly* twelve inches apart.

The tramp collected up his possessions methodically and fitted them into the knapsack. When he'd done that, he rolled up the sleeping bag with practised ease, wrapped it in a piece of cord, and tied the cord with an elaborate knot.

Only when he'd finished his work did he look at Paniatowski and say, 'The threat of being arrested isn't enough.'

'Enough for what?'

'Enough to make me cooperate with you. If you want me to come to the cop shop voluntarily, you'll have to persuade me that there's something in it for me.'

'How about the promise of unlimited cups of tea?' Paniatowski suggested.

Pogo nodded. 'That'll do it,' he agreed.

The basement of police headquarters had been

23

converted into what the chief constable liked to call 'the nerve centre of a major investigation', but as yet there were none of the customary trappings – desks set in a horseshoe configuration, blackboard at the front, dozens of phone lines being installed – because this time most of the area was needed as a holding pen for all the tramps who had been picked up in the police swoop.

There were around two dozen of them, Wood-end noted, surveying the scene. They were all kitted out in a similar fashion – wearing clothing long discarded by others and now encased in grime – but otherwise they were a fairly disparate crew, because while it was true that the majority were between forty and sixty, there were also both older and younger men – and three women.

Thirty years earlier, it would have been surprising to find even two or three tramps sleeping rough in the centre of town, the chief inspector thought. Back then, the tramp was a country-dweller. He would sleep in barns, and sometimes lend a hand on one of the thousands of small farms which were still in existence. And even if he didn't work for his keep, the tenant farmers would give him *something*, because they would have regarded him as much a part of the natural life of the countryside as the rabbits and birds. Now the traditional farms had mostly gone, swallowed up by much larger ones where all the heavy work was done by machinery, and there was little room for casual labour – or even casual acquaintanceship.

Woodend turned to Detective Constable Colin Beresford, who – it was widely believed around police headquarters – had much greater access to his boss's ear than his lowly rank would indicate.

'Did you have any difficulty rounding them up?' he asked.

'A few of them were a bit awkward, mainly the ones who were so out of their heads that they had no idea what was actually going on,' Beresford said. 'But on the whole, they were no trouble. After all, they've taken the line of least resistance for most of their lives, so why should they change now?'

'Until you've had a little more experience of life yourself, don't be so sweepin' in your generalizations, lad,' Woodend said, with an unaccustomed harshness in his voice.

The tone flustered Beresford. 'Sorry, sir, I never meant to suggest...'

'Forget it, lad,' Woodend said. 'But,' he cautioned, 'don't let me catch you jumpin' to conclusions again.'

The chief inspector turned to face the tramps. 'I'm very grateful to you for agreein' to co-operate with this investigation,' he said in a loud voice which caught all their attentions, 'an' I'd like to make one thing clear from the start, which is that none of you are a suspect in this murder, in any way, shape or form.'

Some of the tramps looked relieved, some showed no emotion at all, and some – and Beresford had probably been right about this – were so out of their heads that they had no idea what he was talking about.

'The reason you're all here is because you're potential witnesses,' Woodend continued. 'Now you may think you have nothin' of value to contribute to the investigation – an' maybe you're right – but it's also possible that you might just have noticed somethin' in the past few days which won't mean anythin' to you, but could tell *us* a lot. That's why you'll each individually be taken to another room, an' asked a few questions by one of my men. Once that's happened, you'll be given a packet of cigarettes an' will be allowed to leave. Thank you for listenin'.'

He turned away, and saw Monika Paniatowski looking at him with a troubled expression on her face.

'You're letting them go?' she asked, disbelievingly.

'That's right,' Woodend agreed.

'Even though this could well be nothing more than the first in a series of killings?' Paniatowski asked.

'Even if it is,' Woodend confirmed.

'So it's your intention to put them back out on the street. to be used as live bait?'

Woodend shook his head. 'Nay, lass. I'm puttin' them back out on the street because we don't have the facilities to hold them, an' even if we had, there's no legal justification for doin' it. In other words, I'm puttin' them back out on the street because I have no bloody choice in the matter.'

The more gruesome the murder, the more it

appealed to Elizabeth Driver's readership, and hence to Driver herself. Which was why, even as Woodend was addressing the tramps in police headquarters, she was behind the wheel of her Jaguar, and heading towards Whitebridge at speed.

As she drove, she was thinking not only about the case of the dead tramp – 'Horror of Grilled Vagrant' suggested itself as a headline – but also about her own relationship with Woodend's team in general, and with Detective Inspector Bob Rutter in particular.

The core of that relationship was the book she had decided to write – was *contracted* to write – about the Whitebridge Police. It was going to be a sensational exposé, and the fact that there might be nothing sensational *to* expose about the Force had not bothered her for a second, since she considered truth to be a commodity to be used sparingly.

In order to write that book, she'd needed an insider in the Force, and she'd seen Bob Rutter – weakened first by the break-up of his adulterous affair with Monika Paniatowski, and then by the murder of his blind wife, Maria – as the ideal candidate. When she'd approached him initially, she'd offered the bait of writing an inspirational book about his dead wife, and – wracked with guilt as he was – he'd fallen for it hook, line and sinker.

For the first few months of their relationship, she'd deliberately avoided any physical contact, since she'd felt it would have been unwelcome to a man grappling with his own conscience. But once she'd sensed that the time was right, she'd gone ahead and seduced him.

And it had been so easy!

So very easy!

Other steps in her plan had not run quite so smoothly. Rutter had his daughter living with him now, and the little brat – for reasons of her own – had shown as much disdain for Driver as she'd shown affection for Monika Paniatowski.

And then there had been the career of Chief Inspector Charlie Woodend, who was to be the cornerstone of her book. That had taken a dip which had almost resulted in a fall, and – as much as she hated to do anything to help her old enemy – she'd been forced to write an editorial praising him. Still, she consoled herself, that wouldn't last for long, and when his merely *postponed* fall did inevitably come, it would be all the greater.

She'd made one change to her plans which had quite surprised her. Initially, she'd intended to bring Rutter down with the rest of Woodend's team, but now she found that she didn't actually *want* to. Affection was another of those qualities she didn't have much use for, yet she'd grown fond of Rutter, and liked the idea of keeping him around on a permanent basis.

She wouldn't be faithful to him, of course – the very idea was ludicrous – but it would be nice to have him there when she wanted him, like a particularly comfortable pair of shoes. *He* might baulk at the idea at first, especially after she had just destroyed the careers of his boss and his ex-lover, but she was confident enough in her own abilities to believe that she could twist things round in such a way as to make it look like it wasn't her fault at all.

And if that failed, there was always the bedroom in which to win him over – because, when all was said and done, he was still only a *man*.

The road sign ahead said that Whitebridge was now only twenty miles away. Elizabeth Driver turned her thoughts back to the story that lay ahead of her, and then to THE BOOK, now almost finished, which was nestling comfortably in the boot of her car, next to her portable type-writer.

Three

The man sitting opposite DC Colin Beresford could have been anywhere between forty and sixty years old. He was wearing a tattered overcoat which was far too long for him and dragged along the ground when he walked. The coat had once been brown, but was now so streaked with dirt that the overall effect was grey. Under it was evidence of several other layers of clothing, which looked equally disgusting. The tramp had lost most of the hair on his head, but had grown a long, straggly grey beard to compensate for it. He was blind in one eye, and there were only a few rotting teeth left in his mouth.

And he stank!

'Could you tell me your name?' Beresford asked gently.

'Tommy,' the tramp said.

'And your second name?'

The tramp looked at him strangely, as if he had no idea why the policeman should even want to ask such a question, then said, 'Moores. Tommy Moores.'

'And are you a Whitebridge man, Mr Moores?' Beresford inquired.

'Where's Whitebridge?' Moores asked.

'Here,' Beresford explained. 'You're in Whitebridge now.'

The information seemed to be of no interest to the tramp.

And why should it be? Beresford asked himself. To Tommy Moores, the name of the place he was in was unimportant. When he thought about the town at all, he would think of it in terms that would mean little to people who lived in the mainstream – a restaurant where the bins were particularly worth scavenging, church steps on which he would be likely to find a good number of discarded cigarettes, the cheapest place to buy meths...

'So you're *not* from here?' Beresford asked.

'No, I'm not.'

'Then where *are* you from?'

'Somewhere else.'

Beresford suppressed a sigh. 'But you live here now?'

'Don't live anywhere,' the tramp replied. 'Travel.'

'All right,' Beresford said patiently. 'How long have you been in Whitebridge *this* time?'

'Don't know,' the other man said.

And he probably didn't, Beresford thought. He was probably nothing more than an unthinking force of nature, staying somewhere for a while and then moving on for no other reason than because that was what he did.

'Where do you sleep when you're in Whitebridge?' he asked.

'Here and there,' Moores said vaguely.

'Do you ever sleep in the old Empire Cotton Mill?' Beresford wondered.

The tramp thought about it for a second. 'Big brick building?' he asked. 'Close to the canal?'

'That sounds like the place,' Beresford agreed.

'I've slept there,' the tramp admitted.

'But did you sleep there last night?'

'Might have done. Don't know.'

'And other tramps slept there as well, didn't they?'

'A few.'

'So what can you tell me about them?'

'Nothing.'

'But you must have talked to them, mustn't you?'

The tramp gave him a puzzled look. 'Why would I do that?' he asked.

Indeed, Beresford thought, why *would* he do that? What could he possibly have to say to his fellow tramps, and what could they possibly have to say to him?

'Have you noticed anything unusual recently?' he asked, shifting his line of questioning.

'Like what?' Moores asked.

'Like strangers turning up at the places where you sleep. Strangers who aren't tramps. Norm—'

He'd been about to say 'normal people', but cut himself off just in time. Not that it would have mattered if he hadn't, he told himself. Tommy Moores wouldn't have recognized an insult if he'd heard one. He seemed beyond all that.

'There was a man in a suit,' the tramp said.

'Go on,' Beresford encouraged him.

'The other night, when I was in the big brick

32

building, a man in a suit came in.'

'What did he look like?'

'I told you, he was wearing a suit.'

'Was he young? Middle-aged? Old?'

'Yes,' the tramp said.

Beresford sighed again. 'And what did he do, this man in a suit?'

'He looked at me.'

'And then?'

'And then he went away.'

'And he didn't say anything to you?'

'No.'

'You're not being very helpful, Mr Moores,' Beresford said, chidingly.

'Aren't I?' the tramp asked, with a show of indifference.

'A man's been killed,' Beresford pointed out. 'A tramp like yourself. The killer may well strike again, and when he does, you could be his next victim. Doesn't that bother you?'

'No,' Moores said. 'Why should it?'

'Being burned to death is a very painful way to go,' Beresford said.

For the first time in the interview, Moores looked him straight in the eye, and for a moment Beresford caught a glimpse of the intelligence and interest in life he must once have had.

'And you don't think I'm in pain already?' the tramp asked.

Dr Shastri met Woodend at the door of the police morgue. There was a smile on her face, and the edges of her colourful sari were just visible under her green medical gown.

'My dear Chief Inspector,' she said. 'What a pleasure – though hardly an unexpected one – to see you.'

'The feelin's mutual,' Woodend said.

And he *meant* it, for though he hated the smell of the morgue, he loved spending time with the exotically beautiful – and breathtakingly competent – police surgeon. Shastri, it seemed to him, was the ideal combination of a doctor who approached her work with a soul which was pure and strangely innocent, and yet, at the same time, had a mind which was as sharp and cutting as one of her own finely honed scalpels.

'Oh, what *has* happened to my manners?' the doctor wondered, as she led him into her office.

'Your manners?' Woodend repeated.

'Indeed! Though I have had ample opportunity to do so, I have not yet thanked you for providing me, yet again, with a specimen which would put a lesser woman off her food for days.'

Woodend grinned. 'What can you tell me about this particular appetite-suppressor?' he asked, as he took the seat which Shastri offered him.

'He died of sixth-degree burns,' the doctor said, 'which in layman's terms means not only was his skin destroyed (fourth-degree burning) and his muscular structure irreversibly damaged (fifth-degree burning) but also that his bones were charred.'

'So I assume there's really not much you can tell me about him at all?'

'If, by that, you mean that you wish to know whether he was a concert pianist or an industrial labourer while he was alive, then you are quite correct in your assumption. His hands, or what is left of them, are no more than blackened claws, and provide no clues as to their previous usage. If, however, you wish to know how tall he was before the fire shrunk him, or how old he was when he died, then I might be able to be a little more helpful.'

'So how tall was he?'

'Somewhere between five feet eight and five feet ten. And, in age, I would place him between forty-five and fifty-five.'

'What kind of man can set fire to another human being?' Woodend wondered. 'What could his motive possibly be?'

'You are doing it again,' Dr Shastri said, wagging a playfully rebuking finger at him.

'Doin' what again?'

'Asking me to speculate on something well beyond my own area of expertise.'

Woodend grinned for a second time. 'Yes, that's *just* what I'm doin', isn't it?' he admitted. 'But I'd still like to hear your thoughts on the matter.'

'Very well,' Shastri agreed. 'The first thought that occurs to me is that your killer is a very disturbed individual who enjoys inflicting pain and has chosen to inflict it on tramps because they are the easiest targets.'

'Aye, that had occurred to me, too.'

'Alternatively, he may hate tramps in general because of what one in particular has done to him.'

'For example?'

Dr Shastri shrugged an elegant shoulder. 'He may have been robbed by a tramp of something he held very dear to him,' she suggested. 'He may have been beaten up by a tramp. Or perhaps a tramp raped his wife or his sister.'

'Possible,' Woodend agreed. 'But I've never heard of a tramp bein' arrested for committin' any major offence. The most any of 'em usually get up to is petty thievin'.'

'Then there is a third possibility,' Shastri said warily, 'though, without proof of any kind, I am reluctant to suggest it.'

'Go on,' Woodend urged, 'let's hear it.'

'It could have been the mods,' Shastri said quickly, as if she were in a hurry to get the words out of her mouth before she changed her mind.

'The mods?' Woodend repeated. 'Them lads with puffy haircuts an' sharp suits, who ride around on scooters?'

'Not the *peacock* mods,' Dr Shastri said. 'The *hard* mods. The ones with the short hair and big boots.'

'Are *they* mods, an' all?' Woodend asked. 'Because they don't look like the other lot at all.'

'That is because they can't afford to look like "the other lot",' Dr Shastri said. 'The peacock mods work in offices, and come from prosperous homes. The hard mods are working-class boys who labour in the same factories as their fathers. And since they do not have the money to compete with the peacock mods successfully in terms of style, they have stopped competing altogether.'

'Which is why, given the kind of town this is,

36

we've got more of the hard mods in Whitebridge than we have the other kind,' Woodend said.

'Exactly,' Dr Shastri agreed.

'I've got two more questions for you,' Woodend told her. 'The first is, how come you seem to know so much about these lads? An' the second is, why do you think they might have been involved in the murder?'

'That is not two questions, but two parts of the same question,' Dr Shastri replied. She paused for a second, then continued, 'Though I have not sought out the position, I seem to have become a person who many in the Asian community of Whitebridge come to for advice.'

That was hardly surprising, Woodend thought. Most of the Asians in the town were recent immigrants who held low-paid jobs. Dr Shastri, who, in addition to holding an important post, was brimming with assurance and self-confidence, would be the natural person for them to turn to for help.

'Quite a number of these poor people have either been threatened or abused by the hard mods,' Shastri continued. 'Several of them have been beaten up.'

'An' have they reported it to the police?'

Dr Shastri laughed scornfully. 'Of course they haven't reported it. They remember the brutality of the police in their own countries, and steer well clear of authority whenever possible.'

'So what *are* they doin' about it?'

'They are avoiding the places where the attacks are most likely. They feel that is all they *can* do.'

'You should have reported it to me yourself,' Woodend said accusingly.

'They would not have thanked me for doing so,' Dr Shastri told him. 'And the next time they had a problem they would take it to someone else, who might not be able to deal with it as well as I could.'

'I still don't see why you think these hard mods should have had anythin' to do with the victim,' Woodend said.

'I told you from the beginning that the link was tenuous,' Dr Shastri pointed out.

'Aye, you did,' Woodend agreed. 'But let's hear what you think it is, anyway.'

'It seems to me that what mainly drives these young men is anger,' Shastri said.

'Anger at what?'

'At a world that seems to be offering so many opportunities to other people, while all it shows them is a dead end. And this anger they feel makes them want to strike out at something different to themselves. The Asians offer them a perfect target, but so do the tramps. After all,' she concluded, with a bitter edge entering her voice, 'we are both parasites – and we both stink.'

Her initial contact with Pogo had so intrigued Paniatowski that she'd reserved the job of questioning him for herself, but even before they'd properly sat down at the table in the interview room, he'd begun questioning *her*.

'Tell me about the big sod in the hairy jacket,' he said. 'What's he like to work for?'

38

'Why do you ask?' Paniatowski asked.

'Because I'm interested,' Pogo replied. 'Do I need any more reason than that?'

'I suppose not,' Paniatowski admitted. 'Well, he's a hard task-master, but he's very fair. He expects you to be at your best at all times, but if you deserve any credit, he'll make sure that you get it.'

Pogo nodded. 'That's the impression he gave me,' he said.

'You're about the same age,' Paniatowski said.

'We probably are.'

'Which means, I suppose, that you will have fought in the same war.'

'How do you know I fought in any war at all?' Pogo asked.

'You're not going to deny you were a soldier, are you?' Paniatowski said, smiling. 'Because if you do, I certainly won't believe you.'

'You seem very certain of yourself,' Pogo said wonderingly.

'I am,' Paniatowski agreed.

'And what's that certainty based on?'

'It's based on a lot of things. For example, it can't be easy to keep clean, given the kind of life you lead, but you're a lot cleaner than any of the other tramps we brought in.'

'So I'm fastidious,' Pogo said. 'That proves nothing.'

'When I told you my rank, you practically came to attention, which means that while you were undoubtedly in the army, you never rose above the rank of corporal. So is that what you were? A corporal?'

39

'No comment.'

Paniatowski smiled. 'Not even name, rank and number?' she asked. 'And then there's the question of your possessions,' she continued. 'When I asked you to come to headquarters with me, you collected them all up.'

'Well, of course I did. I wasn't going to leave them there for anybody who came across them to steal, was I?'

'But it was the way you picked them up which was interesting,' Paniatowski continued. 'You did it purposefully, and according to a pre-determined routine. Everything in your knapsack has a designated place – and you made sure that's where it went.'

'You're building something out of nothing,' Pogo said.

Paniatowski smiled. 'If you say so,' she said.

Pogo was silent for a few seconds, then he said, 'All right, it's a fair cop. I was a soldier once. And now I'm a tramp. What of it?'

'What *made* you become a tramp?' Paniatowski asked.

'Next question!' Pogo said, with a vehemence which startled her.

'Can you think of any reason why someone would set a tramp on fire?' Paniatowski asked.

'No.'

'Aren't you worried that the same thing might happen to you?'

'It *won't* happen to me.'

No, it won't, Paniatowski thought. You might not be the man you used to be, but you can still take care of yourself.

'I'd like you to help me,' she said.

'I don't see how I can,' Pogo replied. 'I told you back at ba— back at the place where you found me, that I don't know anything.'

'But you could *find out* things,' Paniatowski said.

'What do you mean?'

'I'm a bobby,' Paniatowski said. 'The moment I'm on the scene, it's not the same scene any longer. My mere presence there *changes* things. But you can go to all kinds of places I couldn't, and not be noticed.'

'So you want me to become a spy? A narc? An informer?'

Paniatowski grinned. 'I prefer the term "undercover operative",' she said.

'And what's in it for me?' Pogo asked.

'A couple of packets of cigarettes,' Paniatowski told him. 'A little money. But, most of all, the chance to be useful again – the chance to earn your own respect and the respect of others.'

For the briefest of moments, Pogo's face began to crumple in self-pity, but then his features hardened again, and became a mask of inscrutability.

'I'll think about it,' he said.

Four

The man sitting at a table near the counter in the police canteen was close to sixty, and had a shock of white hair and a complexion which looked as if it had been constructed out of sandpaper.

When Woodend approached him, it was with a reverence that went far beyond what his position in the police hierarchy merited, because Sid Roberts was not so much a sergeant as an institution.

Roberts was not only the oldest sergeant in the force, but had held the rank for so long that there was no serving officer who could actually remember a time when he *wasn't* a sergeant. And the reason he had never been promoted above that rank was, the chief inspector suspected, largely a matter of his own choice. He was a 'coal-face' policeman, who loved his home town, and loved the perspective on it that the three stripes on his sleeve allowed him. And when people said that he was a *natural* sergeant, what they really meant was that it seemed as if he had been there first, and the title had been invented specifically to fit him.

Woodend sat down opposite him, and said, 'What can you tell me about the hard mods,

42

Sid?'

'Depends what you want to know, sir,' Roberts replied.

'I don't *know* what I want to know,' Woodend admitted. 'Just give me a thumbnail sketch of them.'

'They like to think they're hard, hence the name – and they generally are. Most of them are working-class lads, and the great majority of them have jobs in factories. One of the things that gives them a sense of identity is their taste in music – they're very big on "ska", which is sometimes also known as "rocksteady".'

'I've never heard either of those names before,' Woodend admitted.

'You wouldn't have, sir,' Roberts replied, though not dismissively. 'It's Jamaican music. There's one song in particular, "Rudie Got Soul" by Desmond Dekker, which has practically become their anthem, and I have to say, they could have chosen worse.'

'You're amazing, Sid,' Woodend said, full of admiration.

'Well, I do try to keep my finger on the pulse,' Roberts said. 'I'm a bit like our beloved leader in that way.'

Woodend grinned, then grew serious again. 'You said they were hard. Does that mean they're violent?' he asked.

'You're wondering if they were behind that tramp's murder,' Roberts guessed.

'Exactly,' Woodend agreed.

'It's possible,' Roberts said cautiously. 'Until recently, their main concern has been beating *each other* up, but now they've started to fall under the influence of Councillor Scranton.'

'Oh, that bastard!' Woodend said.

'That bastard,' Roberts agreed. He checked his watch. 'Have you got half an hour to spare, sir?'

'Why?'

'Because if you want to get a closer look at some of the hard mods, I know just where to find you a few.'

The man was standing on the soapbox outside the factory gates of Lowry Engineering. He was small, in his late forties, and sported a moustache which did not stretch far beyond his nostrils. Gathered around him were some of the workers from the factory, who were on their dinner break.

'How did you know this was goin' to happen?' Woodend asked, surveying the scene through the windscreen of his Wolseley.

'It's my *job* to know things like that,' replied Sid Roberts from the passenger seat. 'See that big ugly sod standing close to Scranton?'

'I see him,' Woodend said, studying a youth whose hair was so closely cropped he was almost bald.

'His name's Barry Thornley,' Roberts said. 'I've know his whole family, and there's never been a good one yet. Bazza's got a gang of his own, and he's a great admirer of Councillor Scranton.'

Scranton had a megaphone in his hands, and now he raised it to his lips.

'It's a pleasure to see so many honest working men gathered here today,' he said in a slightly metallic voice. 'And do you know why? Because you're the backbone of this country. You're what made this country great.'

Several members of the crowd cheered, and Scranton looked very pleased with himself.

'But there are forces afoot to rob this country of its greatness,' he continued. 'Have you seen how many Pakis there are on the streets of Whitebridge? And there's more of them every day.' He paused. 'Did you hear me say the name of your town? *Whitebridge!* Not *Brown*bridge! Not *Black*bridge! It's a town built by white people *for* white people.'

'And built on the cotton that the Indians and "Pakis" grew,' Roberts said to Woodend.

'Aye, you're right,' the chief inspector agreed. 'It's funny that Scranton didn't think to mention that, isn't it?'

'And it's not just the Pakis that are bringing the town down,' Scranton said. 'There are the dirty thieving tramps and gypsies who you see all over the place. I hear one of the tramps was burned to death last night. Well, that's one less to worry about, isn't it?'

'Bastard!' Woodend said.

'The rest of the town council is frightened of me,' Scranton told his audience. 'And why? Because I speak the truth! They're *so* frightened of me that they're abolishing my ward before the next election. But if they think that will keep me out of the council chamber, they've got another think coming. I shall stand in another ward. And whose ward do you think I'll stand in?'

'Councillor Lowry's!' someone shouted out.

'That's right,' Scranton agreed. 'Councillor Lowry's. He thinks because he owns this factory, he can do what he likes. But he's wrong. People find it hard enough to be bossed about by men like him *at work*. They don't want to be told what they can and can't do – what they can and can't *think* – once they've left the factory gates behind them. So here is my message to Councillor Lowry – when the votes are counted after the next election, I'll still have a seat on the council. But you won't.'

'He's quite impressive,' Woodend said reluctantly.

'Yes, he is,' Roberts agreed. 'You were a sergeant in the army, weren't you, sir?'

'I was,' Woodend agreed.

'So was I. Seems to me the sergeants are what make the army tick. They're the balancing point between the men and the officers, and if there's harmony, it's largely down to them.'

'Agreed,' Woodend said.

'I've never known a bad sergeant, but I've known bad corporals,' Roberts continued. 'There is some – by no means the majority, but some – who resent not being sergeants themselves, and they try to establish their own positions by stirring up trouble and then posing as the champions of the other ranks. Do you know what I mean?'

Woodend nodded. 'I've seen it myself.'

'Councillor Scranton was a corporal in the RAF, which puts him on a par with his hero,'

46

Roberts said.

'His hero?' Woodend repeated.

'That's right,' Roberts agreed. 'Adolf Hitler was a corporal, an' all!'

Five

The *real* nerve centre of the investigation was not – as the chief constable fondly imagined – the incident room in the headquarters' basement, but a corner table in the public bar of the Drum and Monkey. It was there – over pints of bitter for the men and neat vodkas for Monika Paniatowski – that intuitive leaps were made. It was there that the single shafts of light – which often led them to the murky heart of a case – were produced. And it was there that Woodend found Paniatowski and Beresford when he walked through the door at a quarter to one on the first day of the investigation.

'Where's Bob?' the chief inspector asked as he sat down. 'Slipped out to the bog, has he?'

Monika Paniatowski shook her head. 'He said he'd got something else to deal with first, but he'd be here shortly.'

'An' is this "somethin' else" connected with the case?' Woodend asked.

'I've no idea,' Paniatowski said flatly.

Which meant, Woodend assumed, that though she thought she had a *very good* idea what Rutter was doing, she wasn't about to tell *him* what it was.

That was one of the troubles with Monika. She

was still loyal to her ex-lover, and she still tried to protect him – even when he didn't deserve it.

Woodend signalled the barman to bring another round of drinks. 'Well, even if Inspector Rutter isn't here, I suppose we'd better get started,' he said. 'So what have you got to report, DC Beresford?'

'There's not much *to* report,' Beresford said. 'The tramps all claim they don't know each other, and I think they're mostly telling the truth.'

'I agree,' Paniatowski added. 'They didn't give up one kind of society simply to become involved in another. Besides, they spend their days teetering on the edge of survival, and there's no room for passengers on a journey like that.'

'I wouldn't have phrased it quite like that myself,' Woodend said, 'but I do know exactly what you mean.'

'One of the tramps, a man called Tommy Moores, said he saw a man in a suit in the old cotton mill,' Beresford told the chief inspector. 'Said the man looked at him, then moved on.'

'An' are you inclined to take him seriously?' Woodend asked.

'On balance, I don't think I am,' Beresford admitted. 'He was a bit vague about when he'd seen the man, and I'm not entirely convinced that if he *did* actually see him, he saw him where he said he did. And it doesn't seem likely, does it, that a man intent on that kind of murder would be wearing a suit.'

Woodend laughed. 'So what would he be wearin'?' he asked. 'A jumper with "Arsonist-

Murderer" written across the front?'

'No, of course not,' Beresford said seriously. 'But a suit would still make him stand out, so if there really *was* a man, he was a man who didn't mind being noticed – which would argue for him being some kind of council inspector.'

'Fair point,' Woodend agreed. 'Now let me tell you what *I've* learned this mornin'.'

He outlined Dr Shastri's theory on the hard mods, and what he had seen and heard outside the foundry gate.

'So what do you think?' he asked when he'd finished.

'I think we should lock up Councillor bloody Scranton and throw away the key!' Paniatowski said vehemently.

Of course she did, Woodend thought. She'd grown up as one of the few Polish kids in Whitebridge. She knew what it was like to be part of a minority that a lot of people looked down on.

'I agree with you on that,' he told his sergeant. 'But that's not the issue at the moment. What I want to know is how you feel about the theory that one of the hard mods could be our killer?'

'I think it's a possibility,' Paniatowski said. 'From what I've seen, they're violent enough, and they've got chips on their shoulders the size of boulders. But investigating them isn't going to be easy, because, in many ways, they're a bit like the tramps.'

'They're outsiders?' Woodend suggested.

'Yes,' Paniatowski agreed. 'They live in their own world, and they're very resistant to the idea of anyone who doesn't belong entering it.'

'So maybe we need somebody who *does* belong – or *seems* to belong,' Woodend said thoughtfully. 'An' I may have just the feller.'

'Who?'

'I'll tell you later, when I've had time to think it through,' Woodend promised.

Elizabeth Driver felt her heart skip a sudden – and unexpected – beat as she saw Bob Rutter enter the residents' bar of the Royal Victoria, Whitebridge's swankiest hotel.

Damn! she thought. This shouldn't be happening. This isn't like me *at all* – and it's time I got it under control.

Rutter walked over to her table, kissed her lightly – but not *that* lightly – on the cheek, and sat down.

'It's good to see you, Liz,' he said.

'It's good to see you, too,' Driver agreed.

And it *was*! Despite the warning she'd given herself only moments earlier, it sodding well was!

'You're here to cover the murder, are you?' Rutter asked.

'That's right,' Driver agreed. 'So we must be very careful that whatever we say to each other has nothing to do with the case.'

If only Charlie Woodend could hear this conversation, Rutter thought, he might finally come to accept that Liz had changed, that she wasn't the heartless, unscrupulous woman they'd known in their earlier investigations.

'You don't have to stay here in this expensive

51

hotel, you know,' he said.

'The newspaper's paying for it,' Driver pointed out.

'I appreciate that,' Rutter said. 'But it might be somehow ... cosier ... if you stayed with me. We wouldn't have to share a bed – not if we'd decided not to – but it would be nice to have you around.'

'Louisa doesn't like me,' Driver said, pleased that she finally seemed to be able to remember the brat's name.

'She'll get used to you in time,' Rutter said hopefully.

Elizabeth Driver shook her head. 'She won't. She'll *never* get used to me. And I don't want to put her under the pressure of even having to try.'

Besides, she added mentally, the less time I spend around the bloody kid, the happier I am.

'You're very thoughtful,' Rutter said.

'I try to be,' Driver replied. 'And there are other factors to be taken into consideration as well as Louisa. *We* both know we won't discuss the case, even if we are living under the same roof, but we have to think about how it would look to *other* people.'

'You're right, as you so often are,' Rutter said.

A waiter appeared at the table. 'Can I bring you anything, sir?' he asked.

Rutter nodded. 'A pint of bitter, please.'

A glazed look came to the waiter's eyes. 'I'm afraid we don't serve beer in pint glasses, sir,' he said.

'Pints are far too uncouth for a place like the Royal Victoria,' Elizabeth Driver said, grinning.

She turned to the waiter. 'Isn't that right?'

'I'm afraid I couldn't possibly say, madam,' the waiter replied.

'Would it be all right if I had two halves instead?' Rutter wondered.

'Yes, sir, that would be perfectly acceptable,' the waiter said, deadpan.

As he walked away, Elizabeth Driver giggled quietly. 'What am I going to do with you?' she asked Rutter.

'I don't know,' Rutter replied. 'What *are* you going to do with me?'

'I think we both know the answer to that,' Driver replied, with just a hint of sexiness in her voice. 'But before we get to all that heaving and groaning, why don't you tell me what you've been doing since we last saw each other? And remember, I don't want to hear any police business.'

It was so easy to talk to Liz, Rutter told himself, as he did as she'd asked. The subject of the conversation – even the words they used to express themselves – didn't really matter. It was the very *act* of talking which was important – which had such a soothing effect on him.

And then, belatedly, he realized how much time must have passed, and glancing down at his watch confirmed his suspicion was true.

'I have to go,' he said.

Elizabeth Driver smiled again. 'And where, exactly, are you off to?' she asked. 'Let me guess. You're going to the Drum and Monkey – for another session of that brains' trust that runs on best bitter served in *pint* glasses.'

Rutter smiled back. 'That's right,' he agreed.
'Will I see you tonight?'

Rutter shrugged. 'You know what it's like during an investigation. I can't promise anything.'

'You don't have to be tied down by this job of yours, you know,' Elizabeth Driver said. 'I could hire you as an investigator, to do all my legwork for me. You'd be very good at it, you'd be earning at least twice what you're earning now – and we'd get to spend much more time together.'

'I won't say it's not a tempting idea,' Rutter admitted, 'but how would it look if you employed someone you were emotionally involved with?'

'It would look exactly like what it was – as if I was taking on the best man for the job.'

'You're very sweet,' Rutter said, standing up. 'And listen, I really will try to see you tonight, if I possibly can.'

'I know you will,' Driver told him. 'And if you can't make it, well, I'll understand – and I'll try not to be too disappointed at spending another night alone.'

'You really *are* sweet,' Rutter said, leaning over and kissing her briefly on the lips, before turning away.

It was only as he was walking to the door that it occurred to Rutter that anyone overhearing the latter half of their conversation would have taken them for an old-established, rather happily married, couple.

'So we've agreed we'll get nothin' much of any

value out of questionin' the tramps?' Woodend said to Beresford and Paniatowski.

'Except maybe from the one I talked to – the one who calls himself Pogo,' Paniatowski replied.

'Except for him,' Woodend concurred. 'But even in his case, I wouldn't put too much reliance on him comin' up with anythin' useful.' He paused, to take a drag on his cigarette, then said, 'So what else have we got?'

'It might help if we could find out who the dead man was,' Paniatowski said. 'But since we don't even know what he *looked like*, that seems a very remote possibility.'

'Aye, it's a real bugger,' Woodend agreed.

'Perhaps we'll get some help from the general public on that,' Beresford suggested.

'In what way?'

'We'll ask them to describe all the tramps they *have* seen, compare them to the descriptions of the tramps we've interviewed, and see if there's one that doesn't match up.'

'An' hope that the tramp they describe hasn't simply moved on since the last time they saw him,' Woodend said discouragingly. 'Besides, how many people really *look* at a tramp at all? Most folk just want to get away from them as quickly as they possibly can. An' anyway, given that they've all got long hair an' ragged beards, they pretty much all look alike to anybody who's not studied them in detail. Bloody hell, even I would find it difficult to tell the ones we've interviewed this morning apart.'

'If the public can't help us to identify the

victim, then maybe they'll be able to help us identify the killer,' Beresford said.

'If they can, they'll have been a damn sight more observant than they normally are,' Woodend countered, rather sourly.

The meeting was not going well, and they all knew it, Paniatowski thought. There were a number of reasons for that, but one of them was certainly that the team worked best as a *whole* team, and the second most important member of it hadn't even bothered to turn up yet.

'The best chance we've got is that the killer will try to strike again, an' will be caught by one of the extra patrols I've arranged to be on duty tonight,' Woodend said. 'Or, to put it in much the same terms as Sergeant Paniatowski did earlier, our best chance is that the killer will be caught nibblin' at some of the live bait I've thoughtfully laid out for him.'

'I'm sorry, sir, I was completely out of order talking like that,' Paniatowski told him.

'Aye, you were,' Woodend agreed. 'But then we all make mistakes.' He glanced down at his watch. 'Where the bloody hell *is* Inspector Rutter?'

'Maybe he's caught up in traffic?' Beresford suggested.

'Caught up in traffic?' Woodend repeated. 'For *so* long? This is Whitebridge, not central bloody London.' He sipped moodily at his pint, then turned to Beresford and said, 'You remember what I said earlier – that I'd got an idea about how we could get closer to the hard mods?'

'Yes, sir?'

56

'Well, I've been thinkin' it through, an' I've decided it will work. But before it *can* work, you need to pay a visit to the barber's shop.'

'Why?' Beresford wondered. 'My hair's not that long, sir.'

'No, it isn't,' Woodend agreed. 'But it's too long for the job that I have in mind.'

'Wait a minute!' Beresford exclaimed. 'You want me to ... to infiltrate the hard mods?'

'That's about the size of it,' Woodend agreed. 'Monika's got a source which *she* thinks is reliable among the tramps, I need a man I can trust in among the other buggers.'

'But I'm *twenty-three!*' Beresford protested.

'Aye, but somehow – despite havin' worked for me for over a year – you still haven't lost your boyish charm,' Woodend said, with a smile. He placed an avuncular hand on Beresford's shoulder. 'Look, lad, I realize it'll probably all be a waste of time, but when straws are all you've got to clutch at, you make a grab for 'em.'

'Do you really think I can pull it off?' Beresford said.

'I don't know, but you've certainly got more chance than I'd have,' Woodend told him. 'But I don't want you runnin' any risks. Carry your warrant card with you at all times, an' if it looks like you're about to be rumbled, get the hell away – as quick as you can.'

The bar door swung open, and Rutter walked in.

Woodend gave him the briefest of glances, then turned to Beresford and Paniatowski, and

said, 'Well, murders don't usually solve themselves, so we'd better get back to it, hadn't we?'

The DC and sergeant drained their glasses and
stood up, and Rutter, who had been close enough
to hear Woodend's words, did a half-turn
towards the door.

'Not you, Inspector!' Woodend said loudly.
'You can take a seat – because it's about time
you an' me had a little talk.'

Paniatowski and Beresford made the hurried
exit which had obviously been demanded of
them, but before they reached the door, Paniatowski distinctly heard Woodend say, 'So tell
me, Inspector Rutter, are you still a full-time
member of this team or aren't you?'

It was not like Charlie to speak so loudly, she
thought as she stepped out on to the pavement –
so the fact that she'd heard what he said meant
that she'd been *intended* to hear it.

Or to put it another way, her hearing it had
been part of Rutter's punishment.

Six

The note that Woodend found waiting for him on his desk when he returned from the Drum and Monkey was brief – and very much to the point.

'The chief constable wishes to see you *the moment* you return to headquarters,' it read.

Woodend studied Marlowe's spidery hand-writing for a second, and then found himself wondering just what kind of man it was who needed to write about himself in the third person.

'An' the answer is,' he said aloud to his empty office, 'it's the kind of man who's a real dick-head.'

Then he sat down, lit up a cigarette, and promised himself he would smoke it really slowly.

When he did finally reach the chief constable's office, ten minutes later, he discovered that his boss was not alone – nor even, apparently, in charge. For while Marlowe usually sought to reinforce his position in the pecking order by sitting behind his over-large desk, his chair was at that moment occupied by another man, and the chief constable himself was standing by the window.

The man behind the desk was in his middle

forties. He was square-faced, brown-eyed and had a cleft in his chin. His body had the chunkiness of a rugby player, and if that had been his sport, he'd obviously made an effort to keep in shape after he'd hung up his boots for the last time.

'You know Councillor Lowry, don't you, Mr Woodend?' Marlowe asked.

Woodend nodded in the general direction of the man behind the desk. 'We've met,' he said.

'As you may already be aware, Councillor Lowry is not only the managing director of the highly successful Lowry Engineering Company, but also the chairman of the Police Authority for Central Lancashire,' Marlowe said.

There didn't seem to be much to say in response, so Woodend said nothing. But what he was *thinking* was that Lowry's appearance spelled trouble. Ever since he'd assumed the chairmanship of the police authority the previous year, Lowry had been harrying the Force to produce more results at a lower cost to the ratepayers. And that, in Woodend's opinion, led to bad police practice.

Lowry had been studying Woodend intently for some seconds, but now he turned his attention to Marlowe, and said, 'Thank you, Henry.'

It was as neat – and abrupt – a dismissal as Woodend had ever seen, and in the face of it the chief constable could do no more than nod and reply, 'Well, if you need me for anything, Tel—'

'I'll know where to find you,' Lowry interrupted him. Then he waited until Marlowe had stepped out into the corridor, before continuing, 'Do take a seat, Chief Inspector Woodend.'

Woodend sat.

'Every once in a while, I make it my business to meet one of the officers who work for this police authority,' Lowry said. 'It helps to give me some idea of what the grass roots are thinking.'

'No need to talk to us foot soldiers to find that out,' Woodend said. 'Just ask the chief constable. After all, as one of the most experienced sergeants on the force was tellin' me only this mornin', Mr Marlowe's really got his finger on the pulse of the Whitebridge Police.'

'I don't appreciate sarcasm, Mr Woodend,' Lowry said.

'Sarcasm?' Woodend repeated innocently.

'I know what *you* think of Mr Marlowe, and whilst you could not expect me to openly agree with you, I assume you've also noted that I'm not exactly defending him, either.'

Well, well, well, there was a turn-up for the books, Woodend thought. Marlowe's one real talent was impressing his superiors, and in Lowry's case, he seemed to have failed completely. So maybe there was more to the councillor than met the eye.

'Sorry,' he said. 'I'll cut out the sarcasm from now on.'

'Good,' Lowry said crisply. 'Now let's get down to business, shall we? I've been looking at these overtime requests that you've submitted, and they really are outrageous, you know.'

'I disagree,' Woodend said. 'There's some

kind of nutter on the loose out there, so the streets have to be patrolled.'

'You don't actually know whether or not he's going to strike again, do you?' Lowry asked.

'I know,' Woodend said firmly.

'How?'

'I can feel it.'

Lowry laughed. 'That would be the famous Woodend "gut feeling", would it? I've heard about that.'

'Then you'll also have heard that it rarely lets me down.'

'Interesting that you should use the word "rarely",' Lowry mused. 'I take that to mean that this gut instinct of yours is not *quite* as infallible as you sometimes like to give the impression it is.'

'It's failed me a few times,' Woodend admitted.

'And even if your feeling is correct, there's no saying that the killer will strike again tonight, is there? He might wait a week. Or a month. Or even a year.'

'It won't be as long as a month,' Woodend said.

'That's something else you just *know*, is it?'

'Yes.'

'Then let's say that he waits three weeks. Do you expect to keep all that extra manpower on the streets for a whole three weeks?'

'Yes.'

Lowry shook his head. 'It simply can't be done,' he said. 'The ratepayers would never stand for it. They elected me to reduce the rates, not drive them up to new record highs.'

'And, of course, there are municipal elections coming up soon,' Woodend mused.

'What exactly are you suggesting?' Lowry asked angrily.

'I'm suggestin' there's municipal elections comin' up soon,' Woodend replied.

'I want to keep police costs down,' Lowry said. 'I can do that without your help, but it would be easier if you cooperated.'

'What you really mean is that your committee might think twice about takin' the course of action you were recommendin' if I was known to be strongly opposed to it.'

'Well, exactly,' Lowry said, as if he were pleased that the rather slow chief inspector had finally grasped the point. 'It would certainly be to your advantage to work with me, instead of against me.'

'Would it?' Woodend asked, and those who knew him well would have detected the dangerous edge creeping into his voice. 'In what way?'

'For starters, it would ensure that you kept your job.'

'You mean that if I don't become your monkey, you'll get me fired?'

Lowry laughed. 'No, no, Chief Inspector, you've got things completely the wrong way round. It's that fool Marlowe who wants to get you fired, but he wouldn't dare push for it if I were on your side. Now wouldn't you like to have that kind of protection?'

Woodend shrugged. 'I've put in a good few years' service. I could live off my pension if I retired now.'

'You probably could,' Lowry agreed. 'But there wouldn't be much cash left over for extras, would there?'

Woodend shrugged again. 'I've never been one for drinkin' pink champagne out of chorus girls' slippers.'

'Of course you're not. But there's your daughter Annie to consider, isn't there?'

'What do you mean?'

'She's just graduated from nursing college, hasn't she? She'll be looking to buy a place of her own, and it would be nice if you could give her a hand with the deposit – but you won't be able to do that on a policeman's pension.'

'Now listen to me—' Woodend began.

'And then there's Joan, your wife,' Lowry interrupted him. 'She had a mild heart attack in Spain, a couple of years back. Of course, we all pray she won't have another one, but if she does, wouldn't it be nice to know that as far as treatment went, she was being rushed to the front of the queue?'

'Don't threaten me, you bastard!' Woodend growled.

'I'd be threatening you if I'd said I'd do my best to ensure that she was kept at the *back* of the queue,' Lowry said mildly. 'What I'm offering you is something much more positive. And if I could give you a piece of advice, Chief Inspector,' he continued, his voice hardening, 'you should never forget that while I'm a reasonable man who always tries to reach a consensus, I'm also the chairman of the Police Authority, and, while I am wearing that particular hat, I will simply not tolerate the kind of offensive remark you have just directed at me.'

Woodend stood up. 'If you don't want to be called a bastard, then don't behave like one,' he said. 'An' here's a bit of advice for you – don't try to block the overtime, because if you do, I'll be on the blower to all the local papers before you can say "landslide electoral defeat".'

And then, without waiting for a reply, he marched furiously to the door.

Woodend was back at his own desk. In the ashtray in front of him lay the remains of three Capstan Full Strength cigarettes, which he had not so much smoked as crushed between his agitated fingers.

'The man's a real bastard, Monika,' he told Paniatowski, across the desk. 'A complete bloody arsehole.'

'Yes, sir, I rather gathered that was what you thought of him the *first* three times you said it,' Paniatowski replied. 'But however much of a bastard he is, it wasn't your wisest move to tell him so to his face.'

'He knew about Annie, and he knew about Joan,' Woodend ranted. 'He was using my *family* to put the screws on me.'

'It's a despicable trick, if that's what he was doing,' Paniatowski agreed, 'but even so—'

'Two can play at that game,' Woodend interrupted her. 'I want all the dirt you can dig up on him, so that the next time he comes after me, I'll have something to hit back with.'

'That's a dangerous game to play,' Pania-towski cautioned.

'Maybe – but I'm not the one who started it,' Woodend countered.

'And there's always the very real possibility that there's no dirt on him *to* dig up.'

'There's dirt,' Woodend said firmly. 'I can smell it on the bastard. I can almost see it oozing out from under his fingernails.'

'I'm not sure I feel entirely comfortable with the assignment, sir,' Paniatowski said. 'I am *supposed* to be working on a murder inquiry.'

'In this case, you can't separate the two things,' Woodend told her. 'If Lowry has his way, we won't have the resources to investigate the murder.' He paused, and took a deep breath. 'Look, I know it's a shitty job, and normally I wouldn't ask you to do it,' he said. 'But what choice do I have?'

'You could put Bob on it,' Paniatowski replied.

'Could I?' Woodend wondered. 'Could I really? So tell me, if you were in my shoes, would you put Bob Rutter in charge of it?'

'I'm *not* in your shoes,' Paniatowski replied defensively.

'Which is as good a way of not answerin' the question as any, I suppose,' Woodend said. 'But let's be honest, Monika – at least with each other. Given the way Bob's behavin' at the moment, neither of us would put him in charge of a chip shop.'

Seven

Modern wardrobes were constructed of crisp, light, white wood, but the one in Beresford's bedroom was heavy, clumsy and coffin-brown coloured. It had been bought in the early years of his parents' marriage, and, for that reason, he sometimes viewed it as a time machine which transported him back to a happier time, when his father was still alive and his mother still had her mind. But no such thoughts were entering his head at the moment. In fact, most of his thoughts were concentrated *on* his head – or, to be more accurate, on that portion of his head which had once had hair.

Staring at himself in the wardrobe's full-length mirror, he could not quite get used to the change that the close-cropped haircut had brought about in his appearance. He no longer looked like the rising young detective constable he had come – with Woodend's encouragement – to think of himself as. Instead, he was looking at the face of the sort of young thug who shouts insults at ordinary people as they walk through the shopping centre.

He stepped back, to take a look at the rest of his disguise, which consisted of a buttoned-up flannel shirt, straight-legged jeans, and heavy boots with steel toecaps. He was also wearing braces, which made his shoulders itch and – since the jeans were perfectly capable of staying up without any help – served no useful purpose. Still, he couldn't remove them even though he wanted to, he told himself. The braces *had to* stay – because they were part of the uniform.

As he continued to stand there, wondering if he could really pull the deception off, he became aware that he was not alone, and turning around, found his mother was standing in the doorway.

Mrs Beresford was watching him with a strange, puzzled expression on her face – but that was no more than par for the course, Beresford reminded himself.

'I ... don't remember seeing those clothes before,' his mother said. 'Did I buy them for you...' She paused, as if trying to grasp one of those pieces of information that were constantly slipping from her mind. 'Did I buy them for you, *Colin*,' she continued triumphantly.

'No, Mum, you didn't,' Beresford said gently.

'And didn't you...' his mother asked, grappling for more lost information, '...didn't you used to be a policeman?'

'I still am a policeman, Mum.'

'I don't remember policemen dressing like that when I was younger,' Mrs Beresford said.

Her son sighed. He could explain to her that he was going under cover, he supposed, but he doubted if she would be able to grasp the concept.

'Times change, Mum,' he said.

'Yes, they do,' Mrs Beresford agreed, sighing in turn. 'And never for the better.'

Some of the tramps had been questioned and released, but, Woodend noted, there was still a group of around a dozen of them sitting in the basement of police headquarters and waiting for their turn to come.

'A *group*?' he repeated to himself.

Yes, that was what he'd just labelled them – but he'd been wrong to.

Take most bodies of people waiting for something – a bus queue, for example – and the members of it would strike up small, superficial conversations with those around them. Usually, they would complain about the weather – or the infrequent bus service, or the council's seeming inability to collect dustbins on time, or what rubbish they were showing on television these days – then round it all off with a vague hope that things would improve in the future.

It was a habit born from custom to act in this way. It sometimes felt *almost* like a legal obligation.

But custom and obligation were not binding on these tramps. They had no interest in the people around them. Each one sat alone, a small island protected from the rest of the world by its indifference to him, and his indifference to it.

But there was one thing they did all have in common, the chief inspector thought – they didn't seem particularly concerned by how long it was taking them to get back on the streets.

And why should they? The basement was

warm and dry, there were free cigarettes and cups of tea being handed out. What more could they want?

Drink! That's what they could want.

Most of them had probably already been drunk when they had been collected in the sweep, but were now in the process of sobering up. And being sober would make them – paradoxically – more difficult to interview. Because while it was true that their minds would be clearer, this new clarity would be focused on only one thing – getting their next fix of mind-dulling meths!

All of which meant that the whole process needed to be speeded up, and if Bob Rutter needed reminding of that – which he *shouldn't* – now was the time to do it.

'Which interview room is Inspector Rutter in at the moment?' Woodend asked the WPC who'd been put in charge of watching the men and serving them endless mugs of tea.

'He's not in any of them at the moment, sir,' the constable replied. 'He was here up until a few minutes ago, but now he's gone.'

'Gone?' Woodend repeated, incredulously. 'Where to?'

'He didn't specify exactly. He just said he had some personal business to deal with.'

Personal business to deal with!

You just didn't *have* personal business in a murder inquiry, where the first twenty-four hours could be crucial!

You didn't have any life outside the case!

Yet despite the bollocking Woodend had given his inspector earlier, it was clear that Rutter had forgotten – or decided to ignore – what was the cornerstone of any investigation.

They said there was no point in having a dog and barking yourself, Woodend thought, but what else could you do when the dog in question had buggered off?

'Are all the interview rooms bein' used?' he asked.

'Two of them are,' the WPC said. 'But the third one, the one that Inspector Rutter was using before he...'

'Went off to deal with his personal business!' Woodend supplied.

'Yes, sir. That one's free now.'

Woodend walked over to the area where the tramps were sitting, and picked one of them at random. 'If you'd like to follow me, sir, we can have our little talk an' then you can be on your way,' he told the man.

The discreet coughing sound, coming from somewhere behind her, made Dr Shastri look up from the dissecting table on which the victim of a recent road accident lay, and when she did so, she saw Bob Rutter standing in the doorway.

'My dear Inspector, what a true delight to see you,' she said, with her customary breeziness. 'But what is the reason for this unexpected call? Have I been negligent in my duties? Is there some piece of information which the wise and good Chief Inspector Woodend urgently needs for his investigation, but which I have somehow failed to supply him with?'

'No, no, nothing like that,' Rutter said, in a

71

manner which seemed to Shastri to be slightly awkward. 'The fact is, I'm here for a piece of advice.'

Dr Shastri laughed. 'If it is a medical matter – especially one concerning cadavers – then you have undoubtedly come to the right place,' she said. 'If, on the other hand, you require instruction in some other area of expertise, on how to build a dry-stone wall or re-plaster your kitchen, for example, I suspect you had better look elsewhere.'

'It *is* a medical matter,' Rutter said. 'I was wondering if you could recommend a good doctor to me.'

'But surely you have a doctor already,' Shastri said, puzzled.

'I do,' Rutter agreed. 'But he happens to be the same doctor most of my colleagues use.'

'I do not see that as a problem,' Dr Shastri said, her bewilderment growing. 'Anything that passes between you will be in complete confidence.'

'Yes, but however good the intentions are, things might still slip out,' Rutter said, showing increasing difficulty. 'One of my colleagues might see me entering or leaving the surgery. Or perhaps Doc Taylor might say to one of them, "You should have a full medical check-up, like Bob Rutter had." He wouldn't *mean* to be giving anything away, you see, but that's just what he would be doing.'

'You want a full medical check-up?'

'Yes.'

'But you don't want any of your colleagues to

know that you've had it?'

'That's correct. At least, I don't want them to know about it just for the moment.'

'Might I ask why?' Dr Shastri said.

'Because they might start wondering *why* I've had the check-up.'

As, indeed, I am now, Dr Shastri thought.

'Are you worried that something might be seriously wrong with you?' she asked solicitously. 'Is that why you want to keep the whole thing a secret?'

'Oh God, no, it's nothing at all like that,' Rutter said. 'I have the odd ache and pain – that happens when you get past thirty, and work the hours I do – but, in general, I feel as fit as a fiddle.'

'Well, then?'

'I just think that, before taking any important step, it's the responsible thing to do.'

'I see,' Shastri said – though she didn't.

'I had a medical just before I married Maria, and—' Rutter began, before stopping abruptly again.

'And...?' Dr Shastri prodded.

Rutter grinned sheepishly. 'Is anything I say to *you* confidential?'

'As a doctor, I am only required to keep my lips sealed on medical matters. But as a friend, and I do like to think of myself as a friend...'

'You are. You *are!*'

'...you can rely on my absolute discretion.'

Relief flooded Rutter's face, and it was plain to Shastri that he had been keeping something important bottled up inside himself, and that she had just given him permission to release it.

'Well, the simple truth is that I'm thinking of getting married *again*,' Rutter said.

'How wonderful!' Dr Shastri exclaimed.

'You think so?'

'Indeed I do,' said the doctor, who had heard all the rumours about his affair with Monika, and, liking them both, had been secretly hoping for some time that they would get back together again. 'And I'm sure Sergeant Paniatowski will make an absolutely beautiful bride.'

Then she saw the look of surprise – almost of horror – which came to Rutter's face, and found herself wishing she were as dead as the body on the table.

It wasn't really necessary for Rutter to say, 'It's not Monika I'm thinking of marrying.'

But he said it anyway.

Eight

Monika Paniatowski absolutely loathed this new assignment that Woodend had given her. The job she'd originally signed on for involved catching criminals, not doing background checks into people with no police record in the hope of finding some *hint* of criminal activity.

But Charlie was right, as he usually was. Tel Lowry was attempting to impede the investigation. That made him the enemy – and to fight back, you needed to be properly armed.

And so she had spent an hour or so going through old copies of the local newspapers, putting some flesh on the bones of Lowry's personal history.

She'd learned that the factory had been founded by his father, and that while his brother, Barclay, had studied engineering at college and then obediently followed the old man into the family business, Tel had preferred to travel a different route, and, in 1950, had joined the air force as a helicopter pilot trainee.

He'd seen active service in the Malaya Emergency in the early 50s, where his helicopter had taken a direct hit. In the crash landing that followed, it was generally agreed, it had been a miracle he wasn't killed. He'd been awarded a medal for courage under fire, promoted to the rank of flight lieutenant, and posted back to Britain. It was while he was serving in his new post at RAF Abingdon that he'd received the news of the tragic accident which had occurred at home.

The accident was big news in the *Whitebridge Evening Post*, and the centre of the front page was dominated by a large picture of a mangled Rolls-Royce. There'd been two people in the car when it had spun out of control and crashed into a tree. One of them, Lowry's father, had been killed outright, while the other, his brother Barclay, had had to be permanently hospitalized.

Tel Lowry had resigned his commission immediately.

'It is with great regret that I have done so,' he'd told the *Post*. *'The air force has been my life, and I had hoped to continue serving my country in it for many more years to come. But now a new responsibility has been thrust upon me, and I cannot escape it. Lowry's is, and always has been, a Whitebridge company, and I could not contemplate letting it fall into the hands of outsiders.'*

Even then, he sounded like a politician, Paniatowski thought. And perhaps that had been deliberate. Perhaps, once he'd lost his opportunity to rise in the air force, he'd determined to rise in local government. But that merely made him ambitious – not criminal. And he was a war hero – even if the war in which he'd been heroic had been much smaller than the one in which Charlie Woodend had served.

76

If she went to the boss with nothing more than this, he would throw a fit, Paniatowski told herself. And so, with great reluctance, she was going to have to dig somewhere else for dirt.

The moment he returned to headquarters, Bob Rutter found himself summoned to the chief inspector's office, and he had barely time to close the door behind him before his boss launched into his attack.

'What the hell are you playin' at, Inspector?' Woodend demanded. 'This is a murder case, an' you're supposed to be one of the people leadin' it. Which means that you don't go skivin' off whenever you feel the inclination – you stay on the soddin' job until it's finished.'

'Can I say something, sir?' Rutter asked.

'No, you bloody well can't,' Woodend told him. 'At least, not until you've heard everythin' that *I've* got to say.'

'Go ahead, then,' Rutter told him.

'I don't *need* your permission!' Woodend exploded. 'Listen, Bob,' he continued, calming down a little, 'I know things have been bloody rough for you, an' I could have understood it if you'd said you couldn't continue doin' the same job you'd done before Maria's death. But you didn't say that, did you?'

'No,' Rutter agreed. 'I didn't.'

'What you *did* say was that you wanted your old job back – very badly. So I gave you the chance. I let you in on the Haverton Camp case even before you'd been properly signed off the sick – which was a pretty big risk for me.'

'I know it was,' Rutter told him. 'And I'm grateful.'

'For a while, I thought it was workin' out,' Woodend said. 'You were a bit wobbly on a couple of cases, but, on the whole, you did well.'

'Except that you'd much rather I hadn't got involved with Liz Driver,' Rutter said.

'Elizabeth Driver has nothin' to do with this,' Woodend said, his anger returning.

'Hasn't she, sir?'

'No, she bloody hasn't. What we're talkin' about here is your performance – an' it simply isn't good enough.' Woodend paused. 'You've been almost like a son to me, Bob, an' if I wasn't a northern workin'-class male, who doesn't go in for any such soppiness, I might even go so far as to say I loved you. But I love my job, an' all, an' I need to have people workin' with me who I can rely on. So I'm goin' to have to let you go, Bob. There's no choice in the matter. I'm goin' to have you transferred to some other, less stressful duties.'

Rutter said nothing for perhaps half a minute, then he asked, 'Can I speak *now*?'

Woodend sighed. 'Yes, you can speak now,' he agreed.

'I know who the murdered man is,' Rutter said.

'You know *what*?'

'A couple of hours ago, I found myself wondering if he'd keep whatever valuables he had on him while he slept. And I decided he probably wouldn't, because when you're asleep, you're at your most vulnerable. So what would he have done with them?'

'You tell me,' Woodend said.

'I thought it likely he'd have hidden them, but that his hiding place would probably be somewhere close to where he dossed down for the night. So I went back to the old mill, and looked around. There was a loose brick in the wall, close to where the body was found, and when I took it out, I found these behind it.'

He took a clear plastic envelope out of his pocket, and laid it on the desk. Inside it, Woodend could see a battered wallet, two faded photographs of a woman, and a dog-eared driving licence.

'His name's Philip Turner,' Rutter said. 'He comes from Manchester, and he was fifty-one years old when he was murdered.'

'Is that what you've been doin' since you left headquarters?' Woodend asked. 'Looking for his personal possessions?'

'Yes,' Rutter said.

'Apart from the time I took to visit Dr Shastri, and make an appointment with the doctor she recommended,' he added mentally.

'But the WPC said you'd gone off on personal business,' Woodend told him.

'Perhaps she's right, and that *is* what I told her,' Rutter conceded. 'Possibly I said it because I thought that was easier than explaining what I was actually going to do, or maybe I just said the first thing that came into my head. To tell you the truth, my mind was so wrapped up in the case that I've no idea *what* I said.'

Woodend's face was filled with remorse. 'I'm sorry, lad,' he said.

'Forget it, sir,' Rutter said awkwardly.

'No, I won't forget it,' Woodend replied. 'I should have trusted you. God knows, you've given me reason enough to in the past. An' there was me talkin' about how I'd gone out on a limb for you, an' forgettin' how many times you'd done the same thing for me.'

'Water under the bridge,' Rutter said. He forced himself to smile. 'If it'll make you feel any better, you can buy all my ale at the victory celebration when we've solved this case.'

'I'll buy all your bloody ale for a month,' Woodend promised.

'Then you'd better think about taking out a second mortgage on your cottage,' Rutter said, and though the smile was still in place, it was an effort of will to keep it there. He glanced down at his watch. 'I'd better get back to work.'

'Aye,' Woodend agreed. 'We *both* need to get back to work.'

As he was walking down the steps to the basement, Rutter found himself being assailed by a storm of mixed emotions. On the one hand, he felt guilty about lying to his boss, even if it was only a *partial* lie. On the other, he felt relief that the idea of searching for the dead tramp's possessions had come to him as he was leaving the police morgue, because if it hadn't – if he'd come back to headquarters empty-handed – he had no doubt in his mind that Woodend would have carried out his threat, and had him transferred.

But would it have really mattered if that *had*

happened? Though he'd rejected Liz's idea of working for her when she'd first put it to him, it was now starting to sound more and more appealing. If he took the job, there would be no more guilt – no more attempting to perform the delicate balancing act between what he *wanted* to do and what he *should* do. He and Liz would travel the country together, covering murder cases. Instead of being harassed by the press, as he was now, he would almost be *part* of the press – and every night would be spent with Liz.

It would mean making other arrangements for Louisa, of course, but she would benefit in all kinds of ways from the extra money his new job would be bringing in.

And so what if taking the job meant abandoning his ideals and sinking down into the gutter? Hadn't he *already* done enough good deeds to justify one life? And there was no doubt about it, the gutter was beginning to look like a very attractive place.

Councillor Polly Johnson JP hadn't had much time for the golf-club bar while her husband was alive, and was not exactly over-fond of it now. Nevertheless, she had developed the habit of dropping in for a drink on the way home from the magistrates' court, because there were sometimes people there who she found mildly amusing – and because anything was better than going back to an empty house.

Since she hated the idea of sitting alone at a table, she normally took a seat at the bar, despite the fact that the bar stools had been designed for tall men with long calves, not short women with stumpy little legs. Still, she had perfected the art of making the act of climbing on to the stool look easy, though she was convinced that some night, when she had had one drink too many, she would come tumbling off it with a lack of dignity totally unbecoming in a magistrate.

She had only just completed her ascent of the seat when she felt a light tap on her shoulder and turned to find Councillor Tel Lowry standing there. She was surprised, because though they were both councillors, and both sat on the Police Authority, their relationship could rarely be described as warm, and often reached the intensity of an Arctic chill.

Lowry smiled winningly, and said, 'Buy you a drink, Polly?'

'I've already got one coming,' Councillor Johnson told him.

'Didn't hear you order it,' Lowry said.

'That's because I didn't,' Polly replied. 'Since Jack is a bar steward par excellence, there's no need to. The moment I walk through the door he springs to my aid.'

Lowry turned to look at the steward, and saw he was indeed pouring a Scotch whisky into a glass half-filled with ice cubes.

'Put it on my bill,' Lowry called out, and the steward nodded.

'That's very kind of you,' Polly said, wishing she'd ordered a single malt rather than a humble blend. 'But to what do I owe this sudden burst of generosity?'

Or to put it another way, she thought, if I'm not

expected to pay for my drink with money, how *am* I expected to pay for it?

'Terrible thing, this tramp being burned alive,' Lowry said.

'Terrible,' Polly agreed.

'But I still think we're in danger of overreacting to it,' Lowry continued.

'Really?' Polly asked.

She took a sip of whisky, and wished again that she had asked for a malt.

'Nearly every policeman in Whitebridge will be on the streets tonight. I can't tell you how much that is going to cost us in overtime.'

'You don't need to tell me,' Polly Johnson countered. 'I've seen the balance sheets. I can work it out for myself.'

'Well, there you are, then,' Lowry said. 'And the problem is, you see, that if we use up vast amounts of the police budget on this case, where will we find the resources when we have to deal with a really serious crime?'

'You mean that you don't think burning someone alive *is* a serious crime?' Polly asked.

'Oh, it's *very* serious,' Lowry said hastily. 'And I'm hopeful that the police will make an arrest soon. But, when all is said and done, our main responsibility is to protect our ratepayers – and tramps don't pay rates.'

'True enough,' Polly agreed.

'You'd think the police would see that,' Lowry ploughed on. 'Indeed, some of them do. Henry Marlowe's very sound on the subject. But there's one particular chief inspector who's being very difficult.'

Polly chuckled. 'That would be Charlie Wood-end,' she said.

'How ... how do you know that?'

'Easy. Charlie's made a *career* out of being difficult.'

'You know the man socially, do you?' Lowry asked, sounding a little troubled by the news.

'Not socially, only professionally,' Polly Johnson said.

Lowry visibly relaxed.

Which was a big mistake, Polly thought – because professional bonds, if they were strong ones, could be as binding as love. And her bonds with Woodend *were* strong, since twice before – after the Dugdale's Farm murder and the Mary Thomas case – she had trusted him enough to go out on a limb, and in both those cases her trust had been more than justified.

'I was hoping for your support in—' Lowry began.

'You won't get it,' Polly Johnson said.

'You don't even know what I'm going to ask you yet,' Lowry protested.

'You're going to ask me to help you nobble Cloggin'-it Charlie. Well, you're wasting your time.'

'We won the last election on a promise to reduce council spending,' Lowry pointed out.

'You and your party won it on that promise,' Polly countered. 'I'm an independent.'

'Even so...'

'You've seen the same public-opinion polls that I have, haven't you?' asked Polly, who was really starting to enjoy herself. 'Your party's support's down, and you personally are losing ground to Councillor Scranton, who, if I've heard right, intends to stand in your own ward.'

'You've heard right,' Lowry said glumly.

'All of which means, as I see it, that you have to fulfil nearly all your pledges, or you'll be out on your ear next time.'

'Every party experiences a dip in popularity mid-term,' Lowry said sulkily. 'It doesn't mean that on the day...'

'So in order to protect your seat on the council – and so you can continue to be a big fish in what's really a very small and murky pond – you're prepared to leave these *non-ratepayers* unprotected, are you?'

'As I explained to Chief Inspector Woodend, there's no guarantee that the killer will strike again soon, if ever,' Lowry said.

'And, as I'm sure Cloggin'-it Charlie explained to you, there's no guarantee that he *won't*,' Polly Johnson countered.

'Not much of a story at all, so far,' Elizabeth Driver said, over the phone, to her editor in London. 'The burning-alive bit of it is great, of course, but it's a pity that it couldn't have been someone more sympathetic who got fried. I mean to say, who gives a damn about a sweaty tramp?'

'There's a nice juicy murder in Hampshire I'm thinking of sending you to cover,' the editor said with some relish. 'They've been finding body parts all over the place, but so far they haven't located the head.'

'I'd rather stay here,' Driver said.

'No doubt you would,' the editor agreed. 'But you see, that's not the way it works. I'm the one who pays the piper, so I'm the one who gets to say what tune is played.'

'You might miss a top-notch story if you *do* pull me out,' Driver cautioned. 'After all, the great Chief Inspector Woodend could make an arrest in a day or two – and even if the victim isn't interesting, the murderer could be.'

The editor sniffed. 'More than likely, it'll turn out to be the work of some local yobbo,' he said.

More than likely it would, Driver thought. But she wasn't ready to leave Whitebridge yet. In fact, there were several reasons to stay.

She counted them off on the fingers of her right hand. Her book was nearly completed, and this was the ideal place in which to put the finishing touches to it. She needed to finally work out what her future relationship with Bob Rutter was going to be – and that was easier to work out in Whitebridge, too. And most important of all, she needed to get the town – and especially the town's police – firmly into the public mind through some scandal or other, so that when the book did eventually come out, it would have even more impact. She was not quite sure how she would achieve this third objective yet, but she was confident that something would occur to her in the next few days.

'Are you still there?' her editor asked, impatiently.

'If you let me stay, I'll get you a tremendous headline within the next seventy-two hours,'

Driver said.

The editor sniffed again. 'And that's a promise, is it?' he asked.

'It is,' Driver confirmed.

'Well, it's a promise you'd better keep,' the editor said, 'because one thing you should always bear in mind, Liz, is that you're only as big as your last big story.'

Nine

'Am I speaking to Detective Inspector Charles Woodend?' asked a woman's voice at the other end of the telephone line.

'You are,' Woodend confirmed.

'I'm an anonymous informant,' the woman said.

Woodend grinned. 'Are you, indeed? Well, has anybody ever told you, *Anonymous Informant*, that you sound just like Councillor Polly Johnson, JP?'

The woman laughed. 'Damn it! Rumbled!' she exclaimed. Then, in a more serious voice, she continued, 'You've got trouble, Charlie, and it's in the form of Councillor Lowry.'

'I know all about that,' Woodend said. 'He wants to cut back on overtime, an' I don't. But how did you find out? Has he been tryin' to nobble you?'

'Well, *of course* he's been trying to nobble me,' Polly Johnson said, speaking slowly now, as if she'd just realized she was addressing a simpleton. 'And I told him where he can stick it. But there are other councillors on the authority – especially the ones with small majorities – who might be more than willing to listen to him.'

'Thanks for the warnin',' Woodend said.

'Watch your back, Charlie,' Polly Johnson advised.

'I will,' Woodend told her. 'In fact, I've already sent my sergeant out to collect a bit of body armour.'

When Pogo had left police headquarters, he had determined to put the offer that the blonde sergeant had made to him firmly out of his mind. It was too late to start getting involved in life again, he argued to himself. *Far* too late. He was drifting slowly into oblivion – and that was just fine with him.

And yet, despite his own wishes, Monika Paniatowski's words kept drifting back to him.

'It's the chance to be useful again – the chance to earn your own respect and the respect of others.'

She should never have said it, he thought – should never have reminded him of a time when his opinion was sought and his judgement was valued.

And yet ... and yet what was wrong with the idea of travelling a little way along the road she'd suggested? It wasn't a commitment, it was an experiment, and if he didn't like it, he could always turn back.

'Give it a shot, Percy,' he said aloud.

And then he realized that, for the first time in a long while, he'd called himself by his real name.

The pub opposite Lowry Engineering was called, logically enough, the Engineer's Arms, and by the time the workers knocked off for the day, Monika Paniatowski had already positioned herself at a table in the bar.

She was hoping for information. Useful information. The sort of information that Elizabeth Driver would have gleefully splashed across the front page of her disgusting newspaper.

'Factory owner's three-in-a-bed romp!' would do nicely, she thought.

As would 'Factory owner raids workers' pension fund!'

It would, strictly speaking, be blackmail to use such information against Lowry, of course, but blackmail only in the interests of justice – blackmail to protect the community.

The workers began to pour into the bar. They looked as if they were dying for a drink, and after eight hours' hard work, they probably were.

Paniatowski studied the men, wondering which one she should approach. Then it occurred to her that it might be more interesting – and more productive – to wait and see which of them would approach *her*.

It didn't take long for an approach to happen. As soon as they paid for their pints, three of the men started to make their way towards her table.

Paniatowski studied them, and quickly assigned them into rough – but useful – categories. The one leading the group had carefully quiffed hair, and though he was wearing a boiler suit, he *moved* like a man decked out in his best dancing clothes. He was the Romeo of the group, and the others were only there as padding – a necessary

90

backcloth for his performance. The second man had pale well-meaning eyes – and she instantly labelled him the Nice Guy. The third was red-faced, with a mouth which seemed to be permanently set in a look of disapproval – the Complainer.

Romeo reached the table first, and said, 'Do you mind if we sit down with you, love?'

Paniatowski glanced around the bar, making it plain to him that she was well aware there were still plenty of *empty* tables to be had, then she smiled and said, 'Be my guest.'

The men sat quickly, before she changed her mind, and Romeo said, 'What's a pretty girl like you doin' in a place like this?'

'I'm doing research,' Paniatowski said.

'Are you? That is interestin'. Into what?'

'Into pick-up lines.'

'I beg your pardon?'

'I wanted to find out if there was one man left in the whole country who still used that corny "pretty-girl-place-like-this" line. And apparently, there is.'

Nice Man chuckled, a sour grin filled the Complainer's face and Romeo said, 'No offence meant, love.'

'And none taken,' Paniatowski assured him. 'I'm Monika.'

'I'm Jack,' Romeo said. 'An' this is Teddy,' indicating the Nice Man, 'an' Archie,' pointing to the Complainer.

'Pleased to meet you,' Paniatowski said. 'Do you all work at the factory across the road?'

'We do,' Jack confirmed.

'What's it like?'

'It's a man's life,' Jack said, in a tone that was half-mocking and half-not.

'It's hot, sweaty, tedious work,' said Teddy. 'But we can't really complain – it puts food on the table.'

'And who owns the factory?' Monika asked.

'Well, it's called Lowry Engineering, so chances are it's owned by a feller called Lowry,' Archie said.

Teddy clicked his tongue reprovingly. 'There's no need for that kind of sarcasm,' he said. 'The lass asked a civil question, an' she deserves a civil answer.' He turned his attention to Paniatowski. 'The boss is called Tel Lowry, Monika.'

'Councillor Lowry?' Paniatowski asked, sounding surprised.

'That's right.'

'I saw him on the local news once. What's he like?'

'He's like all bosses,' Archie said. 'Spends most of his time talkin' about his concern for his workers, when the only thing he's really concerned about is Tel Lowry.'

'That's not quite fair,' Jack said. 'He's a better boss than most.'

'An' unlike most bosses, he's not frightened of gettin' his hands dirty,' Teddy added. 'Do you know that when he took over the company he knew nothin' about engineerin'. Now he's got a degree in it – an' he earned that degree by studyin' in his free time, when he'd already put in a day's work at the factory.'

'You make him sound like a saint,' Archie

92

grumbled, 'but the truth is, we hardly see him at all these days.'

'Maybe so, but that's not because he's sailin' round the Med on a private yacht, livin' the life of Reilly, now is it?' Jack countered. 'The reason we don't see him is because he's devotin' all his energy to local politics.'

'I suppose it's all right for them as can afford it,' Archie said.

'If I'm remembering correctly, Councillor Lowry's not married, is he?' Paniatowski said.

Jack nodded. 'No, he isn't.'

'Lives with his mother,' Archie said. 'A *proper* mummy's boy.'

'Now I find that *very* hard to believe,' Paniatowski said. 'He looks to me like the kind of man who'd be having affairs left, right and centre – and a lot of them with *married* women.'

'Well, there's been rumours enough,' Archie said. 'He had this secretary once, who was married to one of the shop-floor foremen, and—'

'You seem very interested in the boss,' Jack said, and for the first time there was a hint of suspicion in his voice.

Even in the light of that comment, it might be possible to squeeze a little more information on Lowry from these men, Monika thought. But it wouldn't be a good idea. In truth, she'd pushed it as far as she dared – perhaps further than she *should have*. Any minute now, they'd start asking who *she* was, which was a short step from one of them – probably Archie – telling Lowry about the encounter. And then the fat *would* really be in the fire.

Besides, this job was leaving a bad taste in her mouth, and though she agreed with Woodend that it might be useful to get the dirt on Lowry, what she really wanted to do was put some flesh on the bones of the *real* investigation.

'I said, you seem very interested in the boss,' Jack repeated.

Paniatowski laughed lightly. 'Do I really? Perhaps I fancy him, and didn't even realize it.'

'There's no accountin' for taste,' Archie said. 'But I'll tell you who I definitely *didn't* fancy – the man I saw standing on a soapbox outside the factory gates, when I drove past earlier.'

'That would be Councillor Scranton,' Teddy said.

'Does he work in the factory as well?' Paniatowski asked.

'Ron Scranton doesn't work in the factory or anywhere else,' Archie said with disdain. 'He's never done a hard day's work in his life.'

'Really?' Paniatowski said sceptically.

'Really,' Archie repeated.

'He surely must do *something* to earn a living.'

'He *calls* himself the regional organizer of the British Patriotic Party,' Archie said, 'so I expect they're the ones payin' his wages. But if they're givin' him more than a couple of bob a week, they must be soft in the head.'

'Now you're not bein' fair, Archie,' Jack said. 'However you feel about him personally, you have to admit he's got some good ideas, don't you?'

'I suppose so,' Archie said.

'What do you think about Scranton, Teddy?'

Paniatowski asked.

Teddy seemed torn between his natural good nature and telling the truth as he saw it. 'I don't like him, either,' he said finally. 'But somebody's got to keep the Pakis and tramps down, haven't they?'

Pogo had been studying the other tramp for some time. The man was standing, with casual nonchalance, against a lamppost which was situated a few yards from the back entrance of the market cafe.

Pogo understood his game, having played it often enough himself. The tramp was trying to pretend that he had no interest at all in the bins, because if the owner of the cafe realized what he was after, he'd drive him away – and then any chance he had of picking up some tempting scraps would be gone.

He approached the other tramp cautiously, because he might – like many tramps – be of a nervous disposition. And he might – like many tramps – carry a knife or a razor.

The tramp spotted him. 'I was here first,' he said. 'And that makes it my pitch.'

'I know the rules,' Pogo said quietly.

'And don't go thinking you'll get my leftovers, because there won't be any,' the tramp warned him.

'Don't want leftovers tonight,' Pogo said. 'I've got money.'

The other tramp's eyes narrowed. 'How much?' he demanded.

'Half a crown.'

'You could buy two bottles of meths with that.'

'I could,' Pogo agreed. 'Or I could go into a proper pub and have a real drink – if I could find one that would serve me. But instead of doing either of those things, I thought I'd blow the money on a couple of bacon sandwiches.'

'What do you want *two* bacon sandwiches for?' the other tramp wondered.

'One for me, and one for you,' Pogo told him.

'I don't know you, do I?' the other tramp asked suspiciously.

'No,' Pogo agreed.

And it wouldn't make any difference even if you did, he thought. Tramps don't share things with their friends. Tramps don't *have* any friends.

'So if I don't know you, what's your game?' the other tramp asked.

'I want information, and I'm prepared to pay for it,' Pogo told him.

'What kind of information?'

'I'm trying to find out who set that bloke on fire last night.'

'Why?'

'Because I might be marked down as the next victim, and I want to know what to look out for.'

Any other explanation would have left the tramp unconvinced, but self-preservation was something he understood.

'And that's worth a bacon sandwich, is it?' he asked.

'Yes,' Pogo agreed.

'How do I know I can trust you?' the other tramp wondered. 'I might tell you everything I

96

know, and all you have to say, to avoid paying me, is that it's not worth anything.'

How did we ever get to this state? Pogo wondered. At what point did we start to mistrust everything our fellow man said or promised?

But he knew well enough what the answer to that was in his own particular case.

'I'll buy you a sandwich whatever you tell me,' he promised.

The tramp thought about it. 'All right,' he agreed. 'There was this lad.'

'What lad?'

'Young. He had very short hair. Almost like he'd shaved his head. And tattoos on his arms.'

'And what did he do?'

'Told me I was making the town untidy. Told me I should think about moving on.'

'Nothing unusual about that,' Pogo said. 'You should be used to abuse by now.'

'But it went further than that,' the other tramp persisted. 'He said if I *didn't* move on, he'd see to me.'

'How?'

'He said the best way to get rid of louses was to *burn* them out.'

'When was this?'

'Last week sometime. Didn't think any more about it until I heard what happened last night.'

'Did you tell the police about this?' Pogo asked.

'Course I didn't. Don't tell the police nothing.'

'What I don't understand,' Pogo said, 'is why, after all that, you're still here.'

'It's hard work, moving on,' the tramp said.

'Before you can do that, you need some food in your belly. But once I've got some, I'm leaving.'

And abandoning the rest of us to our fate, Pogo thought.

Still, he supposed, he shouldn't have expected anything else.

'I've earned my bacon sandwich, haven't I?' the other tramp asked worriedly.

'Yes,' Pogo agreed. 'You've earned your bacon sandwich.'

Beresford knew very little about what went on in America, but what he *imagined* was that when gangs met up over there, they did so in clubhouses – which, in his mind's eye, were dark, dangerous places, the urban equivalent of the Hole-in-the-Wall Gang's hideout. The Whitebridge hard mods, on the other hand, had no such institutions, nor the finances to acquire them. Most of the time – if they had the money and had not been banned by the landlord – they met in pubs. Otherwise, their fall-back plan was to rendezvous outside one of Whitebridge's numerous chip shops.

There were half a dozen mods standing outside Joe's Friary as Beresford approached it. A couple of them were eating fish and chips out of funnels made from rolled-up newspaper, but the rest were just looking vaguely into the distance, as if they were waiting – and hoping – for something to happen.

And they seemed quite comfortable with their braces, Beresford thought, though his were continuing to make his shoulder blades itch damnably.

The group noticed him, and awaited his arrival with something approaching interest. Beresford, for his part, found his eyes involuntarily drawn to their steel-toecapped boots – which had the potential to inflict some very heavy damage – and wished that Woodend had given this particular job to somebody else.

As he drew closer, the mods fanned out, blocking his passage and making it impossible for him to keep an eye on all of them at the same time. The only course of action open to him, it seemed, was to come to a halt. So he did.

'What's your name?' demanded a voice which came from just beyond the edge of his vision.

Beresford turned toward the speaker. He was nineteen or twenty, the DC guessed. He was a big lad with calloused, work-hardened hands, arms covered with badly etched purple tattoos and a scar above his left eye.

'Don't you have a name?' the hard mod demanded.

'Do you?' Beresford asked, feeling his mouth drying up.

The mod grinned unpleasantly. 'Yeah,' he said. 'I'm Big Bazza.'

Barry Thornley, Beresford thought. Worker at Lowry Engineering, and enthusiastic supporter of Councillor Ron Scranton.

'So you're Big Bazza, are you?' he asked, as his heart went into overdrive. 'An' is there a *Little* Bazza?'

Big Bazza scowled. 'Are you tryin' to be

funny?' he demanded.

'No,' Beresford replied. 'I was just askin' a question.'

Big Bazza seemed unsure of what to do or say next. Violence was always a good response to any situation, his expression seemed to suggest, but it might just be more interesting to let things slide a little more first.

'That's Little Bazza over there,' he said, flicking his thumb in the direction of a shorter boy at the other end of the semicircle.

'I'm Col,' Beresford said. 'Not Little Col or Big Col. Just Col.'

'Haven't seen you around here before, *Col*,' Big Bazza said, somehow making the last word sound like an insult.

'Haven't *been* around here before,' Beresford said.

'So why are you here now?' Bazza wondered.

'It's where they told me to come when they let me out,' Beresford replied.

'Where *who* told you to come?'

Beresford sighed, as if he were already becoming bored with the conversation. 'The filth. They said they didn't want me goin' back on my old patch, an' that they'd have me if I did. They said they'd fixed me up with a probation officer in Whitebridge who was tough enough to handle me.'

'Are you sayin' that you've been in prison?' the mod asked.

'You catch on quick, don't you?' Beresford replied.

'What did you do?'

Beresford shrugged. 'Nearly nothin'.'

'What *kind* of nearly nothin'?'

'There was this Paki...' Beresford began.

'Beat him up, did you?'

'Hardly touched him. I think he must have broken that big nose of his when he fell over.'

There was a few seconds' silence, in which all the mods looked to their leader for guidance. Then Big Bazza nodded to Little Bazza, and the smaller youth stepped forward, holding his cone of newspaper out in front of him.

'Fancy a chip, Col?' he asked.

Ten

The town-hall clock chimed eleven times, and in the Drum and Monkey, the Crown and Anchor, the George and Dragon – and countless other pubs around the Whitebridge area – drinkers heard the dread sound of a bell behind the bar chiming in sympathy with the municipal time-keeper.

'It's too late now,' those bars' bells were saying in a language that all the drinkers could understand. 'If you've miscalculated the amount of ale you need to get you properly pissed – if you were so distracted by your chatter with your mates that you failed to order a last pint when you heard the first warning bell ten minutes ago – well, tough! The towel has gone over the beer pumps, and you've missed the boat.'

There were some drinkers, in all the pubs, who went hopefully up to the bar anyway, in spite of the bells' clear message. There *always* were, and always *would be*. They were doing no more than following a long tradition which stretched back into the mists of antiquity, when the very first licensing hours were introduced.

'Any chance of one more quick pint?' they asked, smiling ingratiatingly and playing heavily on their commercial 'friendships' with the landlords.

It had sometimes worked in the past, and the customers had watched with joyous hearts as the landlords slipped a glass under the towels and looked the other way while they were pulling the pint – as if the action had nothing at all to do with them.

But it didn't work that night. All the landlords that night were firm. All of them were absolutely resolute.

'There are a lot of bobbies out on the street tonight,' they informed the hopeful boozers, 'and I'm not about to risk losing my licence for one shilling and eleven pence.'

The landlords had not lied. There *were* a lot of bobbies out on the streets that night, and two of them – PC Roger Crabtree and PC Dave Warner – were driving around the area of the abandoned cotton mills even as the landlords were heartlessly turning down the last desperate requests.

'Foot patrol!' Warner said in disgust, as Crabtree parked the car outside one of the derelict buildings. 'We're on *foot* patrol!'

'True enough,' Crabtree agreed.

'But we're *motor* patrol,' his partner pointed out. 'That's why we wear smart flat caps, instead of big pointy helmets.'

Crabtree chuckled. 'Are your bunions playing you up again?' he asked innocently.

'I don't have bunions,' Warner answered, with mock outrage. 'Bunions are an old man's affliction, and I'm still a slip of a youth.'

A slip of a youth who would be twenty-nine

next birthday and was already developing a beer belly, Crabtree thought, but he kept the observation to himself, and simply said, 'As the duty sergeant pointed out, the reason we're issued with thick boots is so that we can walk if we have to.'

'And we *do* have to?' Warner asked, as if still searching for a loophole.

'Yes,' Crabtree replied firmly. 'We do.'

Warner shrugged. He was not a bad bobby, and he supposed that if that was what the Sarge wanted, then that was what the Sarge got.

He stepped out of the car. The sky above them was cloudless, and the full moon bathed the old mill in a ghostly golden glow.

Warner shivered. 'It's brass-monkey weather out here,' he complained.

'Look on the bright side,' his partner told him.

'What bright side?'

'When all this is over, you've got a nice warm bed to go back to, haven't you?'

'Yes?'

'Which is more than any of the poor buggers we've been sent out to protect can say.'

'I heard in the canteen that Councillor Lowry thinks all this is a waste of time,' Warner said, making one last-ditch stand.

'And I heard in the same canteen that DCI Woodend *doesn't*,' Crabtree said. 'Which of them would you prefer to cross?'

Warner grinned. 'Let's get patrolling,' he suggested.

Beresford had only been a hard mod for a few

hours, but had already decided that it was no life for a man.

The simple fact was that the mods were both bored and boring. What conversation they had was desultory at best. They didn't talk about their jobs – and why should they, when most of them were employed in mind-numbingly repetitive industrial tasks? They didn't talk about their home life, because the very reason they were out on the streets was to forget about all that. And they didn't talk about their prospects, because they were realistic enough to accept that – in a declining industrial town – they had none.

A few years earlier, they would have been conscripted into the armed forces, which would at least have taken them away from Whitebridge for a couple of years, and subjected them to a different *kind* of boredom, but the call-up had been abolished in the early sixties, leaving these lads with nowhere to go but along the streets of their own home town.

From the chip shop, the gang had drifted aimlessly to the shopping centre, but there was very little of interest there, since lads, unlike girls, considered window shopping to be soft. They had eventually found themselves outside the off-licence, where Big Bazza had held a collection, and – armed with the pitiful amount of money that the entire gang could stump up between them – bought a couple of bottles of rough cider.

They'd passed the bottles back and forth. Each member only took a small drink – they were all aware that their leader's eyes were on them – but even with moderation, the bottles were soon empty, and a listless apathy settled over the group again.

At eleven o'clock, the lights in the off-licence went out, and at ten past eleven Big Bazza said, 'Well, I'm off.'

'You're what?' asked another member of the gang, who, Beresford had learned, went by the name of Scuddie.

'I'm off,' Big Bazza repeated. 'Any objections?'

'None,' Scuddie said with a grin. 'I suppose if your mum says you have to be home by a certain time, then you have to be home by a certain time.'

Beresford studied Big Bazza's reaction, and tried to get inside his mind. On the one hand, Bazza has his position as leader to consider, and Scuddie's dig at him would have to be dealt with. On the other, what Scuddie had said clearly amused the rest of the gang, and – for the moment at least – they were on his side.

Bazza had three choices, Beresford decided. He could smash Scuddie in the face and run the risk of also smashing the fragile structure of the gang. He could say he'd decided to stay after all, but that would be seen as a sign of weakness by the others. Or he could tell a lie.

Beresford was putting his money on the third course of action.

'I'm not goin' home at all,' Bazza said. 'I'm meetin' a bint.'

'A bint!' Scuddie repeated. 'What's her name?'

Bazza laughed unconvincingly. 'I'm not goin' to tell you that,' he said.

'Why not?'

'Because I'm not just goin' to *meet* her – I'm goin' to shag the arse off her. An' I'll do the same tomorrow night, as well. An' the night after that. But if she finds out I've been talkin' about it, she won't let me get anywhere near her.'

It wasn't a particularly good lie, Beresford thought, but it was acceptable to a bunch of lads who, having no opportunities of their own, were more than willing to get their pleasures vicariously.

'Good for you,' Scuddie said, with mild envy.

'Give her one for me,' Little Bazza added.

Bazza, confident now that he was back on top, smirked. 'I'll give her one for *all* of you,' he promised.

And then he swaggered off into the night.

For a moment, Beresford considered making his own excuses and following Bazza. Because though he did not believe the story about the girl, he was convinced that the lad was up to *something*.

Then he quickly dismissed the idea. Leaving now was too great a risk, he'd decided. He'd only got the barest toehold in the gang, and to push off immediately would open him up to a great many more jibes than Bazza, the established leader, had had to endure.

'Tell us about this Paki you beat up?' Little Bazza suggested to him.

Beresford forced a grin to his face. 'It was in this pub in Accrington that it happened,' he said.

'I thought Pakis didn't drink,' Scuddie said suspiciously.

'They don't,' Beresford agreed.

'So what was he doin' there?'

'Sippin' lemonade! In a pub! Well, if that isn't askin' to get the shit kicked out of you, I don't know what is.'

The gang nodded their agreement.

'That'll learn him,' Scuddie said.

It was at two minutes past midnight that Tel Lowry, after pacing his living room for several minutes, picked up the phone and dialled Henry Marlowe's home number. It took some time for Marlowe to answer the phone, and when he did it was in a dopey voice which suggested that he'd been asleep.

Lazy bastard! Lowry thought. But aloud, he said, 'Have you been giving any thought to our problem, Henry?'

At the other end of the line, Marlowe groaned. 'It's not that easy, Tel. I've got the press to think about.'

'And I've got my *re-election* to think about,' Lowry snapped.

'You got in with quite a comfortable majority the last time,' Marlowe said weakly.

'*Last time*, I wasn't standing against Ron Scranton, was I?' Lowry countered. 'Look, I'm not concerned for myself...' He paused for a moment. 'All right, *I am* concerned for myself,' he admitted. 'I like being a councillor.'

'Well, of course you do. That's only nat—'

'But I'm *also* concerned about the people of this town – especially the newer arrivals. There's a lot of decent, hard-working Asian families that have moved to Whitebridge in the last few years.'

'Are there?' asked Marlowe, as if it were news to him.

'There are,' Lowry said firmly. 'They want to build a new life for themselves, and I think they should be given that chance. Besides, the town in general will benefit from the influx of new blood.'

'If you say so,' Marlowe replied, unconvinced.

'I do say so,' Lowry insisted. 'But things could go the other way as well, couldn't they? With me off the council, and Scranton still on it and stronger than ever, we could have a race war on our hands. And if that happens, everybody loses. Not just the Asians. Not just the whites. Everybody!'

'I ... er ... rather think you might be overstating the case there, Tel,' Marlowe said.

'Well, I don't! I could lose my seat, Henry, I really could. The riff-raff in my ward have already defected to Scranton, and if I can't deliver on my promise to cut spending, some of the more respectable voters will, too.'

'When you put it like that, it certainly does seem to be something of a problem,' Marlowe said reluctantly.

'And it's not just a problem for me,' Lowry pointed out. 'The next chairman of the Police Authority might not regard your little failings quite as indulgently as I do, Henry. The next chairman might want you out!'

'I'll do what I can,' Marlowe said.

'And do it quickly,' Lowry advised. 'Do it

before there's a hole in my budget you could lose the *Titanic* in.'

The narrow alleyway ran between two industrial buildings, a tannery and a small abattoir. They were connected, on their first floors, by a covered bridge which had once been used to transport the skins of the slaughtered cattle from the one to the other. But it had been a long time since that bridge had been used – a long time since either of the businesses had been a going concern.

Crabtree and Warner walked down the alleyway at a leisurely pace, their torches lighting up the cobbled ground in front of them, their minds searching for something to break up the monotony of this patrol.

'What's the time?' Warner asked.

Crabtree shone his torch on his watch. 'It's just turned five past twelve,' he announced.

'It's goin' to be a long, cold shift, without even a cup of tea to warm us up,' Warner said mournfully. 'Don't you think it's about time that somebody opened one of them American all-night diners in Whitebridge?'

Crabtree chuckled. 'Oh, absolutely,' he agreed. 'And while they're at it, they might as well go the whole hog and start a film studio as well.' He looked around him at the blank, decaying walls, then said, in a bad American accent, 'Welcome to Whitebridgewood – the new home of the movie!'

'Aye, move over, John Wayne – and make way for John Wain*wright*,' Warner said, getting into

110

the mood.

A dark silhouetted figure suddenly appeared from out of nowhere, and stood at the other end of the alley, watching them approach.

It was Warner who noticed him first.

'Police!' he shouted, raising his torch. 'Don't move!'

And then the beam landed on its target, and he saw just who the dark figure was.

'Evenin', lads,' Woodend said. 'Anythin' to report?'

'Not a bloody thing, sir,' said Crabtree, and he was thinking, even as he spoke the words, that it was more than fortunate that he'd insisted he and his partner had followed the duty sergeant's instructions to the letter.

'I couldn't sleep,' Woodend told the two constables, as if he felt that some explanation of his presence was necessary. 'An' rather than lyin' there, tossin' and turnin', I thought I might as well come an' see how you lads were gettin' on. Mind if I join you on patrol for a while?'

'Of course not, sir,' said Crabtree.

Because what *else* was he going to say?

They turned the corner from the alleyway and walked around the front of the tannery. The main entrance had been boarded up when the business closed, but the boards – and the door which they had covered – had long ago been removed for firewood, and now there was just a wide gap in the wall.

'Have you been in here before?' Woodend asked.

Crabtree nodded. 'About an hour ago, sir.'

'Did you find any tramps?'

'Just the one. We asked him if he was all right, but we got no answer. The truth is that he was so drunk he wouldn't have noticed if I'd sung the "Hallelujah Chorus" in his lughole.'

'Still, there's no harm in checkin' on him again, is there?' the chief inspector asked.

It could have been a suggestion or it could have been a question – but the two constables knew it was neither of those things.

'No harm at all, sir,' Warner agreed.

The floor of the tannery's upper storey had long since collapsed, and there were holes in the roof which let in the moonlight, so while the place was dark, it was not quite as dark as it might have been.

In the immediate foreground, Woodend could clearly make out the shape of a huge stone vat which had once been used to soak the cattle skins, and as his eyes adjusted to the new conditions, he was able to see more vats stretching into the distance.

The chief inspector recalled the time when the tannery had been in full production. Back then, the smell of the curing hides had found its way out through the air vents and drenched the whole area around the building with an unpleasant stink. But what he was sniffing now was not tanned skins – or even the olfactory memory of tanned skins.

'Can you smell what I think I'm smellin'?' he asked the two constables beside him.

'It's petrol!' Crabtree said.

'It's petrol,' Woodend agreed. He made a

112

sweeping gesture with his hand. 'Fan out. If we're lucky, we might just have the bastard.'

Warner went to the left, Crabtree to the right. Woodend himself made his way down the centre of the tannery.

'You might as well give yourself up now, because there's no escape,' the chief inspector called out in a loud voice, as his beam, and those of the constables, swept across the room like small searchlights.

Their target was hiding behind one of the far vats, close to the tannery's office. Perhaps – for a while at least – he had been hoping that all he needed to do to escape detection was stay where he was, but the closer the three men got to him, the more he must have realized that that was no longer a possibility.

When he did make his move, it was with stunning speed. One second he had been crouched down, the next he had flung himself forward and disappeared into what had once been the toilets.

He moved so swiftly that none of the policemen actually *saw* him – but they heard the noise he made clearly enough.

'I'll get him! You find the poor bloody tramp!' Woodend shouted, as he ran towards the direction of the sound.

He felt his torch jar in his hand, as he inadvertently struck it against one of the vats. The beam went out immediately, and he let the torch fall to the floor. He didn't need much light for what he had to do, he told himself. And when he caught up with the killer, it would be good to have both fists free.

His quarry had reached the toilets fifteen or twenty seconds before he did, and had used the time to pull himself up to a high window. But it was a *small* window as well, and now he was having to wriggle and squirm to get through it.

Woodend grabbed at his leg, in an effort to pull him back in, but he was just too late. The killer fell through the window, landing heavily in the alley on the other side, and all the chief inspector was left holding was his boot.

Dropping the boot, Woodend pulled himself up to the window, and looked out. He couldn't see anybody in the alley, but he heard the sound of the man running away. It was an odd sound – clump, pat, clump, pat, clump, pat – as first his boot hit the ground and then his bootless foot followed it. It was an awkward way to run – but it was fast enough, and though they would go through the motions of looking for him, they would never catch him now.

'Shit!' Woodend said softly to himself.

He returned to the main tanning room. The two constables were leaning over a drunken tramp, who stank heavily of petrol. The jerry can which had been used to carry the petrol was lying a few feet away.

'You, get on your car radio an' tell head-quarters what's happened,' he said to Crabtree. 'You, get him out of those clothes as quickly as you can,' he instructed Warner. 'An' if the old bugger wakes up an' asks for a cigarette, for Christ's sake don't give him one.'

Crabtree stood up.

'Do you need your torch, lad, or can you find

114

your way without it?' Woodend asked.

'I think I can find my way without it,' the constable told him.

'Then give it to me.'

Crabtree handed over the torch, and Woodend took it back into the toilets. The boot he'd pulled off the killer was lying on the floor. From the feel of the thing earlier, he thought he already had a pretty good idea of what it would look like, and when he shone the torch on it, his suspicions were confirmed.

It was an industrial boot, with a steel toecap.

Eleven

When a new cleaner joined the staff at White-bridge police headquarters, the old hands would take her into a quiet corner and tell her all about Chief Inspector Charlie Woodend's desk.

It might *look* like a disaster, they would explain, and, appearances – in this particular case – were not deceptive. Papers and notes were spread out all over it, and no one had any idea what lay on the lower levels. It would take an archaeologist to do the desk justice, the battle-scarred veterans would tell the novice, and a humble cleaning lady like herself would be best advised to ignore it altogether when cleaning the chief inspector's office.

In fact, the cleaners did Woodend an injustice. It was true that the desk, much like his mind, was strewn with seemingly random pieces of information, but the pieces made sense to him, and were set out in a pattern which, while he could not successfully explain it – even to himself – he knew how to manipulate in order to make the connections he *needed* to make.

On the morning after the attempted murder, however – a morning in which the sky outside was battleship grey and malignant clouds hovered like armed zeppelins – the desk had been cleared of all its customary clutter, and occupying the middle of it, like an actor centre stage, was a heavy boot with a steel toecap.

The team, gathered around the desk, had been staring at the boot for some time when Paniatowski said, 'If only the boffins in the lab could analyse sweat and skin in the same way they analyse blood, this might be a real clue.'

'Aye, an' if only criminals had a switch in their heads which clicked on when they'd committed a crime and forced them to march down to the nearest police station, this job would be a doddle,' Woodend said, with early morning sourness. He looked at the boot again. 'I nearly had the bastard.' He held out his hand, with thumb and index finger almost touching. 'I came *that* close to catchin' him.' He turned to Paniatowski. 'You've talked to last night's intended victim, have you?'

'Yes, sir,' Paniatowski replied.

'An' from your less-than-enthusiastic response to my question, am I to take it that this talk of yours didn't do much good?'

'His name's Lew Taylor,' Paniatowski replied. 'He's originally from down south, and he says he's been on the road since just after the Queen's Coronation. He doesn't have any enemies he knows of, and he hasn't got a clue why anybody would want to burn him alive. The one thing he is sure of is that he's getting out of Whitebridge as fast as his legs will carry him.'

Woodend nodded, as if that was exactly what he'd expected to hear. 'So if we're gettin' nothin' from the victims, let's attack it from the other

117

side,' he suggested. 'Do you think the hard mods – an' specifically your mate Barry Thornley – could have carried out the attack on Taylor, Colin?'

'It's possible,' Beresford said cautiously. 'Bazza left the rest of the gang at just after eleven, so it would have been easy enough for him to get to the tannery by midnight.'

'Then why isn't that possibility excitin' you?' Woodend wondered.

'Well, for a start, the hard mods aren't the only ones who wear this kind of boot. Anybody who works in a factory will own at least a couple of pairs.'

'True,' Woodend agreed.

'And even if Bazza was responsible for the *second* attack, I'd be surprised if he was also responsible for the *first*.'

'What's the thinkin' behind that?'

'I learned quite a lot about the hard mods last night. I'm not saying I'm an expert on them yet, but I've at least got some idea of how they think.'

'An' how *do* they think?'

'Short term. If they see an Asian on the street, they might decide, on the spur of the moment, to kick the shit out of him – but to come up with the idea of burning tramps, sometime in the future, is just not their style. They don't plan – they react.'

'In other words, you think that if Barry Thornley *was* involved in last night's attack, he was doin' no more than copyin' the previous evening's murder?'

118

'That's about it,' Beresford agreed.

'Jesus!' Woodend said. 'That's *all* we bloody need.'

'There is another alternative,' Paniatowski said.

'An' what might that be?'

'That though the hard mods didn't come up with the idea themselves, they're the ones who are implementing it.'

'In other words, there's somebody else behind them, pullin' the strings?'

'That's right.'

'An' do you have any theories as to who this *somebody else* might be?'

'I'd put my money on Councillor Scranton – the tramps' friend and gentle Jesus of race relations,' Paniatowski said.

'That's a bit of a stretch, isn't it?' Woodend asked sceptically. 'I mean, I know the man's a bastard, but that's a long way from accusin' him of bein' a *murderin'* bastard.'

'The two crimes that have been committed are apparently random and meaningless,' Paniatowski argued. 'But once we put Councillor Scranton in the frame, they're not random or meaningless *any more*.'

She had a point, Woodend conceded, and looked across at Rutter, to see what his right-hand man thought about the idea.

But Rutter didn't seem to be thinking of *anything* very much.

Pogo woke up to the sound of birdsong, and for a moment he wondered what all the birds were

doing in the front bedroom of a decaying terraced house. Then he opened his eyes, saw the
evergreen leaves which surrounded him, and
remembered where he was.

The decision he'd made to abandon his usual
base had not been taken lightly. He'd been well
aware that there was a risk he might freeze to
death in the night – but it was a risk worth running when the possible alternative was waking
up in flames.

Pogo knew all about risk. He had spent the last
months of the War behind enemy lines, as part of
a sabotage team. There'd been an officer leading
them at first, but he'd been killed and the sergeant had taken over. Then the sergeant had
died, too, and Pogo reluctantly assumed command, only to discover – to his own amazement
– that not only did he like being in charge, but
that he was good at it.

He crawled slowly out of his sleeping bag. His
back ached, and the muscles in his legs were
clenched tightly, but both those things would
pass. He stood up, put all his weight on his left
foot, and began the painful process of stretching
his right leg. And as he brought slow relief to his
burning muscles, he found his mind drifting
back to the dying moments of the War.

*The raids he led his men on were bolder and
more audacious than any of those either of his
predecessors had planned – and that meant they
were much riskier, too. When he went to sleep at
night, it was always in mild wonder that he was
still alive. And when he woke up in the morning,
it was with the expectation that this would be his*

last day on earth.

These thoughts didn't bother him. He needed no vision of a better future for himself – or any personal future at all – to drive him on. He had a purpose – and that was all the engine he required to drive him on.

He had a purpose now, he realized with surprise, as he transferred his weight to his right foot – a purpose that Monika Paniatowski had given him. He was the champion of men who had so little regard for their own worth that they could not be bothered to champion themselves. He would save them, even though they would not thank him for it – even though many of them had no desire to be saved.

He took his bottle of meths out of his pocket, looked at it for a moment, then put it back again. It wasn't necessary, he told himself – though with not enough conviction to make him drop it in the nearest waste bin.

He thought about the 'bacon sandwich' tramp of the previous night. The man's information might be a valuable starting point for his investigation. On the other hand, he might merely have been making it all up – saying what he did because he had to say *something* if he was to get his reward.

Pogo put his hand in his pocket and jangled the change which was left from the pound note that Monika Paniatowski had given him. Those coins would make his work easier, because having given up almost everything else, money was the one thing that tramps still really wanted.

Emerging from his hideout, he started to make

his way to the public toilets, where there were washbasins which would allow him to clean up a little before he began his day's work.

A young woman, taking her baby for an early morning walk through the park in its pram, saw him suddenly emerge, put the pram into a rapid three-point turn, and walked hurriedly back the way she had come.

She was frightened of him, Pogo thought – and who could blame her?

Rutter looked down at his watch. It was the third time he'd done so in the previous ten minutes, Woodend noted.

'I think I'd better be going,' the inspector said.

'Any particular reason for your hurry?' Woodend enquired. 'Is it that you have something more important to do? Or could it be that we're just startin' to bore you?'

Paniatowski and Beresford exchanged rapid – questioning – looks. *We're not used to this kind of friction,*' Beresford's expression said. *'Bloody right, we're not!'* Paniatowski's agreed.

'I have to go to Manchester,' Rutter said, suddenly very much on his dignity. 'You asked me to go there yourself, sir. Remember? You told me you wanted me to track down the victim's relatives.'

That was accurate enough, as far as it went, Woodend thought. But it wasn't like Bob Rutter to want to miss out on one of the team's brainstorming sessions, *whatever* else he had to do.

Then he found himself wondering if his thought had been strictly accurate. It wasn't like

122

the *old* Bob Rutter to miss out on the brainstorming, but this new Bob Rutter – this *Elizabeth Driver* Bob Rutter – was a different matter entirely.

'Am I being fair?' he asked himself silently. 'After all, it was Bob who uncovered the identity of the first victim.'

Yes, that was true, even if Rutter had left his other duties – his *assigned* duties – in order to do it. But after his initial feelings of guilt had faded, the chief inspector had found himself wondering if Rutter had been entirely straight with him the previous day – if the *whole* of his absence could be accounted for by his search of the cotton mill. And if it couldn't, then what the bloody hell had he been doing the rest of the time?

There really was no room for passengers in a murder inquiry, Woodend thought – and it looked to him as if that was just what his inspector – his almost-son – was rapidly becoming.

'Shall I go or shall I stay?' Rutter asked, with just an edge of impatience in his voice.

'You might as well go,' Woodend told him. 'There's no *point* in stayin' if your heart's not in it.'

Big Bazza was at work. He hated his job – the mindless repetitive nature of the production line, the heat and the sweat, the air clogged with iron filings, and the fact that he *had* to be there in the factory, whether he felt like it or not. Even his pay packet on a Thursday was not much consolation, since he had to hand most of it over to his mother.

Though he was not a deep thinker, his thoughts were deep enough for him to realize that he was trapped. He was like an animal in a cage – powerful in his own right, but made helpless by the thick bars. And outside the cage were the *others* – the ones who had escaped from it themselves, or else, by an accident of birth, had never been in it. These others could do what they liked – laugh at him, poke him with a stick – and he had to take it.

But the nights were different. At night, the bars melted away and he was free to roam as he wished – a dangerous, frightening animal on the loose. At night, *he* was the one outside the cage.

'We pay you to work, not to stand there daydreamin',' said a harsh voice to his left.

Big Bazza looked up. 'Sorry, Mr Hoskins.'

The foreman glanced down at his feet. 'New boots, Thornley?' he asked.

'No, Mr Hoskins.'

'Well, they look new to me.'

'They're my *best* boots, but they're not new,' Bazza explained.

The foreman shook his head wonderingly. 'Wearin' your best boots to work,' he said. 'Whatever will you do next? It seems to me that you young lads have more money than sense.'

'Are you comfortable about the idea of continuin' to hang around with the hard mods, Colin?' Woodend asked Beresford.

'Yes,' the DC replied.

'You don't *sound* very comfortable,' Woodend told him. 'If you're thinkin' that it will put you in too much danger—'

'The thought of danger wasn't on my mind at all,' Beresford interrupted. 'What I *was* thinking about was that, if I'm going to learn anything useful, I need the gang to take me into their confidence.'

'Agreed,' Woodend said.

'But it usually takes time to build confidence – and time is just what we don't have.'

'Agreed again.'

'So what I'm looking for is some kind of short-cut to acceptance. I think I've found one – but to make it work, I'm going to need Sergeant Paniatowski's help.'

'What can Monika do?' Woodend wondered. 'Even if she shaves her head like you've shaved yours, she'll never look like a working-class male thug.' He paused, then chuckled. 'Let's face it, for a start, she's far too *old* to pull off that kind of deception.'

'Thanks a bundle, sir. You've really made my day,' Paniatowski said.

But she did not mind the joke. She welcomed a little levity after the scene with Rutter.

They all did.

'So tell me how you think the sergeant can help you,' Woodend said to Beresford.

The constable outlined his scheme, and when he'd finished Woodend shook his head and said, 'I've heard of some pretty devious, underhand tricks in my time, but I've never heard of that particular variation before.'

Beresford looked crestfallen. 'It was just an idea,' he said. 'If you don't think it will work, then I'm more than willing to—'

'Don't do yourself down, lad,' Woodend interrupted. 'It's a brilliant idea – a real bobby-dazzler of an idea. What do you think, Monika?'

'It's good,' Paniatowski agreed.

'An' I'll tell you somethin' for nothin', young Beresford,' Woodend continued. 'If you carry on in this devious underhand way, you'll have a great future ahead of you in the CID.'

As Bob Rutter left the doctor's surgery, he checked his watch. It had been a very detailed medical examination – which was a good thing when you were considering taking an important step in your life – but it did mean that he had spent longer in the surgery than he'd planned to. Still, if he broke a few speed regulations on the journey between Whitebridge and Manchester, he should be able to make up at least some of the time he had lost.

He didn't quite understand what was happening to him, he thought, as he turned the ignition of his car.

If he'd come up with the plan of marrying Liz Driver two years earlier, he'd have approached things much more slowly, taking his time to consider all the angles and weigh all the implications. Now he was rushing into it like a callow youth, waving all objections aside with a casual flick of the wrist. And while he was well aware of the fact that he was letting down Charlie Woodend – a man he respected and admired like none other – he simply couldn't bring himself to care *enough* about it to throw himself into reverse.

'Yes, you'd have approached it differently a couple of years ago, wouldn't you?' asked a voice in his head, as he slid the car into gear. 'A couple of years ago, you'd never have thought about marrying Liz *at all*. A couple of years ago, you were still married to *Maria*.'

And maybe that was the answer to why he was acting in the way that he was, he told himself. He'd been through hell since Maria's murder. Now he wanted something better. He was choosing the soft option not just for its own sake – but also because the *hard* one had become crushingly intolerable.

Rutter had been gone for over an hour, Beresford had recently left, and now the only two people in Woodend's office were himself and Paniatowski – and it was Paniatowski who was doing the talking.

'So that's all I've got for you, sir,' she said, reaching the end of her account of her investigation into Councillor Lowry. 'He's not a bad employer by all accounts, and while he might include promiscuity and ruthless political ambition amongst his weaknesses, I doubt you can use either of those things to put pressure on him.'

'Then find me something else that I *can* use,' Woodend said flatly.

'But I don't even know where to start looking,' Paniatowski confessed.

'Start right at the beginnin' – from the moment that the midwife slapped his bare arse,' Woodend told her. 'That's the way we've always conducted our criminal investigations in this team.'

'But Lowry's *not* a criminal,' Paniatowski protested.

'You don't know that for certain,' Woodend said. 'You *can't* know it for certain, until you've completed your investigation.'

And I don't know *you*, any longer, Charlie, Paniatowski thought.

Because this wasn't the mentor she'd worked with since he'd been transferred to Mid-Lancs. This wasn't the even-handed Charlie Woodend who she'd wanted to *be* like. Getting dirt on Lowry had ceased to be a means to an end, and had become an end in itself.

And then, in a sudden flash of insight, she realized that this whole thing wasn't about *Lowry* at all – it was about Bob!

Woodend was furious with his protégé, but not quite furious enough yet to lash out at him. So somebody else had to be made to suffer. And the target Woodend had selected for his venom was Councillor Tel Lowry.

'I'm not comfortable about carrying on with this investigation, sir,' she said. 'If you insist on it going ahead...'

'An' I do!'

'...then I'd prefer it if you assigned it to someone else.'

'There *is* nobody else. You're the only one I trust.'

Trust!

The word stabbed at Paniatowski's heart with all the force of a sharp dagger. It was one of those words like love, admiration and gratitude – all of which she felt for Woodend – which she was powerless to resist.

And she knew at that moment that even if she thought he was wrong – and she was *certain* he was wrong – she would go along with what he wanted.

She made one last effort to extricate herself. 'The thing is, sir,' she said, 'I think there are more valuable things I could be doing with my time.'

'Like what, for instance?'

'Like looking into Councillor Scranton's background.'

Woodend nodded. 'Then why don't you look into that *as well*?' he suggested, throwing her a bone.

Henry Marlowe should have been out on the golf course that morning – his game with a local bigwig had been down in his diary for weeks – but instead of artfully and skilfully losing a match to someone who mattered politically, he was stuck in his office, talking to Councillor Lowry on the phone.

'So it looks as if Woodend was right,' he was saying, though he found the words almost sticking in his throat.

'Right?' Lowry repeated.

'About the foot patrols.'

'That's one way of looking at it,' Lowry said ominously.

'And is there another way?' Marlowe wondered.

'There is indeed,' Lowry conceded. 'From what you've just told me, it's clear that if Chief Inspector Woodend had arrived five minutes later, the tramp would have been dead.'

'That's true,' Marlowe agreed. 'But—'

'And how would your Force have looked then? Much worse than if there'd been no policemen on patrol *at all*! Isn't that right?'

'I suppose so.'

'What the ratepayers would be saying is, "You've spent a great deal of our money on this extra police presence, and you might as well not have bothered, because the result has been exactly the same."'

'They *might* say that,' Marlowe agreed.

'And what about the *next* time, when the patrol doesn't manage to get there in the nick of time?' Lowry asked.

'I don't know,' Marlowe said miserably.

'I'm sorry for these tramps. I really am,' Lowry said. 'But it *will* happen again – I see now that DCI Woodend was right about that, at least. Where I disagree with the chief inspector is that I don't think we'll catch him in the act, however many patrols we have on duty.'

'Woodend almost caught him last night,' Marlowe pointed out.

'So next time the killer will be more careful,' Lowry countered. He sighed. 'I hate to say this, Henry, but the resolution to the situation will only come when there *is* a second victim.'

'Are you saying that once the killer has struck twice, he'll give up?' Marlowe asked, mystified.

'I'm saying that once he's struck twice, there

won't be any tramps around as fodder for a third murder.'

'But there are dozens of them...' Marlowe began.

'*Now* there are,' Lowry agreed. 'But when another of their number dies, even the stupidest and most lethargic of them will feel this isn't a safe place to be, and get out of town as quickly as possible.'

'So all we have to do is wait until there's a second murder?' Marlowe asked hopefully.

'No, what we have to do – what *you* have to do – is find a way to stop the night-time patrols before these ruinous overtime payments bankrupt the council,' Lowry said forcefully.

'But I don't see what I *can* do,' Marlowe whined.

'Can I be frank?' Lowry asked.

You're going to be, whether I want it or not, Marlowe thought. 'Yes, you can be frank,' he told Lowry.

'As I think I've said before, you're not the most effective chief constable around, Henry, but at least you've always been amenable to the council's wishes – and that has made you useful. But if you can't deliver on this, then you're neither use nor ornament. Do you understand what I'm saying?'

'Yes,' Marlowe said, almost in tears by now. 'Yes, I understand.'

Twelve

Warner and Crabtree had signed off duty at eight o'clock, and by ten past eight were sitting in the police canteen, munching their way through sausage sandwiches doused in a layer of thick brown sauce.

'Food fit for heroes,' Crabtree announced between mouthfuls.

And though Warner laughed at the comment – as he was expected to – that was how they both secretly saw themselves.

They'd finished their sandwiches, swallowed the remains of their industrial-strength tea, and were walking across the car park when they saw the man standing awkwardly next to Warner's Ford Popular.

'It looks like Mr Marlowe,' Crabtree said.

'It can't be,' Warner scoffed. 'He doesn't really exist.'

'He does, too,' Crabtree countered, falling in with the game. 'I've seen him on the telly, talking to the press.'

'But have you ever seen him in *real life*?' Warner wondered.

'I thought I got a glimpse of him once, but I may have been mistaken,' Crabtree conceded.

'Anyway, even if he *does* exist, he only exists

in his office,' Warner said. 'He doesn't go out into the real world, like ordinary mortals.'

But the closer they got to Warner's car, the more they were forced to admit to themselves it did *look* like the chief constable, and that he was not only loitering, but loitering *uneasily*.

They were almost level with the car when the apparition spoke.

'I just thought I'd come out and congratulate you on the splendid job you did last night, lads,' it said.

The words were yet another hammer blow to Crabtree's and Warner's already weak grip on reality.

It was surreal.

It was bizarre.

Marlowe had called them 'lads', and whilst the word would have sounded fine coming from Cloggin'-it Charlie's lips, to hear Marlowe using it was a bit like hearing the Pope advise you to always use rubber johnnies when having it off with a stranger.

'Yes, a splendid job,' Marlowe repeated. 'And it's because of the way you've performed that I've decided to entrust you with another small task, which I'd like you to complete before you finally turn in for a well-earned rest.'

'Another small task, sir?' Crabtree repeated, cautiously.

'That's right. In a way, I suppose it's almost a *private* task – a sort of personal favour to me. In other words, it wouldn't be part of your normal police duties *as such*, though I think it would certainly be a service to policing in

Whitebridge.'

'I don't quite see what you're getting at, sir,' Warner admitted.

'Then I'd better explain more fully,' Marlowe said indulgently, as if he was doing them *a favour*.

He delivered his explanation, and when he'd finished, Crabtree said, 'We won't get into trouble for this, will we, sir?'

'Get into trouble!' Marlowe repeated, with an irritated edge creeping into his voice. 'How the bloody hell could you get into trouble? I'm the one asking you to do it, aren't I?'

'Well, yes, sir, but...'

'And *I'm* the bloody chief constable.'

'Well, if you're sure it will be all right...'

'I want you to know that I won't forget this,' Marlowe said, as though it were already a done deal. 'And just bear this in mind – it can't do you any harm to have your boss on your side, now can it, lads?'

Marlowe had used that word 'lads' again, Crabtree thought. He wished he wouldn't do that.

The concrete pipe was twenty feet long and had an internal radius of forty-six inches. It had once been intended to form part of an ambitious new sewage system, but then council cutbacks had meant that the project was abandoned. Now it stood on a piece of waste ground, waiting for the next time that local government felt rich again – and slowly crumbling away.

Pogo approached the front end of the pipe

slowly, walking in a straight line. He made enough noise for the man inside to be aware of his presence, yet not so much that the other tramp was likely to be alarmed. When he was a few feet from the pipe, he came to a halt, and said, 'Mind if I join you?'

The tramp inside the pipe considered the matter. 'Why would you want to?' he asked.

Pogo shrugged. 'I feel like a bit of company,' he said. 'And I've got some cigarettes.'

'I don't have anything worth stealing, you know,' the other tramp said.

'I don't steal,' Pogo said angrily. 'However low I've sunk, I've never stolen anything.' And then, realizing he'd just undone all the good work of his careful approach by his show of temper, he continued, in a much quieter voice, 'I don't blame you for being suspicious. There are a lot of bad people about.'

'Have you got a knife?' the other tramp asked.

For a moment, Pogo was tempted to lie, but then he said, 'Yes, I have – but if you let me into the pipe, I'll leave it outside.'

'You do that,' the other tramp said. 'But even without the knife, there's still an entrance fee of three cigarettes for coming in.'

Pogo grinned. 'Three cigarettes?' he repeated. 'To enter a palatial pipe like this one? It's cheap at twice the price.'

The other man returned his grin. 'But you'll leave your knife outside, like you promised?' he said.

Pogo pulled his weapon out of his belt, and placed it on the ground. Then he squatted down and entered the pipe. Once inside, it seemed remarkably easy to get comfortable.

He handed over his entrance fee, then said, 'My name's Percy, but when I was serving in the army everybody called me Pogo, and the name stuck. What's your name?'

'Did you fight in the War?' the other tramp asked, perhaps as a way of avoiding answering Pogo's question.

Pogo nodded. 'And you?'

The other man shook his head. 'Too young. They called me up *after* the War, but then they decided that they didn't want me.' He grinned again, revealing a mouth full of rotting teeth, and tapped his head with his index finger. 'I've got mental problems, you see.'

'Too bad,' Pogo said sympathetically.

'Not bad at all,' the other man contradicted him. 'I never wanted to be a soldier anyway.' He paused. 'Did you ever kill anybody?'

Too many to count, Pogo thought. *Far* too many to count.

But aloud, he said, 'Not as far as I know.'

'I once knew a killer,' the other tramp said softly, as if he were revealing a great secret.

'Did you now?' Pogo asked, trying to sound interested. 'What kind of killer was he?'

'A very bad one. But he didn't go to jail.'

'Why not?'

'I forget,' the other tramp said, seeming to lose interest in the subject. 'It was all a very long time ago.'

'Have the police questioned you?' Pogo asked-ed.

'They did. I talked to a big bastard in a sports coat.'

Monika's boss, Pogo thought. 'Did you tell him anything?' he asked.

The other tramp shook his head. 'Didn't have anything to tell.'

'So you haven't noticed any suspicious characters hanging around?'

'No. Have you?'

'None at all,' Pogo said.

'Shall we be pals?' the other tramp asked unexpectedly.

Pals! It was a long time since he'd had pals, Pogo thought.

And those last pals of his had done something so utterly unspeakable that he still had nightmares about it.

'Yes, we can be pals, if you like,' he heard himself say. 'But if that's what we're going to be, you really should tell me your name.'

'You can call me Brian,' the other tramp replied. 'But that's not my real name. I don't like my real name.'

'Why not?'

'It carries too much responsibility with it.'

'How can a name carry responsibility with it?' Pogo wondered.

'My real name,' said Brian, with a great deal of pomp and circumstance, 'is Brunel.'

There's no wonder the army turned you down, Pogo thought.

The vagrant's name was Terry Dodd, and he was sitting on a bench in the Corporation Park when he saw the uniformed police constable approaching him.

Dodd thought quickly. There were two ways to handle the situation, he calculated. He could either pretend to be asleep, or he could look in the opposite direction. And since the bobby himself had probably already seen that he *wasn't* asleep, looking away was definitely the best option.

He turned creakily, and fixed his eyes firmly on a yew tree in the distance. Behind him he could hear the sound of the policeman's footfalls drawing ever closer.

The constable stopped walking, and the tramp felt a slight tap on his shoulder.

Reluctantly, Dodd turned around and said, 'I haven't done anything wrong.'

Crabtree smiled. 'Nobody said you had,' he replied reassuringly. 'But I'd still like you to come with me.'

'I don't *want* to go to the police station,' Dodd whined.

'And I have no intention of taking you there,' Crabtree replied.

'Then where *do* you want to take me?'

'To the off-licence,' Crabtree told him. 'I'm going to buy you a bottle of cheap wine. Or, if you prefer it, you can have cider.'

'What's the catch?' the tramp asked.

'No catch,' Crabtree lied uneasily.

Rutter was sitting in the living room of a modest semi-detached house in one of the outer suburbs of Manchester, looking across the coffee table at a man who'd appeared to be around forty-five when he'd answered the door, but now seemed much, much older.

Finding Henry Turner hadn't been difficult. In fact, as was so often the case when tracking down members of the respectable working class, it had been an absolute doddle, involving no more than a few phone calls to the relevant government and local council offices.

On the other hand, breaking the bad news of his brother's death to him hadn't been easy at all.

It never was.

'I've been expecting to hear that our Phil was dead for years,' Turner said dully. 'With the kind of life he led, he was never going to make old bones. But to have gone like *that*!'

Rutter nodded sympathetically. 'Did he have any other relatives?'

'There was Edith, his wife, of course, but she was run over by a corporation bus. Broke his heart, it did. It was straight after her funeral that he started hitting the bottle. He never recovered from it.'

'When did he first become a tramp?' Rutter asked.

Turner's eyes hardened. 'Our Phil was never a tramp!' he said with feeling. 'He might have lived a bit rough from time to time, but that didn't make him a *tramp*!'

Didn't it? Rutter asked himself. Then what *did* it make him?

'What would you prefer me to call him?' he asked.

'He was a traveller,' Henry Turner said firmly,

'looking for the peace of mind on the road that he could never have found living in the city where his darling Edith died.'

'Of course, a traveller,' Rutter agreed hastily. 'So how long was he a traveller?'

'Must be eight years now,' Henry Turner guessed. 'For the first two or three, he used to send me postcards from the places he visited – Cardiff, Newcastle, Glasgow – but then even that stopped.'

'Can you think of any old enemies he might have had?' Rutter asked, suspecting, even as he spoke, that it was a pointless question to put.

'Phil wasn't the sort to make enemies, and even if he had any, how would they find him when even his own brother didn't know where he was?' Turner replied, confirming the suspicion. Then he looked Rutter straight in the eyes, and said, 'Who do *you* think killed him? And *why* did he kill him?'

'We don't know,' Rutter admitted. 'Our best guess at the moment is that it was a random act of violence. Somebody wanted to kill a tram— a traveller, and your brother just happened to be the victim he lighted on.'

Turner shook his head. 'It seems such a waste,' he said. 'Can I claim the body?'

'Of course,' Rutter agreed. 'I'll put the wheels in motion as soon as I get back to Whitebridge.'

'I'd like to see him properly buried. It's the least I can do for him.' Turner hesitated for a second, then added, 'I suppose it'll have to be a closed coffin?'

'I'm afraid so,' Rutter agreed. He looked around the living room, at the beautifully polished display cabinets and the framed pictures on the walls, then added, 'Do you happen to have a photograph of your brother? Preferably one that was taken not too long before he started travelling?'

Turner walked over to the display cabinet like an old man, and returned with a photograph in a silver frame. Two people smiled out of it – a woman who could not be called pretty but looked very pleasant, and a man who bore a close resemblance to Henry Turner.

'That's the most recent one I have,' Turner said. 'It was taken about three years before he went away.'

'Can I borrow it?' Rutter asked. 'You'll get it back when we've copied it.'

'Will it help you to catch the man who did this terrible thing to him?' Turner asked.

Probably not, Rutter thought, but aloud he said, 'In an investigation like this one, every single piece of additional information we get can be a help.'

'Then take it,' Turner said. 'Take it with my blessing.'

Though he'd been dying to do so for some time, it was not until he was out on the street again that Rutter looked at his watch.

He was running late again, and for a moment he almost abandoned his plan to do a bit of shopping away from the watchful eyes of his colleagues. Then he told himself that the purchase was important to him, and if his col-

141

leagues didn't like it, they could bloody well lump it.

Elizabeth Driver thought quickly on her feet, but even better when she was behind the wheel of her Jaguar, which was why, for the previous hour or so, she had been driving around the Whitebridge area with no particular destination in mind.

The book was going well, she told herself, as she slotted another piece of its venom mentally into place. Better than well – it was going bloody marvellously.

The town would never be the same again after her book came out. It would do its best to prove her wrong, but the corruption she would expose – some of it, no doubt, true – would leave a stink that would cling to the place like sprayed-on cow piss.

The book would also, of course, make her a figure of hatred in the town, but that wouldn't bother her – not when all she had to do was take the money and run.

She had just turned on to Hardcastle Street when she noticed the big police van. It was parked in front of an off-licence, and though there was nothing at all unusual about that, the behaviour of the uniformed constable standing by the double doors at the back of the van immediately aroused her interest.

She pulled into the kerbside and switched off her engine. She was probably wasting her time, she told herself, but even as her brain was processing the thought, her reporter's instinct was bringing a tingle to the back of her neck.

The back doors of the van were open, and the constable was having a heated discussion with a couple of rough-looking men who looked like tramps. The tramps, it appeared from their gestures, wanted to get out of the van, and the constable was intent on persuading them to stay in.

It was the *persuasive* element of the encounter that interested Elizabeth Driver. If the tramps had been arrested, she argued, persuasion wouldn't have come into it. And if they *hadn't* been arrested, what were they doing in the back of the van, and why was the bobby so keen to keep them there?

The door of the off-licence opened, and another constable stepped out on to the pavement. He had a carrier bag in his hand, and when the tramps saw it, they became even more agitated. And not only them, but the tramps behind them – because it now became apparent that there were at least half a dozen of them inside the vehicle.

The constable with the carrier bag had arrived back at the van, and when his colleague had stood aside, he reached into the bag and produced a bottle of cider. Several hands made a lunge for it, but the constable brushed most of them aside and handed it to a youngish man wearing a threadbare fawn overcoat, who, once having a firm grip on his prize, disappeared into the bowels of the van.

The next bottle the constable produced was sherry, and once again he seemed to know exactly who it was intended for. A bottle of red wine followed the sherry, and a bottle of white wine came after that. Soon, all the tramps had been issued with a bottle of something or other, and had retreated into the van. Once they were gone, the constable closed – and locked – the doors.

He's not only bought all them a drink, he's done it to order, Driver thought incredulously.

The two constables climbed into the front of the vehicle, and the van pulled off.

Driver waited until they were almost at the end of the street and then set off in pursuit.

You never know what's going to happen to you, Bob Rutter thought, as he stood at the counter of a very expensive shop in the centre of Manchester.

Take Philip Turner's case, for example. One minute he was a happily married man – as was obvious from the silver-framed photograph – and the next his wife had been run over by a corporation bus.

Take his *own* case. He *hadn't* been happily married – the guilt he felt over his affair with Monika Paniatowski had ensured that – but he had loved Maria, and he had been devastated when she was murdered.

So what was the moral to be learned from all this?

Simple! When you wanted something that you thought would make your stay on earth a little more bearable, you grabbed it immediately.

Because if you stopped to think about it – even

for a second – it might well be gone.

'Can I help you, sir?' asked the cashmere-clad assistant.

'Yes, you can,' Rutter replied. 'I'd like to buy an engagement ring.'

What Constables Warner and Crabtree really wanted, when they'd finished the task that Henry Marlowe had assigned to them, was a good strong drink – or *several* good strong drinks – but they were still in their uniforms, so they settled for large mugs of tea in the nearest cafe.

The tea helped soothe them – but only a little.

'I just can't help thinking we've done the wrong thing,' Crabtree said worriedly, as he sipped at the dark sweet liquid.

'What choice did we have?' Warner countered. 'When the chief constable says, "Jump!" all we can ask is, "How high, sir?" That's the way things are in this world."

'I know that. But did it feel *right* to you?' Crabtree persisted.

'No,' Warner said gloomily. 'It didn't feel right at all. I knew when I joined the police that there'd be lots of things I'd have to do that I wouldn't like doing, but I *never* expected I'd—'

'Mind if I join you?' asked a voice.

They looked up, and saw a woman standing over them. Crabtree noticed that she was in her late twenties, and rather smartly dressed to be in a place like this scruffy cafe. Warner noticed that she had long black hair and breasts you could drown in. Both wondered why she wanted to waste her time sitting with them.

The woman sat down anyway, without waiting for the invitation.

'I'm Elizabeth Driver,' she announced. 'I'm a reporter for the *Gazette*. You may have read some of my stuff.'

Neither constable said anything, though they were already beginning to fear the worst.

'Well, you have been busy boys, haven't you?' Elizabeth Driver asked brightly.

'Don't know what you're talking about, madam,' Crabtree said.

Driver laughed. 'Even if you were a good liar, that particular line wouldn't work. And you're *not* a good liar. In fact, you're a bloody awful one.'

'Now look here, madam—' Crabtree started to protest.

'I think you should know that I've been following you since you left the off-licence,' Driver interrupted.

'Oh!' Crabtree said.

'Oh!' Warner agreed.

'Oh!' Elizabeth Driver confirmed. 'You're in big trouble, boys. You know that, don't you?'

'We were only—' Warner began.

'Following orders?' Driver interrupted again.

'Well, yes.'

'That's the defence the Nazi war criminals used – and look what happened to them.' Driver tilted her head to one side and mimed being hanged, then continued, 'Somebody's going to have to take the fall for this, and if you don't help me, it could be you. On the other hand, if

146

you decide to cooperate...'

'What do you want to know?' Warner asked desperately.

'Who *issued* the orders that you were "only following"?'

'Mr Marlow,' Crabtree said. 'He's the—'

'Chief constable! I know. And did Mr Marlowe give you these orders *personally* – or were they relayed through a flunky?'

'He gave them personally,' Crabtree admitted.

'So who paid for all the booze that I saw you buying at the off-licence?'

'He did. He gave me a couple of pounds, and said if I needed any more, I'd only got to tell him.'

A look of perfect happiness spread across Elizabeth Driver's face. 'Excellent!' she said.

Thirteen

The Alderman Baxter Retirement Home was housed in what had once been the Whitebridge Workhouse.

A great deal had been done to brighten up the place since those far-off days when it catered for desperate paupers with no choice but to throw themselves on the mercy of the Board of Guardians – liberal applications of pastel paint had all but obliterated the institutional chocolate-brown colour with which the walls had once been coated, gaily patterned curtains somewhat softened the stern windows – and yet, for all that, the building still had an air of Victorian pious self-righteousness and inflexibility which made Paniatowski shiver as she walked through the entrance archway.

She had not seen James Fuller, the person she was there to visit, for nearly twenty years. Back then, viewed through the eyes of childhood, he had seemed a tall, almost godlike figure, but he had probably never been as imposing as she'd believed, and now he was nothing more than a little old man.

'I wasn't sure you'd remember me,' she told him.

'You underrate yourself,' Fuller replied. 'I

never forget any of my star pupils.'

'Is that what I was?' Paniatowski asked, surprised. 'A star pupil? I don't recall doing *that* well at school.'

Fuller laughed. It was a dry, rasping laugh, which was almost a cough. 'Oh, I don't mean you were a star pupil in the *academic* sense,' he explained. 'You were only slightly above average when it came to your school work.'

'Well, then?'

'What made you stand out was that you had a spark. You had character. Look how you fought them when they tried to change your name!'

'When *who* tried to change my name?'

'Your mother and your stepfather. They wanted to change your surname so it was the same as theirs. But you weren't having that. You were eleven years old, living in a country you hardly knew, and with still a trace of a Polish accent, but you still stood firm. And, in the end, it was them who gave way. Do you really not remember that?'

'No, I don't remember it at all,' Paniatowski admitted.

But then, she told herself, she had tried to forget as much as she possibly could about her abused childhood.

'I wanted to ask you about someone else's school days,' Paniatowski said.

'Whose?'

'Councillor Tel Lowry's. He was at the school quite a few years before me, but...'

'You don't need to tell *me* that.'

'...but since he's become such an important

149

man in the community, I expect you remember him even better than you remember me.'

'I remember him *as well as* I remember you,' Fuller said, with just a hint of reproach in his voice. 'But given that it's well over thirty years since he passed through my hands, why have you come to ask *me* about him?'

Because I'm desperate, Paniatowski thought. Because Charlie Woodend – for reasons of his own – wants me to find a weakness where none seems to exist.

'We can learn a lot about people from their childhood,' she told Fuller. 'Don't they say that the child is father to the man?'

'They do say that,' Fuller agreed. 'And they're not far off the mark.'

'So what *was* he like?'

'In a word, unhappy. Parents always have favourites among their children, you know, however much they may deny it, and it was Tel's older brother, Barclay, who was his father's favourite.'

'How do you know?'

'Because Joseph Lowry – hard, unbending man he was – never made even the slightest attempt to disguise the fact. Barclay was the crown prince. He was destined to take over the family firm. He was sent to an expensive school, so that he'd gain a place in one of the top universities. Tel, on the other hand, had to make do with being educated locally.'

'And the mother just accepted that?'

'I don't think she had any choice in the matter. Joseph held the purse strings, and Joseph called the shots.'

'It must have been terrible for Tel,' Pania-towski said with feeling.

'It got worse,' Fuller told her. 'Whatever Tel did – however successful he was – it was never good enough for Joseph. Tel won prizes, and Joseph never turned up to see him collect them. Tel captained the school football team, and had to play without his father there to cheer him on. But he overcame all obstacles, didn't he? Just like you did. As soon as he was old enough, he joined the RAF.'

'And became a hero,' Paniatowski said.

'And became a hero,' Fuller agreed. He paused, to suck a little air into his leathery old lungs. 'I liked most of the pupils I taught, Mon-ika, but there were only a few I actually *admired* – and you and Tel Lowry were both members of that select group.'

Paniatowski sighed. The problem about trying to dig up dirt on Tel Lowry, she decided, was that the more she got to know about the man – and the disadvantages that he, too, had suffered – the more she found herself warming to him.

'Councillor Scranton didn't happen to pass through your hands, as well, did he?' she asked.

Fuller scowled. 'That piece of shit!' he said.

The phrase rocked Paniatowski. She knew, objectively, the teachers must swear, just like ordinary people, but it was still a shock to hear one of them actually do it.

'In what way was he a piece of shit?' she asked, marvelling at her own courage in repeat-ing the words in front of her old teacher, even if

151

he *had* used them first.

'In what way?' Fuller said. 'In any way you'd care to think of. He was a bully and a sneak – and possibly a thief as well. He liked to pick on the children who didn't quite fit in, and, of course, Tel Lowry was one of them. The bullying went on for quite some time, until Tel decided to square up to him in the playground one day. I was on playground duty at the time, and if I'd seen the fight, of course, I'd have been morally – and *contractually* – obliged to stop it.'

'But you didn't see it?'

Fuller grinned. 'No. I could see what was *about to* happen, and I found I had developed a sudden fascination for the cloakroom door. And that door didn't stop being fascinating until Scranton was on the ground, and had no intention of getting up again. When I did finally deign to notice him, I could see he was a real mess, so I told him he'd better be more careful in the future, or he'd fall over again. He got the message clearly enough.'

'He would have done,' Paniatowski agreed.

'Funnily enough, though they obviously didn't plan it, they both ended up not only in the RAF, but posted to the same base. Abingdon, I think it was.'

Paniatowski smiled. 'Where they buried the hatchet, and became great friends?' she suggested.

'That sort of thing might happen in films, but I've never seen it happen in real life,' Fuller told her. 'Besides, Tel was an officer and a hero, while Scranton was nothing more than an enlisted man. And from what I've heard, they weren't on the same base for long, anyway, because Scranton was dishonourably discharged.'

'And now he's a town councillor,' Paniatowski said.

'And now he's a town councillor,' Fuller agreed. 'Makes you think, doesn't it?'

Rutter slid the photograph of Philip Turner and his wife across the desk to Woodend.

The chief inspector studied it for a moment. 'They look as if they were very happy together,' he said. 'An' she was killed in an accident, was she?'

'That's right,' Rutter confirmed. 'And according to his brother, that's when he started to go to pieces. And once he was on the slippery slope, he couldn't make himself stop, until eventually it got to the point where he couldn't do his job properly, and he was fired.'

An' there should be a warnin' in that for you, Bob, Woodend thought.

'So you don't think there's any connection between Turner's former life in Manchester an' what happened to him in Whitebridge?' he asked.

'None at all,' Rutter said. He reached across the desk, picked up the picture again, and slid it into his pocket. 'Well, if that's all, I'll see about getting this picture printed up and circulated,' he continued.

'But *is it* all?' Woodend wondered.

Rutter looked puzzled. 'Well, yes. Unless there

is something else you'd like to add.'

'I was rather hopin' that *you'd* have something to add,' Woodend said heavily.

'I'm afraid I'm not following you, sir.'

Woodend sighed. 'You've been out most of the day, yet all you seem to have done is talk to Turner's brother.'

'Not *just* talked to him,' Rutter pointed out. 'Don't forget, I had to *find* him first.'

'An' how difficult was that?' Woodend wondered.

'Not *too* difficult, but even so—' Rutter began.

'You seem to forget I've done that kind of work myself,' Woodend interrupted him. 'An', even more significantly, I've seen the speed at which *you've* done that kind of work in the past. It shouldn't have taken you nearly all day, Bob. You should have been back here hours ago.'

'I am a *detective inspector*!' Rutter said angrily.

'What's your point?' Woodend wondered.

'My point is that not only have I more than earned your respect by the work I've done for you, but I'm *entitled* to your respect by virtue of my rank – which is only one below yours. So I don't expect to be checked up on all the time, and I don't expect to have to account for every minute of my day to you.'

'Listen, Bob...' Woodend began.

But Rutter had no intention of listening. He had already stood up and was walking towards the door.

'There was a time when I would have taken this kind of crap from you, because I was your

154

boy,' Rutter said as a parting shot. 'But I've grown up, and I'm not your boy any more.'

He stepped out into the corridor, and slammed the door behind him.

Woodend, still sitting behind his desk, shook his head from side to side.

'No,' he said softly. 'No, you're *not* my boy any more.'

It was earlier that afternoon that the chief constable's secretary asked him if he wanted her to schedule a press conference in time for the reporters to meet their deadlines, and Marlowe had replied that he wasn't sure whether he wanted to hold one or not.

'Well, you could have knocked me over with a feather when he said that,' she later confided to her best friend, over an early evening glass of shandy in the local pub.

'Why's that?' the friend asked.

'Because Mr Marlowe *loves* press conferences. They're his favourite part of police work. He thinks they make him look authoritative, and I suppose they do, in a way. Besides,' she giggled, 'it gives him an excuse to put his best uniform on.'

'But he did decide to hold one in the end, didn't he?' the friend asked.

'Oh, yes. About an hour after he'd said he wasn't sure, he told me to go ahead and set it up.' The secretary glanced up at the clock on the wall. 'In fact, it should be starting about now.'

Henry Marlowe stepped on to the podium.

Given all the complications of the case – the lack of progress, Woodend's continued feud with Lowry, and the fact that his own solution to the problem had not yet had time to come to fruition – he was still not sure this press conference was a good idea, but he had decided that *not* to hold one would have invited too much unwelcome speculation.

He looked down at the faces of the gathered journalists, and began to feel more at ease. He was a past master at this kind of thing, he reassured himself, and surely a smart operator like him could find a way to grab some personal glory out of the occasion.

He devoted most of his opening remarks to the second attempted murder, the previous night, and managed – subtly, he thought – to suggest that whilst he had not actually been a party to the *physical* rescue of the tramp, the man would certainly have died but for his own behind-the-scenes work.

When he had finished his prepared statement, he threw the meeting open to questions.

'When do you expect to make an arrest?' asked one reporter, with annoying predictability.

'You should know by now that I never divulge that kind of information,' Marlowe replied reproachfully.

'In other words, you've no idea,' the reporter countered, in a clumsy attempt to goad him into some indiscretion.

'In other words, I am not prepared to prejudice the progress of my investigation simply to give you a story which will help you when it comes to negotiating your next pay rise,' Marlowe said, and was pleased to hear a few amused titters of laughter from around the room. 'Next question?'

Elizabeth Driver's right hand shot up immediately. She was wearing a glove on it, though there was not one on her left, and for a moment Marlowe wondered why that should be. Then he turned his mind to the more pressing problem of whether to allow her to ask the next question, and decided that since he would have to let her speak eventually, it might be best just to get it over with.

'Yes, Miss Driver?' he said.

'Why does the progress of your investigation involve picking up tramps in Whitebridge and dropping them the other side of the borough's border?' Elizabeth Driver asked.

'I beg your pardon!' Marlowe said.

'Why does it involve shipping tramps out of Whitebridge and abandoning them in Accrington?' Driver clarified.

Marlowe was starting to sweat. 'As far as I'm aware, Miss Driver, no such thing has occurred,' he said. 'But if I were to find out that the practice you've just described has, in fact, been going on...'

'Do you deny that you gave Constable Crabtree two pounds?' Driver demanded.

Oh Jesus! Marlowe groaned inwardly.

'It's possible that I may have given one of the men serving under me some money,' he said. 'Now I think about it, I'm certain I did. But I can't recall, for the moment, *why* I gave it to him.'

'Then let me help you remember,' Driver ploughed on relentlessly. 'In order to get the tramps into the van in the first place, you had to bribe them. And what you chose to bribe them with was booze. So you gave the two pounds to Constable Crabtree, who gave them to the owner of the off-licence...'

'This is pure fantasy!' Marlowe exploded.

'...who, in turn, gave them to me,' Driver continued, reaching into her handbag with her gloved hand and producing two pound notes. 'These are the notes in question. My fingerprints won't be on them, of course, because I'm wearing a glove, but I'm sure your police laboratory – which you never tire of telling us is one of the finest in the country – should have no difficulty finding evidence of *your* prints.'

'What the bloody hell did you think you were playing at?' Tel Lowry demanded angrily, down the telephone line.

'I ... I was simply trying to defuse the situation,' Henry Marlowe said. 'Charlie bloody Woodend wanted to keep the bobbies on the night patrol, and you wanted them taken off. Neither of you was going to budge an inch, and I was caught right in the middle of it. And since I couldn't see any way to resolve the problem as it stood, I thought I'd try and make it go away instead.'

'By moving the tramps out of our jurisdiction?'

'Well, yes.'

'How *many* of them have you transported?'

'Probably no more than half a dozen.'

'You're sure about that?'

'Certain. There would have been more, but then that Driver woman stuck her bloody oar in.'

'That's something to be thankful for, at least,' Lowry said. 'Accrington Council's been kicking up a stink since the news broke, but if it *is* only six of them we're talking about, we can probably weather the storm.'

Marlowe let out a sigh of relief. 'Thank you, Tel,' he said. 'Thank you so much.'

'For what?' Lowry asked.

'For saving my bacon.'

'You seem to be labouring under some kind of misapprehension here, Henry,' Lowry told him. 'When I said *we* could probably weather the storm, I was talking about my party in particular, and the council in general. In no way, shape or form was I referring to you.'

'You can't be serious,' Marlowe gasped.

'The Police Authority is meeting this evening with the sole purpose of considering your future,' Lowry said.

'And couldn't you tell them I was only trying to...?'

'But if I was you, I wouldn't bother waiting for their verdict. If I was you, I'd already be clearing out my desk.'

Fourteen

'How you doin', Col?' Scuddie asked Beresford, when he joined the hard mods outside the chip shop. 'Beaten up any Pakis recently?'

Beresford grinned. 'No, I haven't,' he admitted. 'I seem to be losin' my touch.'

'It's easy enough to *say* you've beaten up Pakis,' Big Bazza said sourly. 'Actually *doin'* it is somethin' else.'

The rest of the gang had accepted him easily enough, Beresford thought, but Big Bazza, who was probably starting to see him as a rival, was not so open to the idea – and Big Bazza was the one he really *needed* to get close to. Even so – and however much it was necessary that they become friends – he couldn't let what Bazza had just said go unchallenged.

Beresford squared up to the gang's leader. 'Are you callin' me a liar?' he demanded. 'Because if you are, we know how we can settle it, don't we?'

Big Bazza did no more than grin. He didn't want a fight. Why would he, when he had already planted seeds of doubt about his potential rival in the minds of the other gang members?

'No, I'm not callin' you a liar,' he told Beresford. 'All I'm sayin' is that *so far* you haven't done anythin' to convince us you're *not*.'

'Paki!' Little Bazza hissed, and the whole gang turned to look.

A woman wearing a long tunic with trousers beneath it – and with her head sheathed in a scarf – was passing them on the opposite side of the street.

'Paki bitch!' one of the gang called out.

'Piss off back to your own country, you black slag!' another added.

The woman immediately increased her pace.

'That's right, run for it, you cow,' Little Bazza jeered.

'She's scared,' Beresford said thoughtfully. 'But she's not as scared as she should be. Not *yet*.'

And before any of the others had had time to answer him, he was crossing the road and following the woman.

Once he was in position behind her, Beresford hunched his shoulders, put his hands under his armpits, and adopted the bow-legged gait of a chimpanzee. The rest of the hard mods, still on the other side of the road, thought it was one of the most hilarious things that they had ever seen.

The woman was aware she was being followed and she began walking even faster, but even with his own awkward style of moving, Beresford had no trouble in keeping up with her.

It was not until the two of them had reached the corner of the street that the woman appeared to lose her nerve and glance over her shoulder in order to see just how *serious* the threat behind

161

her was.

It seemed to the watching gang that this was just the signal that Beresford had been waiting for. He lashed out with his right boot, catching the woman on the upper thigh, and kicking her legs from under her. She fell backwards – as she was bound to – and cracked her head on the pavement.

Beresford looked down at the prone figure, as if inspecting his handiwork, then spat on her once, turned and walked back the way he had come.

There was no more laughter and applause from the gang. In fact, a sudden silence had descended on them.

'I don't think you should have done that,' Little Bazza said, when Beresford rejoined the group.

'Oh? An' why's that?' Beresford demanded. 'Afraid we'll get in trouble with the police?'

'No, it's not that,' Little Bazza said, eager to show that thoughts of the police didn't bother *him*. 'But she's ... she's a woman.'

'She's a Paki monkey!' Beresford said.

'Yeah, well, I know that, don't I? But ... but maybe you've killed her.'

'So what if I have?' Beresford asked. 'That'll just stop her bringin' any more Paki monkeys into the world, won't it?'

But he had not killed her. Though the woman had been lying still for a while, she now climbed painfully to her feet, and hobbled away.

'Shouldn't we be movin' on?' Scuddie asked.

'Why?' Beresford wondered. 'She won't go to

162

the police. An' even if she does, they won't listen to her. Because why? Because they hate Pakis as much as we do.'

'Yeah, but what if she tells her family?' Little Bazza asked. 'They might come here mob-handed, lookin' for us.'

'That's what I'm hopin' for,' Beresford said. 'That's the main reason why I did it. I fancy a good punch-up.' He paused, as if he'd suddenly realized he'd been talking out of turn. 'But it's not up to me whether we stay or go, is it?' he continued. 'It's up to Big Bazza. He's the leader of the gang. Isn't that right, Bazza?'

'Bloody right,' Bazza agreed, looking at him with approval, and also – perhaps – with just a hint of gratitude.

'What I don't understand is why you had to open your mouth in that press conference,' Elizabeth Driver's editor said aggrievedly, from the other end of the line.

'I needed to confirm my story before I ran with it,' Driver said.

'Why?' the editor asked, now sounding more puzzled than angry. 'That kind of thing's never bothered you before.'

'Maybe I'm turning over a new leaf,' Driver suggested.

'Well, if you do, you'll be no good to me *or* this paper,' the editor pointed out. 'We could have had an exclusive if you'd just kept quiet.'

'We *do* have an exclusive – of sorts,' Driver told him. 'When all the other papers report on the story, they'll have no choice but to admit that it was the *Gazette*'s star reporter who broke it.'

'That's not the same as having a scoop,' the editor grumbled.

No, it wasn't, Driver agreed silently. It was *better* than a scoop – at least from her viewpoint. Her name would be in *all* the papers, not just her own. She would become a minor national celebrity. And there couldn't possibly be any better publicity for her book than that.

However, the book wasn't out yet, and until it was she still needed her job, so perhaps it was time to extend the olive branch.

'I'm really sorry, Rick,' she said with a mock sincerity that was so practised it sounded better than the real thing. 'Next time I have an exclusive, I promise I won't breathe a word to anybody. And there *will be* a next time, you know – because I'm too good a reporter not to be able to do it again.'

'Well, make sure it's soon,' the editor said, somewhat mollified.

As she replaced the phone on its cradle, Driver found herself wondering who could be cast in the film version of her book.

Michael Caine or Tom Courtney would both be perfect for Bob Rutter, but Woodend would be more of a problem. Perhaps Stewart Granger or James Mason might be able to carry it off.

She hoped Bob wouldn't take it too badly when he found out about the book, and from the way things had been developing recently, she was *almost* sure that he wouldn't.

The hard mods were sitting around the base of

Sir Robert Peel's statute in the Corporation Park when the Town Hall clock chimed ten, and as soon as the sound had died away Big Bazza stood up and said, 'Well, I think I'll take myself off home.'

That night, nobody accused him of wanting to run home to his mum. The truth was, they were all ready to go home, too, because after all the excitement of watching Col in action had faded away, the evening had begun to feel like a bit of a drag.

'Where are we meetin' tomorrow night, Baz?' Scuddie asked.

'Meet where you like,' Bazza said, with careless indifference. 'I won't be here. I'm off on my holidays.'

'Holidays?' Scuddie repeated. 'At this time of year?'

'That's right.'

'Well, rather you than me. I wouldn't fancy lyin' on the beach at Blackpool in this weather.'

'I'm not goin' to Blackpool. I'm goin' to Spain,' Bazza said, obviously relishing the sound of the last word.

The announcement had the bombshell effect on the rest of the gang that he'd known it would. People like them didn't go to anywhere exotic like *Spain*. The whole idea was inconceivable.

'Where'd you get the money from?' Little Bazza asked.

'Been savin' up.'

'On *your* wages?'

'I've been puttin' a little bit away each week. It's surprisin' how quickly it mounts up.' Big

Bazza started to walk away, then turned round and said, 'So I'll see you lot next week – when I'm lovely an' brown.'

'Jammy sod!' said Scuddie, his voice thick with envy. 'Isn't he a jammy sod?' he asked the others.

No! Beresford thought. He's a bastard! A complete bloody bastard!

It was half-past ten when Beresford arrived at the Drum and Monkey, and the only two people sitting at the team's usual table were Woodend and Paniatowski.

'Is Inspector Rutter coming later?' Beresford asked – and the moment he saw the look on Woodend's face, he knew he had made a mistake.

'Inspector Rutter won't be comin' *at all*,' the chief inspector growled. 'Inspector Rutter's got better things to do with his time than consort with the likes of us.'

Beresford sat down, and turned his attention to Paniatowski. 'All right, Sarge?' he asked.

'*All right?*' Paniatowski shot back at him. 'My head's splitting, and by tomorrow morning there'll be a bruise on my thigh as big as a football.'

Beresford looked down at the table top. 'I had to make it convincing,' he mumbled.

'I know you did,' Paniatowski agreed. 'But surely you could have been convincing without being quite so bloody enthusiastic.'

Woodend chuckled. 'She's not really angry, you know,' he said. 'In fact, she was telling me

166

just now how well you did.'

'I was *telling you* how hard his bloody boot felt,' Paniatowski contradicted him, but now she was smiling too.

'Did it work?' Woodend asked. 'Did it convince the gang that you're one of them?'

'Yes, it did,' Beresford replied, 'but I don't know how much good it will do, because my prime suspect's off to Spain tomorrow.'

'Or says he is,' Woodend said cryptically.

'Sorry, sir?'

'People like Barry Thornley have absolutely no idea where Spain is,' Woodend said. 'They probably think it's somewhere up in the sky, which is why they need a plane to reach it. They certainly don't go there for their holidays.'

'He said he was.'

'An' maybe he was lyin'. Maybe it's not so much that he's goin' somewhere in search of the heat, but more a case of just gettin' out of Whitebridge, because after I ended up with his boot in my hand *this* place is too hot for him.'

'If it *was* his boot,' Paniatowski pointed out.

'If it *was* his boot,' Woodend agreed. 'Anyway, there's only one way to find out where he's really goin', isn't there? An' that's to follow him.'

'Me?' Beresford asked.

'You,' Woodend confirmed.

'But he knows me.'

'Then wear a disguise, for God's sake!'

'A disguise?' Beresford repeated, sounding very confused.

'Bloody hell, you're a squeaky-clean detective

constable, but you've passed yourself off as a hard mod,' Woodend reminded him. 'An' if you can manage that, then lookin' a slightly different kind of "normal" should be a piece of piss.'

'I'll help you, Colin,' Paniatowski promised. 'Women are very good at disguises.'

'Too bloody right,' Woodend agreed. 'They're the absolute...'

Then he stopped speaking, and gazed – goggle-eyed – at the television in the corner of the room.

Beresford and Paniatowski, following his lead, did the same – and saw just what it was that had knocked their boss off-balance.

Henry Marlowe! Standing behind his beloved podium, and staring hauntedly at the camera. There was a clock behind his shoulder which showed this was not a recording, but was going out live.

'What the hell's he doing?' Woodend asked. 'The press conference was earlier, wasn't it?'

Paniatowski nodded. 'It was scheduled for seven o'clock,' she said.

'An' how did it go?'

'Probably like most of Mr Marlowe's press conferences – a lot of piss and wind, and very little else.'

'Turn the sound on for a minute, will you?' Woodend called urgently to the barman.

The barman nodded, walked over to the set, turned the knob, and Marlowe's voice filled the room.

'I have been battling with ill health for some time,' the chief constable said in a shaky voice, 'but have stayed in my post because I wished to continue to serve the community as I always have. But today I learned that will no longer be possible. On the advice of my doctor, I have tendered my resignation, effective from seven o'clock this evening. The Police Authority have appointed Deputy Chief Constable Miles Hobson as my interim replacement. He is a good policeman, and I am sure he will continue to follow the high standards I have laid down. Goodbye, and may God bless you all.'

'The high standards he's laid down,' Paniatowski said contemptuously. '*What* high standards? If he had any, *I've* never noticed them.'

'One of the first things I was told when I joined the Force was never to trust Henry Marlowe,' Beresford said. 'The general opinion in the canteen was that he'd sell you down the river as soon as think about it.'

But Woodend himself had said nothing so far, because his mind was still reeling from the news.

His old enemy was gone. The man he had fought a hundred battles with had finally been vanquished.

He found his voice at last.

'It's the end of an era,' he said.

And then he realized that it had been feeling like the end of an era to *him* from the moment the investigation had started.

Fifteen

It felt very strange to be in an attractive single woman's flat at six o'clock in the morning, Beresford thought, especially if you had not previously spent the night there. And it seemed even stranger to be sitting in a straight-backed chair, looking into a mirror, while this same attractive woman fussed over you.

'If I'd had more time, I could have borrowed some more professional make-up from the local repertory theatre,' Paniatowski said. 'As it is, we'll have to make do with the stuff I use myself.'

'I didn't know you used any make-up, Sarge,' Beresford said.

Paniatowski smiled into the mirror. 'Bless you, you sweet naive child,' she said.

She worked on him for half an hour, first applying a foundation, then using an eyebrow pencil.

'It won't fool anybody standing close to you...' Paniatowski began.

'You're not kidding,' Beresford said morosely.

'...but from a distance, which is as close as you *should* get to Barry Thornley, you won't be the least recognizable.'

Beresford could do no more than agree. He

170

certainly didn't look much like himself – but then he didn't look much like anyone else, either.

The morning paper – *Elizabeth Driver*'s paper – was waiting for Woodend on his desk with a note from Paniatowski which ended in several exclamation marks, and it was by reading through Driver's article that he finally learned the true story behind Henry Marlowe's unexpected resignation.

He wasn't sure quite how he felt about it all. The simple truth was, he was finding it hard to believe that Marlowe was actually gone. It was a little like hearing that someone had died, he thought. You knew *objectively* that they were dead, yet you still expected them to come walking into the room at any moment.

He lit up a Capstan Full Strength – his fifth of the morning – and started to think about what the change would mean.

His first worry, he quickly decided, was Miles Hobson, who was now sitting in the chair formerly occupied by Marlowe's fat arse. Hobson was not a bad sort of feller – he had none of Marlowe's underlying viciousness – but neither was he a particularly strong one, and Councillor Lowry would find it even easier to make him jump through hoops than he had his predecessor. And that could be bad – very bad – for the investigation.

Marlowe's sudden demise wouldn't make working with Bob Rutter any easier, either, he thought. Or rather, he corrected himself, it wouldn't make it any easier working with the man Rutter had *become.*

Bob already thought that the sun shone out of Elizabeth Driver's backside, and that the whole team should all fall down and worship her because – for reasons of her own, as yet undisclosed – she had written the article which had saved Woodend's job. God alone knew how he would expect them to regard her now she had actually *removed* the arch-enemy.

A young uniformed constable appeared in the open doorway, and stood there uncertainly, as if he was not sure whether to knock on the door jamb or walk straight in.

'Don't just hover there, lad, you're makin' the place look untidy,' Woodend said. 'Is there somethin' I can do for you?'

The constable stepped cautiously into the office and held out an expensive-looking envelope. 'I was told to bring this to you, sir,' he said.

'Where'd it come from?'

'It was delivered to the front desk by messenger, five minutes ago.'

Woodend slit open the envelope, and scanned the note inside.

I think we need to talk, either at police headquarters or at the factory, he read. *I'm perfectly willing to come to you, but I can't make it until the afternoon at the earliest, so if you can free up the time, I'd much prefer it if you came to me.*

It was signed *Tel Lowry.*

Now that was a surprise, Woodend thought.

A double surprise.

172

Not only did Lowry want to talk to him, but he was setting up the meeting by invitation, rather than summons.

Of course, it was always possible that both the letter and its tone were no more than part of Lowry's devious strategy to get himself re-elected, but nevertheless, it looked like it promised to be a very *interesting* meeting.

The disguised Beresford sat behind the wheel of an unmarked police car, a few doors down from Big Bazza's house. At a quarter past eight the front door opened, and Bazza stepped out into the street. He was dressed in his normal 'uniform', and, instead of a suitcase, he was carrying a bulging duffel bag which was probably stuffed with his clothes. Beresford half-expected someone else to appear in the doorway, to wave Bazza goodbye, but no one did.

The hard mod walked down the street in a purposeful way, and Beresford let him get nearly to the corner before slipping his vehicle into gear and following.

If Bazza was intending to go any distance on foot, it wouldn't be long before he noticed the car slowly crawling behind him, Beresford thought worriedly. But the worry proved groundless. There was a taxi idling at the corner of the street, and Bazza climbed into it.

Why make it wait there? Beresford wondered. Why not have it pick him up at his own front door?

The taxi set off with Beresford in pursuit, and was soon leaving Whitebridge on the A675. It skirted around both Bolton and Manchester, and, an hour and a half after it had set out, pulled on to the car park at Ringway Airport.

Keeping his distance, Beresford followed Bazza into the terminal, and watched him as he walked up to the BEA check-in desk and handed over his ticket. Then, when Bazza had left for the departure gate, Beresford went over to the check-in desk himself, and showed his warrant card.

The woman behind the desk looked at his card, then at his face. And then she laughed.

That wouldn't happen to Woodend, Rutter or Paniatowski, Beresford thought. They *looked* like proper bobbies.

'What's the matter? It's real,' he said, holding out the warrant card for the woman to inspect a second time.

'So you say, chuck, but real or not, the heat in here's started to make it melt,' she told him.

The warrant card looked all right to Beresford. Then he touched his face, discovered how sticky it was – and realized what she was talking about.

The bloody make-up that Sergeant Paniatowski had applied was sodding running!

'It's a disguise,' he said weakly.

'Well, if that's what it is, it's not a very *good* one,' the woman replied, fighting the giggles. 'Instead of making you blend in with the crowd, all it does is draw attention to you.'

'I need information,' Beresford said, adopting his most official-sounding voice.

'Of course,' the woman said, making a valiant attempt to be serious. 'What can I do for you – '

she glanced down at the warrant card, which Beresford was still holding out – 'Detective Constable Beresford?'

'The man with the short hair, who just checked in...'

'That would be Mr Barry Thornley,' the woman said, consulting her passenger list.

'That's right,' Beresford agreed. 'I want to know where he's gone, and how long he's gone for.'

'He's gone to Malaga in Spain, and he'll be there for a week,' the woman said.

'Thank you for your cooperation, madam,' Beresford said with dignity, before turning and walking away.

'When you get home, I'd apply some Boots No.7 cleansing cream, if I was you,' the woman called after him. 'That's what I always use. It takes make-up off a treat.'

The woman waiting for Paniatowski in the interview room was in her late sixties, and even the expensive tailored clothes she was wearing could not disguise the fact that she was carrying a lot of excess weight. But strip away the fat – and strip off the years – and you could see that she must have been a real stunner when she was younger, Paniatowski thought.

'They said at the desk that you were most insistent that you wanted to see me – and *only* me – but that you refused to give your name,' the sergeant said, sitting down.

'That's right.'

'Would you mind telling me *why* you wouldn't

give your name?'

'I didn't give it because I didn't want to lose the element of surprise.'

'I beg your pardon?'

'As well you might. My name's Lucinda Lowry. I'm Councillor Lowry's mother.'

'Oh!' Paniatowski said.

'Now you see, if you'd known my name in advance, I'd never have got that reaction from you, and I'd never have known for sure that you were the woman I was after,' Mrs Lowry said.

'The woman you were after?' Paniatowski asked, playing for time. 'Why should you be "after" me?'

'Nice try, but you must have realized it was never going to work,' Mrs Lowry said.

Yes, I did realize that, Paniatowski admitted silently.

'If you could be more specific about why you're here...' she said.

'Specifically, there was a blonde woman called Monika in the Engineer's Arms the other night, and she was asking some of our workers questions about my son. Now when I heard about it from one of those men, I asked myself who this blonde was, and I decided she had to be either a journalist or a policewoman. And the more I thought about it, the more convinced I was she was a policewoman, because on the one hand, there's nothing about Tel that could possibly be of any interest to the press, and on the other, Tel's the chairman of the Police Authority, so he's bound to have made some enemies in the Force.'

Spot on, Paniatowski thought, admiringly.

'Of course, if you hadn't been stupid enough to use your own name, it would have taken me longer to find you,' Mrs Lowry continued, 'but I would have found you eventually.'

'Yes, I believe you would,' Paniatowski conceded.

'And now I'm here, I have one simple question I'd like to ask you,' Mrs Lowry said. 'And can you guess what it is?'

'You want to know why I was asking questions about your son?'

'Exactly.'

'I'm afraid I can't tell you that.'

'Then let me try you with another one. Were you doing it off your own bat, or because you were told to?'

'I'm afraid I can't answer that either,'

'So you were *told* to do it. Who by? Chief Inspector Woodend?'

'I—' Paniatowski began.

'I know, you can't tell me that, either,' Mrs Lowry interrupted.

'That's correct,' Paniatowski agreed.

'It'll have been Woodend,' Mrs Lowry said confidently. 'He'll have *made* you do it, whether you wanted to or not. Men are such bastards – and I should know, because I was married to one of them for over thirty years. So, bearing that in mind, I'm not blaming you for what's happened – I'm just telling you that it has to stop. Is that clear? I will *not* tolerate a police vendetta against my son.'

'Does he know you're here?' Paniatowski

177

asked.

'He does not. He knows nothing about this whole sordid business. He's got enough on his plate, trying to make this town a better place to live in, without having to deal with matters I can perfectly well manage myself.'

'I can't make any promises,' Paniatowski said.

'Of course you can't,' Mrs Lowry agreed. 'You're nothing but a minor cog in the wheel. So I'll make a promise myself. I've lived in this town for over sixty years, and I've got to know a lot of important people in that time. In some ways, I have much more influence than my son does – and I'll use that influence if DCI Woodend doesn't call off his dogs.'

'I'll pass your message along,' Paniatowski said.

'Thank you, I'd appreciate that.' Mrs Lowry stood up and walked over to the door. 'There is one more thing I'd better make clear before I leave,' she said.

'Yes?'

'I said I don't blame you for what's happened, but that shouldn't lull you into thinking I admire you as a plucky little woman keeping her head held high in a man's world. The simple truth is that I disliked you on first sight, and that I never expect to see you, or hear from you, ever again. Have I made myself clear?'

'More than clear,' Paniatowski said.

'This is Mr Lowry's office,' said the secretary with the blue-rinsed hair, as he pushed open the large double doors. 'He asked me to apologize for not being here to greet you personally, but something's come up on the shop floor that he had to deal with immediately. If you don't mind waiting, he shouldn't be more than a few minutes.'

'No problem,' Woodend told her.

'Well, then, please go inside and make yourself at home.'

Woodend stepped into the office, and looked around him with frank curiosity. It was a big room, but even so, the rosewood desk in the centre managed to dominate it. The walls were lined with books, many of them leather-bound, and close to the picture window were two leather chairs and an inlaid coffee table.

It was a room designed to impress, the chief inspector decided, and – despite his best efforts – it was doing just that.

Hanging on the wall behind the desk was a large oil painting of a man standing in the foreground, with the factory behind him. He was dressed in the style of an earlier generation, but it was not his clothes which caught Woodend's attention. Rather it was the eyes, which were intense and ice-cold.

'When Oliver Cromwell had his portrait painted, he instructed the artist to portray him as he was – warts and all – and I rather suspect that my father gave his painter exactly the same instruction,' said a voice from the doorway.

Woodend turned, and saw that Tel Lowry had entered the room.

'Your note said you wanted to see me,' he said, neutrally.

'It was the eyes you were drawn to in the picture, wasn't it?' Lowry asked.

'Yes, it was,' Woodend agreed.

'It's the eyes that draw everyone,' Lowry said. 'My father was a hard, unrelenting man, and he didn't care who knew it. He was a firm believer in the adage that if you were determined enough – and ruthless enough – you could achieve anything you desired. But one thing he *couldn't* do – though he desperately wanted to – was get elected to the council. He stood several times, you know, but despite the fact that he had a lot of clout in this town, he never even came close to winning a seat.'

'An' you did,' Woodend said.

'And I did,' Lowry agreed. He walked across the room, and sat down in one of the easy chairs. 'Please join me,' he said, gesturing to the other one.

Woodend sat.

'Tea?' Lowry asked. 'Coffee? Something a little stronger?'

'Nothing,' Woodend replied.

'Then I suppose we'd better get down to business,' Lowry suggested. He cupped his left knee with both his hands, then continued, 'We seem to have got off on quite the wrong footing the last time that we met, and that was probably mostly my fault. I've been under a lot of pressure over the council budget, you see, and I may have slightly over-reacted to the idea of a sudden huge increase in police overtime payments.'

'Is there an apology hidden in there, somewhere?' Woodend wondered aloud.

'You're not an easy man to handle, are you, Chief Inspector?' Lowry asked. 'Most of the people I deal with would have seen where I was leading the conversation by now, and made at least a token effort to smooth my path for me.'

'Ah, but then, you see, most of the people you deal with are probably *politicians*,' Woodend replied. 'An' I'm not especially noted for my skill in that particular area.'

Lowry frowned, and then the frown turned into a smile. 'You're quite right,' he said. 'That's the very root of the problem. I dealt with you as one politician would deal with another.'

'So politicians use each other's families as leverage, do they?' Woodend asked.

'Politicians use *anything* they can as leverage,' Lowry said airily. 'But it's a game, you see. A simple tactic on the chessboard of municipal affairs, which nobody involved ever takes seriously. Your ex-boss, the largely unlamented Henry Marlowe, knew the rules, and would have responded pretty much as I expected him to – but I should never have tried that kind of approach on a down-to-earth straightforward bobby like you.'

'Down-to-earth straightforward bobbies aren't very susceptible to flattery, either,' Woodend said.

'I wasn't flattering you, I was merely stating an obvious fact,' Lowry told him. 'And since you, quite rightly, don't like apologies which are hidden in a thicket of other words, here's one out in the open – I'm very sorry I tried to bully you, Chief Inspector, and it won't happen again.'

'Excuse me for bein' suspicious but—' Wood-end began.

'But you're wondering what's behind all this? You're wondering, specifically, what's in it for me?'

'Exactly.'

'A chance to put things right. I should never have tried to cut back on the night-time patrols. It almost cost another life, in addition to giving Henry Marlowe a reason – at least by his lights – for doing something which was *quite* unacceptable.'

'An' which landed you right in the shit with Accrington Council,' Woodend said.

'And which landed me right in the shit with Accrington Council,' Lowry agreed. 'But that's all ancient history now. You want to maintain the night-time foot patrols, and I'm more than willing to agree to that. But they can't go on indefinitely. They'd bankrupt the town if they did.'

'So how long *can* they go on?'

'Another week,' Lowry said.

'Two weeks,' Woodend countered.

'All right,' Lowry agreed. 'But if they're going to be running for a fortnight, they'll have to be gradually scaled back.'

'Meanin' there'll have to be less men in a patrol in the second week than there are in the first?'

'Just so.'

'Could I borrow your phone for a minute?' Woodend asked.

'Of course,' Lowry agreed.

* * *

182

Beresford had only just walked through the door of police headquarters when the duty sergeant informed him that his boss was on the phone, and wanted to talk to him.

'Well?' Woodend asked, without preamble.

'Big Bazza really has gone to Spain,' Beresford said. 'He'll be away for a week.'

'So he wasn't lyin' after all,' Woodend said. 'Right, I'll see you in the Drum at one o'clock.'

The line went dead, and Beresford handed the phone back to the duty sergeant.

'Have you got anythin' planned for tonight, young Beresford?' the sergeant asked.

'That depends on Mr Woodend,' Beresford replied. 'Why do you ask?'

The sergeant grinned. 'Well, if you are free, I thought we might go dancin' an' have a bite of supper,' he said. 'An' after that,' he winked suggestively, 'who knows what might happen?'

The bloody make-up! Beresford thought.

He'd been sure he'd got it all off, but the sergeant's piss-take was a clear indication that he hadn't. Maybe he'd better follow the advice of the woman behind the BEA counter, and apply a little Boots No. 7 cleansing cream.

When Woodend put down the phone, he saw that Lowry was smiling.

'I couldn't help overhearing some of that,' the councillor said, 'and from *what* I heard, it would seem there's a lot of truth in the Woodend legend.'

'The Woodend legend?'

'It's widely believed, in certain circles, that

183

you and your team do some of your best work in the public bar of the Drum and Monkey. Henry Marlowe always thought it was a disgrace, and would have put a stop to it if he'd dared.'

'An' what do you think about it?'

'I think that I do some of *my* best work at cocktail parties and in the golf-club bar,' Lowry said. 'Shall we get back to the issue of the foot patrols?'

'Good idea,' Woodend agreed. 'If I can have full strength for one week an' reduced strength for another, then I'd prefer to have the full strength at my disposal in the *second* week.'

'May I ask why?'

'You can *ask*,' Woodend said. Then he realized how churlish he must sound, and continued, 'My prime suspect has just left Whitebridge. We expect him to stay away for a week.'

'I see,' Lowry said. 'Well, as far as I'm concerned, it's the amount of money you spend which matters, not *when* you choose to spend it. But that amount of money *is* fixed, Chief Inspector. And if, after two weeks, you've still not caught the killer, we'll have to assume that you'll *never* catch him unless there's another incident which might yield further information.'

Or, to put it another way, we'll go back to usin' what Monika Paniatowski called live bait, Woodend thought.

'There is *one* small condition attached to my support for you in this matter,' Lowry said.

He should have been expecting this, Woodend thought. He should have – but he hadn't been.

'*What* small condition?' he asked.

'You may have noticed a number of rather unsavoury young men, wearing braces and big boots, have started hanging around the streets,' Lowry said.

'They call themselves the hard mods,' Woodend told him.

'Do they indeed,' Lowry replied. 'And is it your opinion, Chief Inspector, that these young men are not only violent, but violently *anti-immigrant*?'

'They've a growin' tendency to be,' Woodend agreed.

'That sort of thing simply cannot be tolerated in a town like Whitebridge,' Lowry said. 'The Pakistani and Indian members of our community are entitled to protection, and it is our job to see that they are given it. Which is why, when the officers on your foot patrols come into contact with these young men, I want them to make it clear to them that violence against the darker-skinned members of the community will not be tolerated.'

'I think I'm beginnin' to get the hang of how this politics lark works,' Woodend said.

'Oh? You think so?'

'Definitely. Councillor Scranton's erodin' some of your white workin'-class support in your ward, but by the time the next elections come around, you'll have a fair number of Pakistani voters livin' there. Now if you can show these new voters that you're concerned about them, you might just keep your seat. An' what you've just asked me to tell my lads to do is the first step in showin' just how concerned

185

you really *are*.'

Lowry was silent for a moment, then he said, 'You would accept, wouldn't you, that my doing the right thing for *me* could also be doing what is simply the right thing *in general*?'

'Yes, I'd accept that,' Woodend said.

'What I've just asked you to do is the right thing in general, don't you think?'

Woodend thought about Councillor Scranton, and the vile speech he had delivered outside the factory gates.

'Yes,' he said. 'I believe it *is* the right thing.'

'Then we're agreed?' Lowry asked.

'We're agreed,' Woodend confirmed.

'I have to go away for a while,' Elizabeth Driver told Bob Rutter in the breakfast room of the Royal Victoria.

'But I thought you told me you were planning to stay until this case was over,' Rutter said, disappointedly.

'That *was* my plan, and my editor agreed to go along with it. But then he changed his mind.'

'Why?'

'Because he wants to punish me,' Driver said, speaking in a light, off-hand way, as if to demonstrate that whatever adversity she was faced with, she would handle it bravely and cheerfully.

'Punish you?' Rutter repeated.

'He's furious with me for not keeping the Henry Marlowe story to myself. *That's* why he's making me go.'

'Why *didn't* you keep the story to yourself?'

'I seriously thought about doing just that. It

would have been a wonderful feather in my cap if I had done. But, you see, if the story had only run in one newspaper, there was a chance that Marlowe would have somehow weathered the storm. And I knew how it important it was – both to you and Cloggin'-it Charlie – to get rid of the bloody man.'

Rutter smiled. 'You're far too good to be true, you know,' he said.

But he didn't mean it. There was no hint of suspicion in the statement, and if she *was* too good to be true, then all he could be was eternally grateful for it.

'I'm a better person for knowing you,' Driver said. 'In fact, I think I'm getting better every day, if that doesn't sound too arrogant.'

'It doesn't,' Rutter said. 'So where is this bastard of an editor sending you to?'

'Oxfordshire,' Driver told him. 'There's been a double murder down there. I have to admit that it does seem quite juicy, but ... you know...' she shrugged helplessly, '...I'd rather stay with you.'

'I *do* know that,' Rutter replied.

Wearing his hard-mod gear again, Beresford had returned to the road on which Big Bazza lived. It was a depressing street, he thought, but it was not the actual buildings themselves which made it so.

In fact, there was nothing at all wrong with terraced houses like the ones he was walking past, as long as they were properly cared for. But these weren't. The paint on the doors and window frames was worn and faded. Where windows had been cracked, the panes had been repaired with sticky tape, rather than replaced. And it wasn't lack of money that led to this dilapidation, he knew from his own experience as a beat bobby – it was lack of care.

The people who lived in these houses had *given up* caring. As long as they had the cash for a drink in their pockets, nothing else bothered them. And aside for the fact that they had roofs over their heads and that some of them occasionally had jobs, there was very little difference between them and the tramps.

He had reached the right door, and knocked. The woman who answered the knock was over-weight, with pendulous breasts and scraggy hair. She was wearing a loose smock which looked far from clean, and had an untipped cigarette dangling from the corner of her mouth.

'Yes?' she said, in an ungracious rasp.

'I'm callin' for Bazza,' Beresford said. 'Are you his mum?'

'Yes I am, an' he isn't here,' the woman replied.

'Do you know where he is?'

'He said he had some holiday time due, so he's gone away. I don't know where, exactly – I didn't ask, an' he didn't tell me – but it can't have been far, 'cos I keep most of his wages to pay for his food an' board.'

'Thanks, you've been very—' Beresford began, but he was only talking to the door, because the woman had gone back inside.

Big Bazza wasn't like his mother, or most of the other residents of this street, Beresford thought, as he turned and walked away. His appearance might frighten little children and old ladies, but at least he took some pride in it. And it was possible that if he had been born into some other family, on some other street, he might have made something of himself, instead of growing into a man who measured his own worth by the number of people he hated.

It was really no surprise that Bazza hadn't told his mother where he was going, Beresford thought. But it was surprising that he had chosen to go there at all.

What *had* put the idea of Spain into his head?

And how the hell had he managed to *pay* for it?

Sixteen

Woodend had not been expecting to see Bob Rutter at the Drum and Monkey, but not only did Rutter turn up, he was actually on time for once. So maybe the heated exchange between them earlier had served a purpose, Woodend thought hopefully, as he sat down at the usual table – maybe fences could still be mended, and Bob could regain his rightful place on the team.

After he had taken a sip of his pint, he told the rest of the team about his meeting with Councillor Lowry.

'I think we can work with him,' he concluded, after he'd spelled out all the detail. 'I really do.'

'Talk about going into reverse gear!' Paniatowski said, almost under her breath.

'What was that, Monika?' Woodend asked.

'I was just saying that your attitude to Lowry seems to have changed,' Paniatowski replied. 'And I mean changed *more than somewhat.*'

'Why shouldn't it have changed?' Woodend wondered. 'He's not given me everything I want – no chairman of the Police Authority would ever have done that – but at least he's made an effort to meet me halfway.'

'So yesterday he was the devil incarnate, and now he's a knight in shining armour?'

Woodend shook his head. 'You should know me better than to imagine I'd ever think like that. Tel Lowry's a politician down to his boot straps, and that little trick that Marlowe pulled has damaged his own standing more badly than he's willing to admit.'

'I still don't see...'

'An' if he's ever to regain the ground he's lost as a result of it, he has to be seen to be distancin' himself from our beloved ex-chief constable – an' that means him gettin' closer to me. So no, Sergeant Paniatowski, I don't see him as a knight in shinin' armour, but for the moment, at least, it's in his interest to ally himself to us – an' we need all the allies we can get.'

'So all the work that I did on his background has been wasted?' Paniatowski said.

'You never *wanted* to do that background check in the first place,' Woodend pointed out.

That was true enough, Paniatowski thought, and after the session she'd had with the formidable Mrs Lowry, it was perverse of her to be annoyed. But the simple fact was that she *was* annoyed. Bloody annoyed!

'Right,' Woodend said, 'if Sergeant Paniatowski's willin' to concede that we've spent enough time on Councillor Lowry, we can move on to Barry Thornley? Up until this mornin', Bazza was no more than a *possible* suspect, because he's not the only lad in Whitebridge who wears big boots an' hates Pakistanis an' tramps. But as a result of his takin' this trip, he's become our *prime* suspect, hasn't he? An' why is that, Colin?'

191

'Because he'd never have raised the money himself, and even if he had, it would probably never have occurred to him to spend it on a holiday in Spain,' Beresford replied.

'Exactly,' Woodend agreed. 'It was somebody else's money, an' somebody else's idea. An' it wasn't *family* money or *family* ideas, because you've already checked out that possibility, haven't you, Colin?'

Beresford nodded. 'His mother could never have raised the cash – even if she'd wanted to – and she has no idea where he's gone.'

'So the way I see it, the holiday was both a reward for what he'd already done, an' a way of gettin' him out of Whitebridge until the heat died down a bit.'

'Why do you keep talking about *somebody*, when we all know you mean Councillor Scranton?' asked Paniatowski.

'Because *I* don't know it *is* Councillor Scranton,' Woodend countered. 'He's certainly a possibility, but there are more right-wing middle-class nutters in Whitebridge than you could shake a stick at.'

'Scranton was dishonourably discharged from the RAF,' Paniatowski said. 'He was stationed in Abingdon at the same time as Lowry. You might ask your new pal, Tel, about that.'

She was still feeling as if her feathers had been ruffled, Woodend thought, and as illogical as that feeling might be, he could understand it.

'Look, I'm not rulin' Scranton out of the picture, by any means,' he told his sergeant, in a placatory tone. 'I'd even go so far as to say that if it's *not* him who's financin' Barry Thornton, it's likely to be one of his friends or associates – or at least somebody he knows well.'

Paniatowski shot him a look which suggested she thought he was doing no more than humour her.

'If you really believe that, it follows that it's as important for us to get as close to Scranton as it was for Colin to get close to the hard mods,' Paniatowski said challengingly.

'Yes, it is,' Woodend agreed, rising to the challenge. 'An' I was thinkin' of usin' young Beresford for that job, too, since the hard mods seem to be some of Scranton's closest supporters.'

'Colin would have to get to him through Bazza, and Bazza isn't here,' Paniatowski pointed out. 'Besides, the hard mods are no more than Scranton's foot soldiers. He's never going to take any of them into his confidence.'

'Then who do *you* suggest we use?' Woodend asked.

'Me,' Paniatowski said.

'An' how do you propose to get close to him?'

'I don't,' Paniatowski said. 'I'm going to make him want to get close to me.'

'An' how do you propose to do that?' Woodend wondered.

'How do you *think* I propose to do that?' Paniatowski countered.

'If he's going to be a primary target, we need to do a very deep background check on him,' Rutter said, out of the blue.

Woodend was surprised, not so much by the suggestion itself as by the fact that it had been

193

made by a man who, for the previous half an hour, had been sitting at the edge of the table like a ghost at a banquet – a man who, despite his earlier hopes, seemed scarcely a part of the team any more.

'Go on,' he said encouragingly.

'The key to a man's present often lies in his past – especially in some big event in his past,' Rutter continued. 'That was one of the first lessons you drummed into us.'

'Aye,' Woodend agreed cautiously. 'It was.'

'A big event in Ron Scranton's past, as we've just learned from Monika, is his dishonourable discharge from the RAF. That needs to be looked into in much more detail.'

'You're right,' Woodend agreed. 'I'll give the Abingdon police a call, an' see what they can turn up.'

'No disrespect intended to the Abingdon bobbies, but I think you need to do more than that,' Rutter said.

'What have you got in mind?'

'Send one of *us* down there. We know how to ask the right kinds of questions. We know about the need to clog it around and get a feel for the place – because that's *another* thing you've drummed into us.'

'You've got a point,' Woodend agreed. 'But since Beresford's tied up with hard mods, an' Monika will be workin' on getting' close to Councillor Scranton, the only person available is you.'

Bob Rutter smiled. 'I'd already managed to work that out for myself, sir,' he said.

Woodend chewed the idea over in his mind.

It was a long shot that Bob would turn up anything useful in Abingdon, he argued – but then long shots had been known to work before. Besides, since the two strongest leads in the case were already being handled by Beresford and Paniatowski, there was little to keep Rutter busy in Whitebridge – for the moment, at least.

He pulled himself up short, recognizing the arguments he was making were just window-dressing, and that the *real* reason the idea was so appealing was that the inspector seemed so enthusiastic about it himself – and letting him follow it through might just be a way of pulling him back from the brink.

'All right, Bob, you go down to Abingdon,' he said, and was gratified to note that Rutter seem-ed delighted at the prospect.

'Where exactly *is* Abingdon?' Beresford ask-ed.

'Somewhere down south,' Rutter said vaguely, giving him, Woodend noted, an unexpectedly hostile look.

'I think it's in Oxfordshire,' Paniatowski said. 'About twenty miles from Oxford itself.'

Barry Thornley had never really believed in heaven – at least, not a heaven for the likes of him – but now he realized he'd been wrong about that all along. There *was* a heaven – and he'd landed in it an hour and a half earlier.

Standing on the promenade, watching the palm trees sway in the breeze, he was still not sure it was anything but a dream. Except he had never

– *could never* have dreamed anything like this.

The sea was so blue, and so was the cloudless sky. The people on the promenade were dressed in bright, casual clothes – shorts or white trousers, sandals and brilliantly coloured shirts – and for the first time in his life, he felt out of place in his drab industrial clothing.

Not that there was any real *need* to feel out of place, he realized. These holiday-makers, if they noticed him at all, neither pointed him out for ridicule nor tried to shy away from him in fear. They didn't *care* what he looked like. They were there to enjoy themselves – dipping in the sea, sitting on the pavement in front of the small cheery bars which made the pubs and off-licences of Whitebridge seem so incredibly dingy – and that was all they were interested in.

The Boss had said he would like it here, and the Boss – as always – had been right.

As the gentle breeze caressed his cheeks, Bazza closed his eyes, and found himself thinking about the day the Boss had recruited him.

'You are a warrior of purity and freedom, operating within a secret army,' the Boss had told him. 'And it is because the army is secret that you must have a code name. I will call you the Avenger.'

Bazza had liked the sound of that. 'An' what should I call you?' he'd asked.

'Since you will report only *to* me, and talk to no one else *about* me, I leave that up to you. What would you like to call me?'

'I don't know.'

'You may, if you wish, address me as the

Leader, which is how Hitler's and Mussolini's followers addressed them.'

But Bazza hadn't cared for that name. It seemed to him to sound very *un-English*.

The Boss, seeing his obvious discomfort with the name, had smiled and said, 'Or, if you prefer it, you may call me the Boss.'

'Yes, I'll call you the Boss – because that's what you *are*,' Barry had said.

He admired the Boss more than any other man he had ever met. He would die for him, if needs be. And yet, he thought guiltily, despite all the admiration and devotion he felt, he had shown weakness and disobeyed the Boss's direct orders the previous night.

'As long as you're in England, the White-bridge police can find a way to get at you,' the Boss had said. 'You'll be much safer abroad. But you must tell nobody where you're going. Not your mother. Not your friends. Nobody! Do you understand, Avenger?'

'Yes, Boss,' Bazza had said obediently.

And he'd meant it. He really had. Yet some-how, when he'd been with the lads the previous night, he'd found himself unable to resist telling them.

He still wasn't sure quite *why* it had happened. Perhaps there was a part of him that wanted to make them jealous. But there was also a part of him, he had convinced himself, which had want-ed to give them *hope*.

To dangle the idea of escape in front of them.

To plant in their minds the idea that maybe, one day, they could follow in his footsteps.

There was another order that the Boss had given him over the phone, just before he took off.

'Don't get yourself noticed out there, Avenger,' he'd said. 'Don't look for trouble, and don't get into any fights.'

And that was one order that Bazza was now sure he would have no difficulty following. Because why would he *want* to get into any fights in Malaga? He had found something that was perfect, and he was not about to do anything that might damage that perfection.

In one short week he would be going back to England to complete his mission, he reminded himself. But when that mission was over, he would not stay in Whitebridge. Instead, he would come straight back to Spain.

He would have a new life!

He would become a new man!

For the purposes of his investigation, there were still a great many tramps he needed to talk to, Pogo told himself. Yet here he was, not looking for fresh sources of information at all, but heading towards Brian's pipe.

He wondered why he was doing it, and tried to convince himself it was because he might have missed some piece of vital information the first time they talked.

But he knew, even as he was making the argument in his head, that it didn't hold water.

The fact was that Brian was too simple to be able to tell him anything useful, and lived too much in a world of his own to have noticed anything significant happening around him.

So why, then, was he wasting his time making this second visit?

As the pipe came into sight, Pogo found himself coming to the reluctant – and surprising – conclusion that he must be doing it because he *liked* the man.

Brian smiled when he saw Pogo approaching. 'You can come in if you want to,' he said. 'And this time there'll be no charge.'

Pogo squeezed into the pipe. 'Are you planning to spend the night here?' he asked.

'Maybe,' Brian replied, noncommittally.

'I wouldn't, if I was you,' Pogo told him. 'You're too much out in the open. Too exposed.'

'That sounds like army talk,' Brian said.

'It is,' Pogo agreed. 'And there's a lot of good solid sense behind it. When there's a maniac on the loose, you need all the protection you can get. That's why I'm sleeping in the park.'

'Don't like the park,' Brian said. 'You see, what I need is a roof over my head, and a solid wall against my back.' He tapped the pipe gently with his knuckles. 'This place is ideal.'

This place is a *death trap*, Pogo thought.

'There must be plenty of pipes like this in other towns,' he said. 'Maybe even nicer than this one.'

Brian sniffed. 'There probably are,' he agreed.

'So why don't we go and look for them – you and me,' Pogo suggested. 'We could start out now, and by tomorrow we could be in Bolton or Burnley.'

'Can't be done,' Brian said flatly.

'We don't have to walk,' Pogo cajoled. 'I've still got a bit of money left. We could take a bus.'

'They won't let *us* on a bus,' Brian said dismissively.

'Maybe not on the first two or three we try,' Pogo agreed. 'But eventually we'll find a kind-hearted bus conductor with a nearly empty bus, and he'll say it's all right. And even if we have to walk, we can take our time, and it's not that bad once you get used to it.'

'It's not the walking that bothers me about going,' Brian said.

'Then what is it?'

'I can't leave this town until I've done my bit of business.'

'And what bit of business might that be?'

'I can't remember. That's the problem. But it will come back to me, in time.'

'And what if it doesn't come back?'

'It will. I remembered it before. That's what brought me here. But somehow, on the way, it slipped out of my mind.'

'Are you sure it was this town you meant to come to?' Pogo asked. 'It could have been one of the others.'

'It was *this* town,' Brian said firmly. '*Whitethorpe.*'

'Whitebridge,' Pogo corrected him.

'That's what I meant.'

Pogo turned his head, and looked around him. The pipe was in the middle of a piece of wasteland, and the nearest house was more than a hundred yards away. It would be so easy for the Germans ... for the *killer*, he corrected himself ... for the killer to sneak up on poor un-suspecting Brian and drench him with petrol.

'Would you mind if I hung around tonight?' he asked.

'Thought you said that you wanted to spend the night in the park,' Brian replied.

'I can change my mind, can't I?'

'Suppose so,' Brian agreed. 'Only, the thing is, there's not enough room in this pipe for both of us to sleep.'

There was *plenty* of room, Pogo thought. But despite their blossoming friendship, Brian still wanted a little privacy in the night. And why wouldn't he?

'I'd make room if I could, but it just can't be done,' Brian said.

'I didn't say I wanted to stay in the pipe,' Pogo pointed out. 'I just asked if you minded if I hung around.'

'But where will you sleep?'

'I've no intention of sleeping,' Pogo said.

Nor had he. His plan was to stay awake all night, keeping watch over Brian – protecting a holy innocent who seemed incapable of protect-ing himself.

Seventeen

The lawn outside the Woodend's kitchen window was covered with a layer of shimmering frost, and the robin redbreasts, perched on the bare branches of nearby trees, shivered and ruffled their feathers.

It was a cold, bleak start to what promised to be a cold, bleak day, and as Joan Woodend flicked fat over the breakfast eggs in the frying pan, she found herself wishing – not for the first time – that she and Charlie could spend their winters somewhere a little warmer.

She turned around to face her husband, who was enjoying a pre-breakfast cigarette.

'Food on the table in two minutes,' she warned.

'Grand,' Woodend replied. 'I'm really lookin' forward to it.'

And there was no doubt he was, Joan thought. But despite the fact that she knew he genuinely loved her cooking, she calculated that, in all their years of married life, she had made less than a couple of hundred such meals for him.

It wasn't that Charlie didn't eat breakfast – like many northern men, a fried heart-attack special was his favourite meal of the day – but he normally had it on the job, either in the police canteen or at a cafe close to the scene of his latest murder investigation.

Which was why she found it strange that, that morning, he was not only eating his breakfast at home, but had not glanced at his watch once.

'There's a bit of a lull in the investigation – at least in the part that I'm involved with,' Woodend said, seeing the questioning look in Joan's eyes as she transferred the fried egg, bacon, sausage and black pudding from the frying pan to the plate which she'd laid in front of him.

'Does that mean that you don't know what to do next?' Joan asked.

'Far from it,' Woodend replied. 'I've got a lot of ideas, but until my prime suspect comes back from Spain, they're pretty much left floatin' in the air.'

He said no more, and she didn't want him to. They had never discussed his work. It was something he did – something that was a big part of him – but, like muddy shoes, Joan had always felt his investigations should be left in the doorway of their home.

'How's young Colin?' Joan asked, going back into the kitchen to cook up some fried bread before the lard in the frying pan had had time to cool down.

'I'm very pleased with him,' Woodend told her between mouthfuls of sausage dipped in egg yolk. 'He's comin' on really well.'

Joan smiled to herself as she turned the bread over in the pan. 'He's become a bit of a protégé of yours, hasn't he?' she said.

'I suppose he has,' Woodend agreed.

'You've taken him under your wing, just like you took Bob under it, years ago. An' how's Bob doin'?'

'He's goin' down to Oxfordshire, to see if he can get any leads there,' Woodend said, avoiding the question. 'Anyway, to get back to Beresford, he's doin' *so* well that I'm thinkin' of pushin' for him to be made up to sergeant as soon as I possibly can.'

'Won't that put Monika's nose out of joint a bit?' Joan asked, with a hint of concern in her voice.

'I shouldn't think so,' Woodend said. 'Monika's not the kind of girl to resent other people gettin' on, if they deserve to.'

And anyway, he thought, by the time Beresford was ready to be made up to sergeant, it was more than likely, despite Bob's recent surge of interest in the case, that there would be an inspector's post going spare on the team for Monika.

Beresford was as uncomfortable with the trilby hat as he had been with the hard mods' braces, though for a different reason.

The braces – apart from itching damnably – made him look far too young, and robbed him of the gravitas he wished to display as an officer of the law. The hat, on the other hand, was something that old men wore, and did not at all fit in with the image of a rising young detective constable he was attempting to cultivate.

Yet the hat had to stay – there was simply no choice in the matter – because while he was just about credible as a plainclothes policeman in the trilby and his best suit, there was no way he could have carried it off with his best suit and a shaven head.

His assignment that morning was to track down the travel agency which had sold Big Bazza's ticket to Spain, and it was at the third agency he visited that he struck lucky.

'Yes, I remember it,' the rather sweet girl behind the counter said. 'Be hard not to, wouldn't it?'

'Why's that?' Beresford wondered.

'Well, most of our clients book their holidays *months* in advance. Some even book the next one the moment they get back from the one they've just been on. But this gentleman...' She paused and looked around the agency.

'Yes?' Beresford said.

'To tell you the truth, he wasn't much of a gentleman at all,' the girl continued, in a much lower voice. 'In fact, he seemed like a bit of a lout, to me.' She paused again, looked at him sideways, then said, 'It's a bit hot in here. Wouldn't you be more comfortable if you took your hat off?'

'I'm fine,' Beresford said, unconvincingly. 'So he asked for a ticket to Spain, did he?'

'No,' the girl said. 'He asked for a ticket to anywhere, as long as it was abroad.' She lowered her voice again. 'I don't think he had much of an idea about foreign travel.'

'So what made you choose Spain for him?'

'We'd just had a cancellation, so that was easiest and quickest. And to be honest with you,

I didn't want to spend a lot of time on him.'

'Why was that?'

'Because I was sure that when it came to actually paying, he'd make some excuse and leave.'

'But he didn't?'

'No, he didn't. He reached into the pocket of those tight jeans of his, and pulled out a wad of notes. Well, you could have knocked me over with a feather. Anyway, he paid, I issued the ticket, and that was it.'

'He didn't say anything else?' Beresford asked hopefully.

'Like what?'

'Like where he'd got the money from?'

'No, he didn't. I think he found the whole process a bit intimidating, and he couldn't wait to get it over and done with.'

Of course he couldn't, Beresford thought. Big Bazza understood the discipline of the workplace and the violence of the streets, but an agency like this one was a totally alien world to him.

'Can I ask *you* a question now?' the girl said.

'All right,' Beresford agreed.

'Have you got some kind of scalp infection? I mean, is that why you're wearing a hat inside?'

'No, it's nothing like that,' Beresford told her. 'I had my hair cut very short, and I feel rather awkward about it.'

'Well, that's all right, then,' the girl said, sounding relieved. She took a deep breath, pushed out her chest and produced what she obviously considered to be her sexiest smile. 'So when your hair's grown back, why don't you come and see me again?' she suggested.

They had arrived in Oxford in the previous evening, and booked into the hotel under the name of Mr and Mrs Robert Rutter.

'It's the best hotel in town,' Elizabeth had said, as they had lain naked on the bed, after a late-night session of passionate lovemaking. 'I always go for the best.'

Rutter had smiled. 'I rather got that impression,' he'd admitted.

'The best hotel, the best cars – and the best men.'

'Is that what I am? The best man?'

And Elizabeth had tickled him lightly under the chin, and said, 'You know you are.'

Now it was morning, and they were sitting in the hotel's breakfast room, looking out on a wide elegant street framed by impressive spires.

'I meant what I said last night,' Elizabeth told him, between mouthfuls of scrambled eggs with prawns.

'About what? The hotel?' Rutter asked.

'About *you*,' Elizabeth answered.

A waiter appeared at the end of the table. 'More coffee, Mrs Rutter?' he asked discreetly.

But Rutter could tell from the look in his eyes that he knew she wasn't *Mrs Rutter* at all – knew, in fact, exactly who she really was.

And that was inevitable, he supposed. She was a celebrity. Her picture appeared at the head of her column in the *Gazette*, and sometimes even on the front page.

If things went as he hoped they would, he told himself, he'd have to accept the fact that Elizabeth would not so much become Mrs Bob Rutter, as he would become Mr Elizabeth Driver.

The thought didn't really bother him. He had carried the burden of responsibility for so long that now he was quite prepared to let Elizabeth bear the weight.

'I expect you'll be off to Abingdon as soon as you've finished eating,' Elizabeth said.

'Yes, I will,' Rutter said, speaking automatically. Then he thought again, and shook his head. 'No, I don't think I will go to Abingdon today. I think I'll tag along with you, if you don't mind.'

Elizabeth smiled. 'Mind?' she repeated. 'I'd be delighted.'

He supposed that at some point he *should* do the work that Charlie Woodend imagined he was already doing. But he did not feel like starting yet, because though he still hadn't proposed to Liz – there were just a few details he had to tie up first – he couldn't help thinking of this as their honeymoon.

Big Bazza was standing in a telephone kiosk on the promenade. He was wearing a flowery shirt, shorts and sandals. He was still not entirely comfortable with his new outfit – sandals felt strange after boots, and he was conscious of how pale his legs were in comparison to those of the other people on the promenade – but he was getting there. His hair, too, would soon be starting to

208

grow, and though, for a while, his head would look like a billiard ball which had mysteriously sprouted peach fuzz, it wouldn't be long before he'd have hair he could actually run his fingers through.

He supposed it was time to make the call. He picked up the phone and dialled the Whitebridge number.

Monika Paniatowski was sitting on a high stool in the saloon bar of the Dog and Whistle. A mirror ran along the wall behind the counter, and through it she had been watching Councillor Ron Scranton – who was sitting at a table near the window with a couple of hard mods – for over ten minutes. And Scranton had been watching her – she was almost certain of that.

The phone rang behind the bar, and the landlord picked it up.

'There's a call for you, Councillor Scranton,' he shouted across the room.

'Switch it through to the phone in the corridor,' Scranton said.

He stood up, and so did one of the hard mods. The two of them walked across the room like men on a mission.

Scranton disappeared into the corridor, but his minder did not follow him. Instead, he closed the door, and positioned himself in front of it.

Another customer – a chunky young man in a donkey jacket – had been heading for the corridor himself, and now found his way blocked.

'Can I just squeeze past you?' he asked.

The hard mod shook his head. 'No.'

'But I need to go to the toilet.'

'You'll have to wait till the Leader's finished with the phone.'

'The leader? Who the bloody hell's the leader?'

The hard mod said nothing.

'I've simply *got* to go,' the donkey-jacketed man said, half-crossing his legs.

'An' I've just said you can't,' the hard mod told him.

'Look, I don't want to have to resort to violence, but...'

The hard mod sneered. 'Think you could take me?' he asked.

'I'd be willin' to give it a try.'

'Think you could take me *and* him,' the hard mod wondered, gesturing towards his mate who was still sitting at the table.

'I...' the donkey-jacketed man said, and then, lost for any suitable reply, he turned to the landlord and complained, 'This feller won't let me go to the bog, Mr Hoskins.'

The landlord shrugged. 'Nothing I can do about it,' he said. 'Councillor Scranton needs his privacy.'

Paniatowski clutched the bar counter tightly. As a police officer, she'd been itching to intervene from the very start, and it was taking a tremendous effort of will to stop herself now.

Bazza had become wrapped up in the colourful life that was going on outside the telephone kiosk, and when a voice at the other end of the line said, 'Yes?' he almost jumped.

210

'It's me, Boss,' he said.

'Avenger!' the other man replied, sounding delighted. 'How are you liking Malaga?'

'It's great!'

'I'll bet it is. No Pakis or tramps to mess things up for you in Spain, are there?'

'No, Boss,' Bazza replied.

Although, in some ways, he wouldn't have minded if there *had* been. Because this wasn't Whitebridge, where it was a question of 'them' and 'us'. On the coast, everybody seemed to know what they wanted to do themselves, and were perfectly happy to let everyone else do what *they* wanted to do.

'I was driving around the city centre last night,' the Boss said. 'The police have cut down on their foot patrols. I knew they would.'

Why did he have to say *that*? Bazza wondered. Why couldn't he just let me forget about White-bridge for a while?

'I've been thinkin', Boss...' he began.

'Yes?'

'An' I'm not sure I want to do it any more.'

'You are a warrior,' the Boss said. 'Isn't that right?'

'I suppose so,' Bazza replied, doubtfully.

'And like all warriors, you need to rest after a battle. But that rest must have a purpose. It must serve to build up your strength for the *next* battle.'

'I know all that, but...'

'The Movement is growing stronger every day. In a few years' time, when it has become unstop-pable, our followers will look back on these early days, and see you as the hero that you are.'

But Bazza was not sure he wanted to be a hero any more. 'Haven't I done enough already?' he asked.

'We can never do enough,' said the Boss, in a voice growing increasingly hard. 'The Movement demands we serve it unceasingly – to death, if that is what is necessary.' He paused, and when he spoke again, his voice was gentler, more persuasive. 'One more mission, Avenger. That's all I ask of you. One more mission, and then you may retire to the glory you deserve.'

'Really only one?' Bazza asked dubiously.

'Really only one,' the Boss confirmed. 'After that, there will be other warriors – inspired by your example – who will be more than ready to take your place. Will you do that for me, Avenger? Will you carry out one more mission?'

'Yes,' Bazza said, though his heart was not in it. 'Yes, I will.'

The door to the corridor swung open, and Scranton re-entered the bar.

Paniatowski waited until he was halfway across the room, then turned to the landlord and said loudly, 'Where's my next bloody drink? I asked for it five minutes ago.'

'I'm sorry, love, but if you asked, I didn't hear you,' the landlord said.

'Do I *look* like a bloody Paki?' Paniatowski demanded.

'No, you—'

'Then don't treat me like I bloody was one.'

'Now listen to me, love—' the landlord began

angrily.

Then Paniatowski heard a voice to her left say, 'The lady's upset at being kept waiting for her drink, Jack. Why don't you serve it to her, then we can all have a bit of peace?'

'Oh, all right, then, Councillor Scranton,' the landlord said, all signs of anger completely drained from his voice and replaced with an oily obsequiousness.

'And put it on my account,' Scranton said.

Paniatowski turned to face him. 'I buy my own drinks,' she said.

'And you seem to have bought yourself quite a few already,' Scranton said mildly.

'First of all, how much I drink is none of your bloody business,' Paniatowski told him. 'And second of ... second of all, you'd drink a lot too, if you had my job.'

'And what job might that be?' Scranton wondered.

'I'm the Filth,' Paniatowski said. She fumbled in her handbag, and produced her warrant card. 'Detective Sergeant Monika Paniatowski.'

'Paniatowski,' Scranton mused. 'Is that a Polish name, Monika?'

'I don't recall giving you permission to use my first name,' Paniatowski said.

'Quite right, you didn't,' Scranton agreed. 'Is that a Polish name, *Miss* Paniatowski?'

'It most certainly is not,' Paniatowski said firmly. 'The Poles are the scum of the earth.'

'I would agree with you on that, just as Adolf Hitler would have done. Though, I must admit, they have serious competition for the title of

213

'scum' from some other quarters – especially in Whitebridge,' Scranton said.

'Bloody right,' Paniatowski agreed.

'So if you're not a Pole, what are you?'

'I'm a *White Russian*!'

'Indeed?'

'Indeed! My grandfather was a *count*. I could have been a countess, but for the bastard Bolsheviks.'

'And *now* you're a policewoman.'

'And now, I'm a police *sergeant*.'

'And one who evidently doesn't like Pakistanis.'

'Do *you* like them?' Paniatowski demanded. 'Because you wouldn't if you came into contact with them as much as I do. They'll take over in the end, you know. Unless we do something to stop them, they'll bloody take over.'

'Do many police officers share your views?' Scranton wondered.

'More than you think,' Paniatowski told him. 'And more – a lot more – than would dare to admit it.' She looked down at her vodka glass, and seemed surprised to find it empty. 'I've probably said too much. I'd better be going.'

With some apparent effort, she clambered down off her stool, only to find that Scranton had placed a restraining hand on her arm.

'Do you know who I am?' he asked.

'You're a rather short, middle-aged man,' Paniatowski said. Then, before Scranton could reply, she held up her hand to silence him. 'For God's sake, don't be offended,' she continued. 'I've always had a very soft *spot* for rather short, middle-aged men.'

Scranton smiled. 'Well, it is a relief to hear you say that,' he said. He reached into his pocket, took out a leaflet, and handed it to her. 'Have you ever seen one of these before?'

Paniatowski squinted at it. 'British Patriotic Party,' she read.

'Have a look at it, and if you like what it says, we'll talk more,' Scranton told her.

'But where will you...?'

'You can usually find me here. And if I'm not here, the people behind the bar will know where I am.'

Paniatowski scrunched the leaflet awkwardly into her handbag. 'Thanks,' she said, and began to walk slowly, and with great concentration, towards the door.

'And even if you're not too keen on what you read, I'd *still* like to see you again,' Scranton called after her.

Part Two

Laying Down the Burden

Eighteen

The calendar on the wall of Woodend's office already had five days crossed out, and now, with a frustrated slash of his pen, the chief inspector made it six.

'It's Tuesday!' he said in disgust.

Paniatowski and Beresford nodded. They knew it was Tuesday, and were already anticipating what the chief inspector would say next.

'On Wednesday – which is tomorrow – Barry Thornley gets back from Spain,' Woodend continued. 'It would be nice to arrest him at the airport, wouldn't it? Only we don't have anything like enough evidence for that, do we?'

The other two shook their heads. They had *all* been hoping that while Big Bazza was away, they would get their big break in the investigation – finally have the tool in their hands that they needed to open the can of worms. But the big break was yet to appear, and the simple truth was that while the wheels of justice had undoubtedly been turning in Bazza's absence, the only thing they'd really been grinding against had been each other.

'Tell me what's been happenin' with the hard mods, Colin,' Woodend said.

'To be honest, there's not much *to* tell,'

Beresford admitted. 'I never realized how much of a leader Bazza was to them until he went away. They're quite lost without him.'

'And Councillor Scranton?' Woodend asked Paniatowski.

'I'm going to nail the bastard!' Monika said vehemently.

'But you're not close yet?'

'I'm getting there. He's so eager to find his way into my knickers that eventually he'll tell me everything I need to know.'

'Neither of you have asked me how Inspector Rutter's gettin' on,' Woodend said.

'We ... er ... thought if there was anything we needed to know, you'd tell us,' Paniatowski said awkwardly.

'It appears that he's gone down with a bad case of the flu, so he hasn't been able to do much actual investigatin' as yet,' Woodend said.

'Well, let's hope he's soon back on his feet,' Paniatowski replied.

From the way she'd said it, it was clear she didn't really believe that Rutter was sick at all, Woodend thought – and neither did he.

'Bazza's the key,' he said aloud. 'He always has been. Once we've cracked him, we've cracked the whole case. And that's mainly down to you, Colin.'

'I can handle it,' Beresford said confidently.

'I'm sure you can,' Woodend agreed.

And he hoped to Christ that was true – because if things went wrong, they would go *badly* wrong.

* * *

The personnel officer in RAF Abingdon had a large bushy moustache which served as a more than adequate thatch for the generous, amiable mouth which lay beneath it. But he was also graced with bureaucrat's eyes – narrow and distrustful – and looking at him across the desk, Rutter realized that getting anything out of him was going to be uphill work.

That was the problem with choosing to cut things fine, the inspector thought. You had to assume, when you made that decision, that once you finally got around to doing the job you'd been sent to do, everything would go without a hitch.

But the truth was, he had not been *consciously* cutting things fine at all. The truth was that he had been having such a good time with Elizabeth that the days had just slipped by, and it had come as a shock to him to realize there was only one left before Barry Thornley returned from Spain.

'The problem is, I don't quite see how I can help you,' the personnel officer said.

'I'm sorry if I didn't make myself clear,' Rutter told him. 'We're conducting a murder inquiry, and I'm doing a background check on one of our prime suspects.'

'Yes, yes, I quite understand that,' the officer agreed. 'But these are *military* records, you see.'

'Which means, I'm sure, that they are both comprehensive and clear,' Rutter said ingratiatingly. 'I'm always telling my chief inspector that we could learn a great deal from the way the military keeps its records.'

'They're *confidential* records,' the officer said, in case Rutter had missed the point.

It was time to lay it on with a trowel, Rutter decided.

'A man has been murdered,' he said.

'So you've already explained.'

'And not *just* murdered, but murdered in one of the most horrible ways imaginable. Set on fire! Can you imagine the fear he must have felt before he finally died? Can you imagine the *pain*?'

The personnel officer shuddered. 'One of my best friends in Fighter Command crashed his kite,' he said. 'He wasn't killed on impact, though it might have been better if he had been, because by the time they'd pulled him out of the burning cockpit...'

'It must have been terrible,' Rutter said, sympathetically.

'It was.'

'Quite as terrible as it was for our murder victim. But, you see, we can't do anything for *either of them* now. What we *can* do, however, is prevent the same thing from happening to some other poor soul.'

'If you could get a court order...' the officer said hopefully.

'We can't,' Rutter told him. 'We haven't got enough evidence yet. But we *know* that Scranton is our man.'

'I'm sorry, but without a court order, there's nothing I can do,' the officer said. He paused for a second. 'Have you had the chance to visit any of the local pubs while you've been here?'

'No,' Rutter said, uninterestedly.

'You should,' the officer urged. 'Some of them are very fine indeed. I'd particularly recommend the Foresters' Arms.'

'I don't think I'll—'

'The landlord was one of our chaps before he retired. Name of Trubshawe. Now I think about it, he served here at the same time as your chum Scranton.'

'I see,' Rutter said.

The personnel officer smiled. 'I rather thought you would.'

Paniatowski was having lunch with Councillor Scranton in the Dirty Duck – and hating every minute of it.

It might have been easier to take if she hadn't read the British Patriotic Party pamphlet that he'd given her, she thought. But she *had* read it – every loathsome word of it.

Councillor Scranton and his party, it seemed, had a violent dislike of Africans, Asians, Eastern Europeans, Catholics, Jews, gypsies and *tramps*. If only these undesirable elements could be purged from British society for ever, the country would again become the earthly paradise it had once been. The pamphlet did *not* make any clear concrete suggestions as to how this purging might be done, but anyone reading between the lines would have no difficulty in discerning what it *thought* would be the right approach.

'You're very quiet, Monika,' Scranton said.

'I was thinking,' Paniatowski replied.

'I've been thinking, too,' Scranton told her.

'I've been wondering how it came about that we suddenly started spending so much time together.'

Paniatowski laughed. 'That's down to you,' she said. 'You're the one who keeps issuing the invitations.'

'But you're the one who keeps *accepting* them. And I find myself asking *why* you accept them.'

'I believe in what you stand for. I think that people like you—'

'That might explain why you would come to meetings and offer to work for the party, but it doesn't at all explain these more intimate moments we've been having.'

'What's the matter? Do you think I'm some kind of police undercover agent?' Paniatowski asked.

Scranton shook his head. 'No, if that had been the case, you'd never have told me you worked for the police in the first place. But looking at you across the table, I see a beautiful woman. And looking at myself in the mirror, I see a rather homely middle-aged man. *Now* do you see what I'm getting at?'

'I think so,' Paniatowski said. 'You're fishing for compliments.'

Scranton looked sheepish. 'It was more a case of seeking an explanation,' he said unconvincingly.

'Well, firstly, you may be no Hollywood star, but you're certainly not homely,' Paniatowski said. 'And secondly, and much more importantly, I'm not too interested in purely physical appearances. What draws me to a man is a sense of his power.'

Scranton smiled – almost smirked. 'And you think I have that sense of power, do you?'

Yes, she was supposed to say. Yes, Ron, of course you have!

Instead, she frowned and said, 'I haven't quite made up my mind about that, yet.'

Scranton looked crushed. 'But you know that my men call me the Leader, don't you? And that I have bodyguards,' he said.

'Hitler's early followers called him the Leader. And he had bodyguards right from the start, even when most people thought of him as nothing but a clown,' Paniatowski said. 'You don't demonstrate your power by what you've got – you show it through what you *do*. It was only when his SS troopers began smashing Jewish shops and beating up gypsies that people really started to take him seriously. That's when he really started to *emanate* power.'

'Do you want *me* to start beating up gypsies?' Scranton asked lightly, trying to turn it into a joke.

'Not necessarily,' Paniatowski said in a serious tone, 'although it would be no bad thing if *somebody* did. But if you want me to really admire you, you'll have to show me that there is something beyond the mere words. After all, even the captain of a school debating team can make a good speech – and he has got no real power of any kind.'

'Something beyond the mere words,' Scranton mused. 'Something *violent*, you mean?'

225

'Violence *is* power,' Paniatowski said. 'Or if not violence itself, the ever-present threat of violence.'

'Do you really believe that?' Scranton asked.

'I *believe* that if Tsar Nicholas had crushed the peasants and workers as he should have done, I'd be at my country estate in Russia right now,' Paniatowski said.

'There *is* more to me than words, you know,' Scranton told her.

'Then I'd certainly like to hear about it.'

'There have been certain things which have happened in Whitebridge recently which would not have happened had I not issued the order,' Scranton said.

'Like what?'

'Oh, I think you can guess like what.'

'I'd still prefer to hear it from you.'

Scranton glanced around him. 'Not in such a public place. And not today. But soon, when we have a little more privacy, I promise I'll give you all the details.'

Paniatowski forced her sexiest smile to her lips. 'I'll look forward to it,' she said.

The Foresters' Arms was a traditional country pub. Its windows were leaded, old oak beams ran the length of the ceiling, and there were horse brasses on the walls. The landlord was standing behind the bar when Rutter entered, and immediately introduced himself as *Tubby* Trubshawe, which left the inspector wondering if Trubshawe had always been on the plump side or whether – given his second name – he had felt under some sort of obligation to develop his substantial girth.

In Rutter's experience, pub landlords fell into one of two categories, the loquacious and the morose, and as they got talking it soon became clear that Trubshawe was a master of loquacity.

'Ron Scranton and I were both corporals,' Trubshawe said. 'Now normally, you try to get on with men of the same rank as yourself – it's a bit of the us-against-the-world mentality, I suppose – but I couldn't get on with him.'

'Why not?'

'To be honest with you, he was a bit right-wing for my tastes. Don't get me wrong, I'm a staunch Conservative myself, but you have to draw the line somewhere, don't you?'

'And where did *you* draw the line?'

'He had this thing about racial purity. Said that Hitler might have had his faults, but that he'd had some good ideas, too. And this – mark you – was just five years after we'd fought a bloody war to defeat the swine.'

'Must have been hard to take,' Rutter said.

'It was,' Trubshawe agreed. 'Didn't like gypsies, either. There was a camp quite close to the base, and he was always going on about them. Saw them as vermin. Parasites. Said we should burn them out.'

'How did he feel about tramps?' Rutter wondered.

'Much the same, I would imagine.'

'He was dishonourably discharged, wasn't he?'

'I believe he was.'

227

'What was the reason for that?'

'You can never be entirely certain why the RAF does things the way it does,' Trubshawe said. 'The army's perfectly prepared to admit it's got some riff-raff in its ranks, but we like to think we're a cut above that, and when we wash *our* dirty linen, we make damn sure we don't do it in public.'

'But you could probably make a good guess at why he was discharged, couldn't you?' Rutter coaxed.

'Well, I certainly have my suspicions,' Trubshawe conceded, 'but I'm not sure I'd like to be quoted on them.'

'You won't be,' Rutter promised.

'There was this Indian restaurant that opened in Abingdon. It was called the Taj Mahal, if memory serves,' Trubshawe said. 'You see them all over the place now, but back then they were a bit of a novelty. In fact, I think the Taj was the first one in Oxfordshire. Anyway, it hadn't been open for more than a week when it was burned to the ground. As luck would have it, nobody was hurt – but they quite easily could have been.'

'And you think it was Scranton who set the fire?' Rutter asked.

'Wouldn't go that far, old boy,' Trubshawe replied, suddenly cagey. 'But I will say *this* – the very next day, the powers that be whisked Scranton out of the camp as if he had the plague, and we heard no more about him until we were told he'd been given a DD. No idea what happened to him after that.'

'He went back home to Whitebridge,' Rutter said.

'With his tail between his legs, no doubt.'

'Not really. He's on the town council now.'

'Extraordinary how things turn out, isn't it?' Trubshawe said. 'There was another chap from Whitebridge here at the same time as Scranton. Name of Lowry. If anyone was going to be a town councillor, I'd have thought it would be him.'

'I take it that you got on better with Lowry than you did with Scranton,' Rutter said.

'Didn't really know the man, to be honest. He was an officer, you see, so our paths very rarely crossed. The only reason I remember him at all is because of his mother.'

'His mother?'

'Flight Lieutenant Lowry was being presented with a gong for conspicuous bravery under fire, and his mother came down here for the ceremony. She must have been in her forties then – as old as my own mother was at the time – but, by Christ, she was a stunning bloody woman. She positively oozed sex appeal.'

'There are some women who can't help doing that,' Rutter said.

'Maybe there are, and maybe they can't,' Trubshawe agreed. 'But that certainly wasn't the case with Mrs Lowry. She knew what she was doing, all right. She was like a lioness on the prowl, stalking her prey.'

'Did she stalk you?' Rutter asked.

Trubshawe laughed. 'There'd have been no *need* to stalk me. I'd have jumped at the chance if it had been offered. But she didn't seem very interested in the other ranks.'

'So it was the officers who attracted her, was it?'

'Let me put it this way,' Trubshawe said. 'After she'd gone back home, there were a couple of wing commanders who couldn't wipe the smiles off their faces for a week!'

Nineteen

It was the rain, that Wednesday morning, which was the start of Barry Thornley's black mood. It was pelting down as his plane landed at Ringway Airport, and it continued to fall in bucketfuls as the bus took the passengers to the terminal. And even inside the building – which was dry and cheerfully lit – there was a smell of dampness and a general feeling of depression.

The taxi ride back to Whitebridge didn't help, either.

'The ring road's a bugger for traffic when it rains like this,' the driver said, 'so, if you don't mind, we'll take a route that's a bit less direct.'

'I don't mind,' Bazza said morosely.

'It'll put a bit more on the clock, but it'll be quicker,' the cabbie told him, as if he still felt the need to make his case.

'I said I don't mind!' Bazza snapped.

The cabbie's quicker route took them through parts of Manchester that Bazza had never seen before – rundown areas of drab grey streets, populated by drab grey people.

'I expect it's a lot nicer where you've just been,' the cabbie said, noticing that his passenger was looking out of the window.

'A lot nicer,' Bazza agreed.

'Yes, there's no arguing that this is a bit of a rough part of the world,' the cabbie continued. 'You'd not catch me picking up passengers here after dark.'

The taxi driver was right, Bazza thought, it was a bit of a rough part of the world. But, he was also slowly coming to realize, this was *his* world they were passing through – a world he had been born into, a world he understood.

A world he would die in.

Spain had seemed like a dream, and now he understood that was actually what it *had been*. And it was a dream which was not for him.

Spain – like heaven – was reserved for someone else.

Woodend was standing in the corridor outside his office and looking through the window at the man who was sitting at his desk.

Bob Rutter was staring blankly at the wall. He did not seem to be aware that he was being observed – he did not seem to be aware of *anything* that was going on around him.

There was a twitch in the inspector's left eye that Woodend could detect even from a distance, and his hands, which were resting on the desk, were performing an erratic drumbeat.

God, he looked rough, Woodend thought. But then, feelings of guilt – and betrayal – could do that to a man.

The chief inspector opened the office door, and stepped into the office. 'So you're back, then,' he said.

'Yes,' Rutter agreed, in a flat, deadened voice.

232

'I'm back.'

'What can I do for you, lad?'

'I thought you might like to hear my report,' Rutter said.

'Might as well,' Woodend agreed, aiming for indifference but falling just short of anger.

'Ron Scranton was discharged from the RAF just after a fire in an Indian restaurant in Abingdon,' Rutter said. 'He was never charged with anything, but I think we can draw our own conclusions.'

'*Is that it?*' Woodend asked.

'Yes, it is. And I would have thought it was a pretty *significant* piece of information,' Rutter countered.

'Aye, it is,' Woodend conceded. 'But it's not much to show for a whole week's work.' He paused. 'Still, it hasn't *been* a whole week's work, has it? Because you've been ill.'

'That's right,' Rutter agreed. 'I've been ill.'

'You must think I've gone bloody soft in the head,' Woodend exploded. Then he reached for a copy of the *Gazette* that lay at the corner of his desk, and slammed it down in front of Rutter. 'Read that to me.'

Rutter picked the paper up. '"Crazed grandma goes on murderous spree",' he read in a flat voice.

'An' the next bit,' Woodend ordered.

'By Elizabeth Driver, Oxford.'

'Oxford!' Woodend repeated. 'That's where you were, isn't it?'

'You know it was.'

'I wondered at the time why you were so keen

233

on havin' that particular assignment, but I never thought your reasons could be as bad – as bloody outrageous – as they turned out to be.'

'I'm sorry,' Rutter said.

'Sorry isn't good enough!' Woodend barked. 'Do you remember what I said last week? That I thought you should transfer to some less stressful area of police work? Well, I don't think that now. Now, I think you don't belong in the police at all.'

'You're quite right, of course, sir,' Rutter said. 'I'd already accepted that myself, which is why I've decided to resign,'

Although it was what Woodend wanted to hear – although he knew it was what *had to* happen – he still felt a wave of sadness wash over him.

'What will you do once you've left the Force, lad?' he asked.

'That's really none of your business, sir,' Rutter replied.

As if he were speaking to a comparative stranger. As if they hadn't shared so *much* over the years.

'I assume Elizabeth Driver's offered you some kind of job,' Woodend said.

'She has.'

'But if you take it, what will happen to Louisa? Constantly travellin' around the country from one sensational crime to the next is no life for a little girl. An' the alternative – leavin' her behind – is just as bad. She doesn't need a dad who she only sees once every few weeks. She needs one who's there to tuck her in at night.'

'That's a bit rich, isn't it, coming from a man

who continually belly-ached if I wasn't there at the precise second he wanted me?' Rutter asked. He stood up. 'As I told you just before I set off for Oxford, I'm not your lad any more, Charlie.'

'Bob—' Woodend said.

'I'm my own man now,' Rutter interrupted. 'And what happens to me – and to Louisa – is really no concern of yours.'

Bazza told the taxi driver to drop him off at the corner of his street, and walked the last hundred yards home. He found his mother in the kitchen – a grease-encrusted hole where cooking pans went to die.

'So you're back, then,' she said.

She was standing over the stove, lethargically stirring a lumpy stew. There was a cigarette in the corner of her mouth, and when some of the ash fell into the pot, she either didn't notice or didn't care.

'How'd it go, Barry?' Big Bazza asked.

'You what?' his mother asked.

'Did my little darlin' have a nice time on his holidays?' Bazza said.

Mrs Thornley stopped stirring, and looked up at her son for the first time. 'I think you must be goin' off your head,' she said.

'Yeah,' Bazza agreed, 'I think I must.'

He turned and walked into the front room, with its dilapidated furniture – with its oilcloth-covered floor sticky from so many beers which had been spilled and never properly mopped up. He went over to the window and looked through the dirt-streaked glass at the street outside. And suddenly he felt an overwhelming urge to hurt somebody.

Rutter was still searching for his keys when Janet, Louisa's nanny, opened the front door and said, 'Welcome back, Mr Rutter. Did you have a good trip?'

'Not bad,' Rutter replied, looking over her shoulder and down the hallway. 'Where's Louisa?'

'She's out in the garden, playing with Sergeant Paniatowski,' Janet told him.

'Does Sergeant Paniatowski come round here often?' Rutter wondered.

'When you're not here, she comes around really every day.'

And when I *am* here, she hardly comes at all, Rutter thought.

He walked into the living room, and looked out through the big picture window on to the garden. Monika and Louisa were crouched down, studying something that was obviously of immense importance to his daughter, and though it must have been cold out there, neither of them seemed to notice.

His relationship with Monika had followed a twisted, unpredictable path, he thought. Once they had been rivals, vying with each other for Charlie Woodend's approval. Then a sharp bend had been turned, and suddenly they were lovers, wrapped up in their mutual passion. His guilt over that relationship was still with him – had survived Maria's murder. It was one of the things he and Monika still shared.

And what else did they share? Not the passion any more – at least from his side.

They shared, he supposed, a job in which they had both invested so much of themselves – and soon even that bond would be gone.

And Louisa, of course. They shared Louisa. But for her, they'd probably see nothing at all of each other, except when they were working on a case.

The door to the garden opened, and Louisa rushed into the room and flung her arms around his leg.

'Daddy, Daddy!' she screamed with delight.

Rutter picked her up. 'How are you?' he asked. 'And what were you doing out in the garden?'

'We found a dead robin,' Louisa said. 'I was very sad at first, but then Auntie Monika told me I shouldn't be, because all life had a natural cy ... cy...'

'Cycle,' Paniatowski supplied.

'Cycle,' Louisa agreed. 'And she said that when it's your time to go, it's your time to go.'

Rutter looked questioningly at Paniatowski.

'She asked,' Monika told him.

But what she really meant was, 'I'm sorry if you'd have preferred me to tell her something else, but you weren't here to consult.'

Rutter gently lowered his daughter to the ground, and Louisa immediately whirled round to face Paniatowski.

'Can we read a book, Auntie Monika?' she asked.

'Not with the state your hands are in, we can't,' Paniatowski said sternly, then laughed to show she wasn't to be taken seriously.

Louisa held up her hands, and gave them an earnest inspection. 'What's wrong with them?' she asked innocently.

'You know what's wrong with them,' Paniatowski said. 'They're filthy dirty, aren't they?'

'Maybe they're *a little bit* dirty,' Louisa conceded.

'So before we go anywhere near a book, you're going to have to wash them,' Paniatowski told her. 'And do it properly – the way I showed you.'

Louisa nodded obediently, 'Yes, Auntie Monika,' and headed for the stairs.

Paniatowski was so much better with his daughter than he was himself, Rutter thought. She seemed to connect with the girl in a way that he was completely unable to.

With Louisa's departure, an awkward silence had descended on the room. For perhaps a half a minute, Rutter stood perfectly still, then he walked over to the window and looked out on to the garden again. A robin had died out there, he reminded himself – but that was all right, because its time had come.

He turned again, to face Paniatowski.

'What's wrong?' she asked.

What was wrong, Rutter told himself, was that there was something he needed to say to her, but he had no idea of how to say it.

He took a deep breath. 'I renewed my house-contents insurance last week,' he told her. 'Everything's very well covered.'

'I'm not surprised,' Paniatowski said flatly.

'You've always been a very careful man.'

Except for that one occasion – when we became lovers – a voice screamed in both their heads. Except for that!

'In fact, the only thing that's not properly insured is Louisa,' Rutter ploughed on.

God, this is awful, he thought. And God, you're making a real bloody mess of it.

'Is it normal to take out insurance on children?' asked Paniatowski, who, having none of her own – and without any prospect of *ever* having them – didn't know how these things worked.

'I wasn't talking about life insurance,' Rutter said. 'I was talking more about insurance *for* life.'

'You're not making much sense.'

'No, I suppose I'm not. The thing is, most children have two parents, so if anything happens to one of them, they've always got the other in reserve. But it's not like that for Louisa. She's only got me.'

'And what do you think is going to happen to you?' Paniatowski asked, starting to sound alarmed.

'Nothing,' Rutter said.

'Well, then?'

'But we can never be entirely *sure*, can we? I could get run over by a bus, like poor Philip Turner's wife did. I could go completely off my head – God knows, I've felt as if I've been going mad often enough, in the last year or so – and have to be locked away. And if one of those things – or anything else, for that matter –

occurred, what would happen to Louisa?'

'I don't know,' Paniatowski said. 'I haven't given it much thought.'

'Well, I have. So what I'd like to do is to name you as Louisa's guardian, should circumstances mean that I can't take care of her myself,' Rutter said, in a rush.

'I see,' Paniatowski said, in a deadpan voice.

'Is that all you've got to say?' Rutter demanded. 'I thought you'd be delighted.'

Delighted? Paniatowski repeated silently to herself. At what?

It hadn't been easy for her to learn to accept the inevitable. But how much harder it would be to be given some hope of attaining what she most wanted in the world, and yet still know – deep down inside herself – that that hope would never be fulfilled.

'You don't have to make a decision right away,' Rutter told her. 'Take a day or two to think it over.'

'A day or two?' Paniatowski repeated, in disbelief. 'What's the rush?'

Rutter smiled. 'You know me,' he said. 'Once I've made up my mind about something, I like to set the wheels in motion as quickly as possible.'

Twenty

Night had fallen, and the gang had congregated outside the chip shop. Bazza had been given a hero's welcome – as befitted a man who had been *abroad* – and for well over an hour the rest of them listened, as Bazza talked about clear blue skies, pubs right on the beach and – most importantly – birds with big knockers who wore hardly anything at all.

Yet even though he spoke with great enthusiasm about the whole experience, it seemed to Beresford that – underneath it all – he was not happy *in himself.*

And perhaps that was because he didn't actually know who *himself* was, any more.

Beresford had come to the chip shop armed with a plan – or maybe, he admitted to himself, it was not so much a plan as a line of approach – but it was another hour before he could get Bazza far enough away from the rest of the gang to be able to put it into effect.

And even then, he hesitated.

'Tread very carefully,' Woodend had warned him, and he'd promised he would.

What he was about to do was not *careful* at all. It was fraught with dangers and pitfalls, and if it went wrong, he would get a stomping which could cripple him for life. But he still wanted to please his boss – wanted to prove that the faith Woodend had put in him had been justified – and sitting on a wall with Bazza, both of them with legs dangling down, he decided that if he didn't force himself to do it now, he would never find the courage to do it at all.

He took a deep breath. 'Where'd you get the money from to go to Spain, Bazza?' he asked.

Bazza grinned. 'That would be tellin'.'

Beresford looked troubled. 'It's none of my business what you get up – or who you get up to it with,' he said.

'Too right,' Bazza agreed.

'But I'm startin' to think of you as a good mate, Bazza, even if you are a bit ... a bit...' He hesitated for a second, then finished off weakly with '...well, you know.'

'No,' Bazza said, slightly menacingly. 'I don't know.'

Still time to back out, Beresford told himself. Still time to smooth over the cracks.

'It's *because* you're a mate that I want to warn that you shouldn't believe everythin' that people have written on the bog walls in the bus station,' he ploughed on.

Bazza started to relax a little, and grinned again. 'You mean all that stuff about which girls will give you a shag an' which girls won't?'

'No,' Beresford said. 'I mean the other stuff. The stuff that says homos can't catch VD.'

One second they were sitting a good three feet apart, the next Bazza had pulled Beresford off the wall, and had him by the throat.

242

'Are you sayin' I'm a poof?' he demanded.

The rest of the gang had noticed what was going on and started to move towards them.

'Stay out of this,' Bazza called to them. 'I can handle it.' He tightened his grip on Beresford's throat and moved his head closer, so that their faces were almost touching. 'Are you sayin' I'm a poof?' he repeated, in a hoarse whisper.

'Not me, no,' Beresford gasped. 'I didn't start the rumours that have been goin' round since you went away.'

'What rumours?'

'That you've got a rich boyfriend. That's he's the one who took you on holiday.'

'Who said it?' Bazza screamed. 'What's their names?'

'Don't know,' Beresford gasped. 'It's on the wall in the bus-station bogs, like all the other stuff.'

Bazza relaxed his grip a little. 'You'd better not be makin' this up,' he said. 'If I go down to the bus station myself, it'd better be there on the bog wall for me to see.'

'It's there,' Beresford promised.

At least, it had been there three hours earlier, when he'd just finished writing it, he thought.

Bazza's hold loosened even more, so that his fingers were hardly pressing on Beresford's neck at all.

'You read it, an' you believed it,' he said, and now there was more sorrow than anger in his voice.

'Of course I didn't believe it,' Beresford assured him. 'Not at first, anyway. But then the more

243

I thought about it, the harder it was to think of any other way you *could* have got the money.'

Bazza stepped back. 'If I tell you how I got it, you'll have to promise not to tell anybody else, not even the lads in the gang,' he said.

'I promise,' Beresford agreed.

'Most of the fellers who run things in this town care more about Pakis, gyppos an' tramps than they do about their fellow Englishmen,' Bazza said. 'But there's one important man who thinks differently – who wants to purge the town of the scum, an' give it back to the ordinary decent white people.'

'Purge' was not a word that Bazza would normally use, but Beresford could think of one 'important' man who used it regularly.

'You're talkin' about Councillor Scranton,' Beresford said.

'I'm explainin' how I got the money for my holiday, not namin' names,' Bazza said.

'So it was this "important" man who gave you the money?'

'That's right. An' he didn't give it to me because he was havin' me up the bum, he did it because I'm helpin' him to purge this town.'

'It ... it was *you* that set that tramp on fire, wasn't it?' Beresford said, feigning amazement.

'An' how would you feel about it if it was?' Bazza asked.

'I'd ... I'd ... I'd think you were a bloody hero.'

'Honestly?'

'Honestly. I mean to say, I've beaten up a few Pakis in my time, but I don't know if I'd have the balls to actually kill anybody. An' what a

244

brilliant way to do it – burnin' the tramps alive. Was that your idea? Or was it his?'

'It was—' Bazza said, stopping himself just time.

'It was...?' Beresford prompted.

'If I said whether it was my idea or his idea, that'd definitely be admittin' I'd done it, wouldn't it?'

'You've already *as good as* said you did.'

'But I've not said nothin' that would stand up in court,' Bazza said craftily.

It wasn't working, Beresford thought. He still didn't have enough to take to Woodend. He was going to have to push Bazza even harder.

He grinned, and said, 'You had me goin' there for a minute.'

'What do you mean?' Bazza asked.

'I really thought you'd done it.'

'I ... I...' Bazza said helplessly.

'I should have known you were only havin' a laugh.'

'I wasn't. I was dead serious,' Bazza said – sounding like a hurt child.

'But serious about *what*?' Beresford wondered. 'Listen, do you remember when I told you that I'd beaten up that Paki in the pub in Accrington?' he asked.

'Yes?'

'An' you said it was easy enough to *talk about* havin' beaten up Pakis, but that wasn't the same as actually *doin' it*?'

'What's your point?'

'So I beat up the next Paki who came along, didn't I? Just to show you that I wasn't just full

245

of piss an' wind!'

Bazza licked his lips. 'Look, you showed me, an' I admire you for it,' he said. 'But this is different.'

'Is it? How?'

'You, you're your own boss. But I'm not. I'm workin' for the Movement. I'm the Avenger!'

The Avenger! What pride he took in saying those two words, Beresford thought. It was pathetic, and for a moment he almost felt sorry for Bazza – and then he reminded himself of what the hard mod had done to the tramp.

'You understand what I'm sayin'?' Bazza asked, with a pleading edge to his voice. 'I want to tell you all about it, but I can't.'

'Then I suppose I'll just have to take your word for it,' Beresford said dubiously.

'Maybe ... maybe if I ask him, the Boss will let me tell you more,' Bazza said desperately.

'Why would he?'

'Because I've got one more job to do, then I'll be retirin'.'

'So?'

'So somebody else has to take over from me – an' that somebody could be you.'

'Just give me the chance! Do that, an' I promise that I won't let you down,' Beresford said.

And now the hectoring tone had quite vanished from his voice, and had been replaced by one of pure admiration.

Bazza smiled. 'I know you won't. The rest of the lads are my mates, an' I'd do anythin' for them. But you – you're somethin' special. I knew that the first time I saw you.'

'So when are you goin' to do this last job before you retire?' Beresford asked. 'Tonight?'

'No, not tonight,' Bazza said.

'Then when?'

'When the time is right. When I'm *told* to do it.'

In the distance, the town hall clock struck ten.

'What say we go an' have a beer – just you an' me?' Bazza suggested.

'Can't,' Beresford told him. 'I'm meetin' somebody.'

'A bird?'

'A feller.'

'Why are you meetin' *a feller*?'

'Because we've got a little breakin' an' enter-in' that needs doin'.'

'Better go an' do it then, hadn't you?' Bazza said, trying not to sound too impressed.

The gang had moved on from the chip shop, and ended up in the Corporation Park, but there was nothing much happening there.

Bazza was almost tempted to go home, except there was nothing there for him, either. Besides, it didn't seem right to quietly crawl into his bed while Col was out doing something as exciting as breaking and entering.

'Anybody got a fag?' he asked.

The rest of the gang shook their heads. It was the day before payday, and if they'd had a couple of bob between them, it would have been a miracle.

Bazza reached into his pocket, and pulled out a pound note. He held it up against the light –

well aware that everyone's eyes were fixed hungrily on it, then said, 'Well, I've got the money for fags, but I don't feel like walkin' all the way to the pub for them. So what *are* we goin' to do?'

'I'll go,' Scuddie said, hardly able to restrain himself from grabbing at the money. 'I don't mind a bit of a walk.'

'Will your mum *let you* buy cigarettes?' asked Bazza, who had still not quite forgotten – nor quite forgiven – Scuddie's suggestion that he might himself be under a curfew.

Scuddie shrugged. 'Do you want me to go, or not?'

'You might as well, I suppose,' Bazza said lazily. He held out the note. 'Get three packets, so there'll be enough for everybody. An' make sure you get the right change – 'cos I'll count it.'

'An' you're sure Barry Thornley's not just spinnin' you a line?' Woodend asked, reaching across the table for his fresh pint of best bitter. 'You're sure he's not just lyin' about his involvement in the murder, to make you think he's tougher than he is?'

'I'm sure,' Beresford said. 'When I asked him whose idea it was to set the tramps on fire, he didn't have to think about it for a second. The answer was on the tip of his tongue.'

'Maybe he'd worked out in advance that you'd ask that question, and had it prepared.'

'Bazza doesn't plan in advance,' Beresford said firmly. 'He didn't even *plan* to tell me that he was involved – I tricked him into it.'

248

'How did you do that?'

'By accusing him of being a homo.'

Woodend looked concerned. 'That was a bloody big risk to run, wasn't it?'

'I was confident I could handle it,' Beresford said airily, although he still remembered the feel of Bazza's hands clamped tightly around his throat.

'What would happen if we pulled him in?' Woodend asked. 'Would he crack?'

'He might, if we charged him and then told him we'd go easier on him if he gave up his boss.'

'But we haven't got *enough* on him to charge him,' Woodend said.

'Then we'll get nothing out of him at all.'

'So all we'd be doin' is alertin' the feller who's pulled his strings that we've found his weak link. What a bloody mess!'

'That's what it is,' Beresford agreed.

'An' you're sure he's plannin' to commit another murder?'

'I'm sure *he's* sure.'

'Right then, we've not much choice but just to watch an' wait,' Woodend said. 'Or rather, we've no choice but to have *you* watchin' an' waitin'. I want you out there with Bazza every night. I want you stickin' to him like a second skin. But I don't want you takin' any more big chances like you did tonight. If you think there's any danger they're startin' to become suspicious of you, get the hell out of there as quick as you can.'

'But that would leave Bazza free to do what-

249

ever he wanted,' Beresford protested.

'Maybe it would,' Woodend agreed. 'But it's a question of balancin' one risk against another. I don't want another tramp to die, but I don't want one of my team battered to death, either.'

'Oh, sir, I didn't know you cared,' Beresford said, in a camp voice.

It was his first ever attempt at humour with his boss, and he was really quite proud of it.

Woodend gave him a hard stare, and then slowly a grin spread across his face. 'Cheeky young bastard!' he said affectionately.

There were other pubs closer to the Corporation Park than the Drum and Monkey, but Scuddie had been banned from all of them, and so it was the Drum that he went to for the cigarettes.

He entered the pub through the door into the lounge bar, and walked up to the counter. He was aware that the other customers – mostly respectable middle-aged couples – were watching his progress with some anxiety, and he rather liked that.

The landlord appeared at the other side of the counter.

'Wouldn't you be more at home in the public bar, son?' he asked, pointing with his thumb to the area behind him.

'I don't want a drink,' Scuddie said. 'I've only come for ... come for...'

'Come for what?'

'Fags. Three packets of Embassy Tipped.'

'No problem,' the landlord said, stepping away and allowing Scuddie an even clearer view of the two men sitting at a table in the corner of the public bar.

One of the men was Col, the Paki-basher. The other, a big bugger in a sports coat, looked very familiar, though Scuddie didn't quite know where from.

And then it came to him – he had seen the feller's picture in the paper.

'So, do you want these cigarettes or not?' a voice asked.

'Sorry,' Scuddie said, handing over the pound note and picking up the packets of cigarettes.

He turned and left the pub, his mind in a whirl, and it was not until he was halfway back to the Corporation Park that he realized he had forgotten to wait for Bazza's change.

Not that that really mattered, he told himself. Bazza would be far too interested in what he'd seen in the Drum to even ask for it.

Twenty-One

It was ten o'clock on Thursday morning, and two tramps were standing at the edge of the busy outdoor market.

Pogo was idly and aimlessly watching the ordinary people going about their ordinary business, and remembering a time when he was ordinary too. And though Brian appeared to be doing exactly the same thing, Pogo knew he wasn't. Brian was looking for something – for *one* thing – on which to focus.

'Time to move on,' Brian said.

'So there's nothing here?'

'Not a sausage.'

This was the pattern of their days now. Wandering around the town apparently without purpose, but searching – always searching.

'You see, what I'm doing is keeping a lookout for something which will remind me of why I'm here,' Brian had explained in the first days of their friendship.

'Like what?' Pogo had asked.

'I couldn't tell you. But I'll know it when I see it.'

All sorts of things had *almost* seemed about to provide the aid to memory that Brian so desperately wanted.

One day, when they had been in the more expensive part of town, Brian had been transfixed by a big shiny Bentley Continental.

'Maybe you used to drive one of these for a living,' Pogo had suggested. 'Maybe you were some fat cat's chauffeur.'

'Don't think so,' Brian said dismissively.

'Or maybe you worked in a garage that serviced them.'

'Not that either.'

So Pogo had fallen silent, and Brian had studied the car for another half-hour before shaking his head and saying, 'That's not it. It's not quite the right shape.'

'The right shape for what?' Pogo had asked as they walked away.

'Don't know,' Brian had admitted.

On another occasion, he had expressed some interest in one of the pubs – the Engineers' Arms.

'Does it seem familiar?' Pogo had asked.

'Maybe.'

'Did you use to drink in there?'

'I don't think so.'

A street, a shop, a stretch of the canal – all these had brought a flicker of interest to Brian's eyes, but that flicker had soon faded away.

Perhaps they were looking in the wrong town altogether. Perhaps there was no such thing as the *right* town, because Brian only *thought* he was looking for something.

It didn't matter, Pogo told himself. None of it mattered.

Though guarding the sleeping Brian through

the night meant he got little sleep himself, and following Brian around the town during the day was bringing him almost to the point of exhaustion, Pogo didn't begrudge any of it.

When he had first rediscovered a purpose in life, that purpose was to help Monika Paniatowski catch the killer. But it wasn't any more. Now, his purpose had been honed down to something much simpler, and – in a way – much purer. All he wanted to do was keep Brian alive.

Elizabeth Driver was sitting in the residents' bar of the Royal Victoria Hotel. The clock on the wall said it was twenty-five past two, which meant that Bob Rutter would arrive in the next five minutes, because he was never late – at least for her.

They'd had a wonderful time together in Oxford, she thought.

They'd visited the same student pubs that Oxford undergraduates had been visiting for hundreds of years – and for hundreds of years had been chased out of them by the bowler-hatted members of the special university police force known as Bulldogs, when they'd had too much to drink.

They'd walked hand-in-hand along the banks of the River Isis, making up names for the swans as they glided by.

'Ermintrude,' Rutter had suggested, pointing at one of them.

'Ermintrude!' she'd mocked. 'It's not a *pig*! It's a regal bird. I shall call her Giselle.'

'Whatever you say,' Rutter had agreed happily.

'You're the boss.'

'And you'd better not forget it,' Elizabeth had cautioned him.

One day, they'd even – God help them – taken a punt out on the river, and though it had been almost unbelievably cold, they'd had a hell of a good time.

And slowly it had begun to dawn on Driver that perhaps she'd been wrong about the nature of the future relationship she'd planned with Rutter. That perhaps he wouldn't be just like a pair of comfortable old shoes she made use of from time to time. That perhaps she wouldn't need to have other men on the side. That perhaps Bob Rutter was actually – and incredibly – everything she wanted.

It was true, she admitted, that things hadn't been quite the same since they'd returned to Whitebridge. In fact, Bob had been moody and almost secretive. But that was understandable. Though he hadn't told her himself, she knew he was about to break his links with his past – and that was never going to be easy.

She suddenly felt a gentle kiss on the back of her neck, and heard a voice say, 'You shouldn't be wasting your time here, you idle woman. You should be working on the book.'

For a moment her heart faltered, and then she realized that it wasn't the book which would make her fortune he was talking about, but the wholly imaginary *Maria* book.

Rutter walked around her chair, and sat down opposite her.

'Just as a matter of interest, how *is* the book

going?' he asked.

He was trying to keep his tone light – almost disinterested – but there was an underlying seriousness to his words.

'It still matters, doesn't it?' Elizabeth Driver asked.

'Of course it still matters,' Rutter replied. 'Why wouldn't it?'

'Well, I just thought that given how much your circumstances have changed – how much *our* circumstances have changed – it wouldn't be quite so important to you any more.'

'It's *because* circumstances have changed that it's important,' Rutter said. 'I need to make my peace with the past. And that's why I really *would* like to know how it's going.'

'It's going fine,' Driver lied. 'Another couple of months and it will be finished.'

'Can I see what you've done so far?' Rutter asked hopefully.

Elizabeth Driver shook her head. 'I never let anyone look at my work in progress.'

'Why not?'

'Because if I knew that someone had seen it in its unpolished form, it would disrupt the creative process – and the book would never be the same again.'

'Couldn't you let me see it, and then pretend to yourself that I hadn't?'

'It doesn't work like that.'

Rutter looked disappointed, but then he said, 'Well, we both want what's best for the book, don't we?'

'Indeed we do,' Driver agreed.

It looked like she was actually going to have to *write* the bloody book, she told herself.

And maybe that would be no bad thing, if it made it easier for Bob to accept that she'd had to write the *other* book as well.

Even when he was still thirty yards from the chip shop, Beresford knew that something was wrong. The gang wasn't doing any of the sorts of things they usually did – watching the street for girls to ogle and Asians to abuse, playing cards for matchsticks, or kicking around a tin can and pretending they were star performers in White-bridge Rovers FC.

That night they were all sitting on the wall, as stiff as boards, as silent as the dead.

They were waiting for something, Beresford thought – and that something could only be him.

'*If you think there's any chance they're startin' to become suspicious of you, get the hell out of there as quick as you can,*' Woodend had told him the previous evening.

But what if he *did* get the hell out? That would leave Bazza free to do whatever he wanted to do.

Beresford forced himself to keep on walking, and when he reached the chip shop he said, 'All right, lads?'

'*We're* all right,' Big Bazza said ominously.

And the rest of the gang said nothing at all.

Beresford swallowed. 'So what are we doin' tonight?' he asked. 'Are we stayin' here, or goin' somewhere else?'

'We thought we might go down to the town centre, an' cause a bit of trouble,' said Bazza, in a flat emotionless tone that chilled him to the bone.

'What kind of trouble?'

'If I tell you that now, it'll only spoil the surprise.'

'Get the hell out,' Beresford heard Woodend's voice say in his head. *'Get the hell out* now*!'*

'I've ... er ... just remembered, there's somethin' else I've got to do,' Beresford said. 'So, if you don't mind, I don't think I'll come with you tonight.'

'But I *do* mind,' Bazza said. 'We *all* mind, don't we, lads?'

The others nodded, and despite the cold night air, Beresford realized he was starting to sweat.

'Honestly, I'd come with you if I could,' he said, 'but—'

'But nothin'!' Bazza interrupted.

And the rest of the gang, who had been operating a flanking movement on Beresford, now moved in so that he was surrounded.

'If that's what you want, Bazza, fair enough,' Beresford said. 'After all, you are the leader of this gang.'

'So I am,' Bazza agreed. 'Well, you'd better get goin', hadn't you, lads?'

'Aren't you comin' with us?' Beresford asked.

Bazza grinned unpleasantly. 'No, I've ... er ... just remembered there's somethin' I've got to do,' he said, imitating Beresford. Then a sudden and totally unexpected look of hurt came into his eyes, and he added, 'We could have been real mates, you an' me.'

* * *

258

The hard mods set off down the street in a tight bunch, with Beresford at the centre.

There was no escaping from them, the detective constable told himself. If he tried to break free, they would have him on the ground in a split second, and then the kicking would start.

The only hope he had was that they'd come across a police patrol, and he could find some way to signal to it that he was a fellow officer in trouble.

But he knew the chances of that happening were virtually non-existent, because most of the available manpower was being concentrated on the rundown areas where the tramps slept at night.

The gang reached the outdoor market. Earlier in the day it had been a busy, bustling place. Now, the tubular steel stalls were bare, and the whole area was quite, quite deserted.

'This is far enough,' Scuddie decided, and the gang came to a halt.

'Why are we stoppin' here?' Beresford wondered.

'Because I say we are,' said Scuddie, who seemed, overnight, to have been promoted to the position of Big Bazza's second-in-command.

'But there's nothin' goin' on,' Beresford protested.

'No,' Scuddie agreed. 'There isn't. Not yet!'

The hard mod took a watch out of his pocket, and studied it with all the care and attention of someone who is not used to telling the time.

How long had Scuddie even *had* a watch? Beresford wondered. He was almost certain he'd never *seen* him with one before.

'Another ten minutes,' Scuddie announced.

'Another ten minutes before *what*?' Beresford asked.

Scuddie grinned. 'Like Bazza said, I can't tell you that without spoilin' the surprise.'

Earlier in the day – and acting on the Boss's orders – Bazza had visited the telephone kiosk near the old mill to make sure it was still working. Now, after first checking his watch, he entered the kiosk, picked up the receiver, and dialled 999.

'Emergency. Which service do you require?' said the operator in a calm, neutral voice.

'Police!' Bazza told her. 'An' make it quick.'

A new voice came on the line almost immediately. 'Whitebridge police headquarters,'

'Do you know Detective Constable Beresford?' Bazza asked.

'Yes, but I don't see—'

'Friend of yours, is he?'

'This line is for emergencies only,' the bobby said. 'If you wish to report one, then you must—'

'If Beresford *is* a friend of yours, you'd better get down to the outdoor market as quick as you can,' Bazza interrupted. 'Because any minute now he's goin' to be gettin' the shit kicked out of him.'

'Now you just listen to me...' the policeman said.

But Bazza *wasn't* listening. With a grin on his face, he was already hanging up the phone.

The gang were no longer so tightly bunched around Beresford. Now, while they still had him encircled, they had spread out.

And that was a bad sign.

'We didn't like what you did to that nice Paki lady,' Scuddie said. 'We thought that was very bad.'

It was almost as if he was reading the words from a script, Beresford thought. And, in fact, that *was* basically what he was doing. They were all in a play that Bazza had written, and they were coming to the end of the final act.

'What do you mean, you thought it was very bad?' he asked. 'You all laughed like drains when I did it.'

But there was no more conviction in his words than there had been in Scuddie's.

'We didn't laugh, did we, lads?' Scuddie asked.

And the others chimed in that no, they certainly hadn't.

'It was so bad what you did to her that we all think you need punishin' for it,' Scuddie continued.

There was no point in pretending any more, Beresford decided.

'It's obvious that you all know who I am,' he said.

'Course we do. You're Col the Paki-basher.'

'I'm Detective Constable Colin Beresford.'

'A bobby?' Scuddie scoffed. 'I don't believe you. If you're in the Filth, where's your warrant card?'

Beresford realized that reaching for his card was a mistake almost as soon as he'd started to do it – but by then it was already too late. The moment's distraction, as his attention shifted from Scuddie to the card, was the signal the gang had been waiting for.

A heavy boot slammed into Beresford's right knee. The agony was indescribable, and he felt his legs collapse beneath him. And then he was on the ground, instinctively wrapping his arms around his head as the boots found easier, more vulnerable targets.

He was going to die – he *knew* he was going to die – and he wondered vaguely, when the pain allowed him to, who would look after his mother when he was gone.

He was aware of a sudden screaming in the distance, but before he had time to identify it as a police siren, he lost consciousness.

Twenty-Two

Woodend was sitting at his desk. His face was grey, and the hand which held the inevitable cigarette was shaking.

When Paniatowski entered the room, he looked up and said, 'How's Beresford?'

'Still in a coma,' Paniatowski told him.

'But he's goin' to be all right, isn't he?'

For a moment Paniatowski searched around for some way of softening the blow. Then she decided that since the truth could not be hidden, he might as well be told it straight away.

'The doctors don't know anything for certain,' she said. 'Colin's taken a lot of punishment, and it could go either way.'

'This is all my fault,' Woodend groaned. 'I should never have given the lad the job in the first place.'

'You did what you had to do,' Paniatowski told him. 'Colin knew the risks, and he *wanted* to do it.'

'Bollocks to that as an excuse!' Woodend said. 'An' bollocks to my feelin' sorry for myself.' He stood up, and suddenly seemed more like himself. 'We've a job to do, so let's get at it.'

'A job to do?' Paniatowski repeated.

'That's right,' Woodend agreed. 'I can't do

anythin' for Colin, but I can certainly do somethin' about the bastard who put him in hospital.'

Cloggin'-it Charlie had always seemed a big bugger, the sergeant in charge of the holding cells thought as he watched Woodend approach him, but at that moment he looked like a bloody giant.

'Barry Thornley!' Woodend said.

'I beg your pardon, sir.'

'I want to talk to Barry Thornley. An' if you happen to hear any screams while I *am* talkin' to him, I'd advise you to keep well out of it.'

The sergeant consulted his list. 'But we don't have any Barry Thornley in custody, sir.'

'Of course you do,' Woodend said impatiently. 'He was one of the hard mods who was pulled in earlier.'

The sergeant looked at his list again. 'Sorry, sir, but you're wrong. We've got the names of all the lads arrested, an' none of them is Barry Thornley.'

For a second, Woodend was silent, then he raised his hand to his head and said, 'Dear God!'

The patrols were being reinstated, but it was probably already too late, Woodend thought, as he drove his battered old Wolseley at what was almost racing-car speed towards the derelict part of town.

The police switchboard operator had confirmed that the person who made the call about Beresford had been a young working-class male, and the chances of that being anyone but Bazza were just about nil.

So kicking the shit out of Beresford had had two purposes. The first, most obvious one, was that it had been a punishment beating. But the second – and more important – was that Bazza had thought it would be a distraction.

He'd been right, of course. There wasn't a police force in the whole country that wouldn't instinctively drop everything else when one of their own was in trouble. And in Whitebridge, every officer within striking distance of the outdoor market had immediately rushed to the scene – leaving the tramps to take care of themselves.

'I should have seen it comin',' he said, furious with himself. 'I should have bloody seen it comin'.'

He had reached his destination, and slammed on the brakes. All around him stood dark empty buildings – sad monuments to Whitebridge's former industrial might – and the chances were that in one of those buildings he would find a tramp, burned to a crisp.

It was as he was getting out of his car that he heard the first scream, and only a few seconds later – when a man came rushing out of the black-lead factory – that he understood what the scream was all about.

The man was on fire! Flames engulfed his legs and his torso, and were licking around his head. And he was running as fast as he could – as if in that way he could escape the agony that the fire was bringing him.

Woodend stripped off his jacket, and began

running towards the human torch. The man stumbled, then fell, then began rolling around on the ground. And still he would not stop screaming.

By the time Woodend had reached him, his face was starting to melt, and though he was attempting to protect it with his hands, they were on fire, too.

Woodend threw his jacket over the man's head and upper body, and pressed down hard. It was not an easy task, because the victim, not understanding that this would help, was still attempting to twist away. And even when Woodend had managed to prevent the trunk from moving, the legs, still blazing, were kicking in the air.

There were others on the scene now – two constables who, following Woodend's lead, were attempting to smother the fire around the man's stomach and legs.

And finally, it had some effect. Finally all the flames were extinguished, and the victim just lay there, groaning weakly.

Stepping away, Woodend looked down at his own hands, and noted – almost objectively – that they had been quite badly burned.

'It'll be the shock that's makin' me take it so calmly,' he told himself.

'Are you all right, sir?' one of the constables asked.

Woodend winced with pain. 'No, I'm bloody not,' he said. 'But I'll live – which is more than this poor bugger will probably manage.' He wished he had a cigarette, but knew that it would probably be too painful to hold it. 'Let's have a look at him, shall we?'

The constable shone a torch on the dying man. The flames had burned away most of his clothes, but his boots were still largely intact, and enough of his face had escaped the fire for Woodend to see that he was a young man with a shaved head.

'Misjudged it this time, didn't you, Bazza?' Woodend said softly. *'Badly* misjudged it.'

It did not take the uniformed constables long to find the second victim of the fire. He was in the black-lead factory from which Barry Thornley had run screaming, and there was no question that he was dead.

'There's a poetic justice in what happened to that lad, isn't there, Sarge?' asked the constable who was showing Paniatowski the body. 'Sort of like, "Them that live by the flame shall die by the flame" – an' quite bloody right, in my opinion.'

'It's certainly hard to feel any sympathy for Barry Thornley,' Paniatowski agreed.

'So that's it, then,' the constable said. 'We've got our murderer, an' he's dead himself. End of story.'

If only it was that simple, Paniatowski thought. But it wasn't. The puppet might be dead, but the puppet-master was still very much alive, and Bazza's death was going to make it harder – *much* harder – to pin his crimes on him.

The smell of cooked meat had suddenly become almost unbearable, and Paniatowski realized just how close she was to throwing up.

'Time for a breath of fresh air,' she said, almost gagging on her words.

'Know what you mean,' the constable replied sympathetically.

Emergency floodlights had been erected outside the factory, and it was as bright as day – *brighter* than most Lancashire days. Paniatowski glanced down at the roped-off section of the road where it looked as if someone had been having a camp fire – and reminded herself that the camp fire in question had been called Barry Thornley.

She needed a cigarette, she thought, but the moment she lit the match – and smelled the burning – she started to feel sick again. She dropped the cigarette and the match on to the floor, and stamped on them. Then, because she didn't want to contaminate the crime scene, she bent down and put them in a plastic envelope, which she placed in her handbag.

It hadn't been a good day, she told herself. It hadn't been a good day at all.

Police barriers had been erected ten yards each side of the factory, and standing behind the one to the left was a tall tramp who looked as if he wished he were dead.

'There you go, Monika,' she said softly to herself. 'However bad you feel, there's always someone worse off than you.'

She walked towards the barrier, and the closer she got to it, the more she could see just what a terrible state Pogo was in. Both his cheeks were badly bruised, and his left eye was almost closed. His moustache was caked in dried blood, and from the way he was holding himself, it was obvious that something else – probably his ribs – hurt like the devil.

'What happened to you?' she asked, horrified.

'We need to talk,' Pogo said.

'Yes, we do.'

'But not here,' Pogo told her, glancing at the factory door, then turning quickly away again.

'My car's around the corner,' Paniatowski said. 'Will that do?'

Pogo merely nodded.

They were sitting side by the side in the MGA. There was a hip flask of vodka between them, and they had both already taken a swig.

'So what *did* happen to you?' Paniatowski said.

'We'll get to that later,' Pogo replied. 'Before that, I'd like to tell you the story of my life, or anyway, the only part of it that matters.'

'Why?' Paniatowski asked.

And the moment the word was out of her mouth she was cursing herself for being an insensitive bitch.

Pogo did not seem to take offence. 'Why?' he repeated. 'Because it's a long time since I've told it to anybody but myself.'

'Fair enough,' Paniatowski agreed.

'The last time I had friends was 1944,' Pogo said reflectively. 'How long ago was that?'

'Over twenty years,' Paniatowski told him.

'Over twenty years,' Pogo echoed, sounding almost surprised it had been as little as that. 'We were all part of a sabotage unit operating behind the German lines. After the officer and the sergeant were killed, I was next in line to take charge, so I did.' He smiled at Paniatowski. 'You said right from the start that I'd been a corporal, didn't you?'

'That's right, I did,' Paniatowski agreed.

'Anyway, what with facing death together, day in and day out, we grew to be as close to each other as any group of men could possibly be. We were closer than brothers. We were closer than a married couple. It wasn't just that we were friends and comrades – we became *a part* of each other.'

'I can see that,' Paniatowski said.

'At any rate, that's what I *thought* we were,' Pogo continued. 'We were living off the land. You've no idea what it's like, Sergeant, to live off a diet that's mostly made up of raw turnip.'

Yes, I have, Paniatowski thought. When my mother and I were on the run, that's what we ate, too.

But this was Pogo's story, and so she said nothing.

'There were *some* Germans who helped us,' Pogo continued. 'People who were sickened by what Hitler had done to their country, and who wanted the war over as soon as possible. And we were staying in the farmhouse of some of these Germans on the particular night I'm talking about. They were an old couple who owned it – even at that stage of the war, when they were desperate enough to draft almost anyone, the man was considered too old for military service. And they had their granddaughter staying with them, a sweet little lass of fifteen.'

'Go on,' Paniatowski encouraged, although she'd already guessed it would be a story she'd rather not hear the end of.

'We'd been hiding there for about three days, and I went out on recce. When I got back, there was blood everywhere, and the farmer, his wife and his granddaughter were all dead.' Tears had begun to run down Pogo's face. 'What had happened, you see, was that while I was out, one of my men – my comrades, my brothers-in-arms – had raped that sweet little girl. Then, once he'd had his share, the others wanted theirs, too. And they couldn't let the family live after that, could they? They would have been a danger. It would have been most *unmilitary* to let them survive to tell the tale.' He shook his head despairingly. 'I should have shot the bloody lot of them right there on the spot.'

'But you didn't,' Paniatowski said.

'But I didn't,' Pogo agreed. 'There was a war going on, and we still had a job to do. But *after* the war, I promised myself, I'd get justice for that girl and her grandparents.'

'And did you?'

'Of course I bloody didn't! Nobody was interested – not my superiors, not the military police. Hundreds of thousands of Germans had been killed – so what did three more matter? But I still cared, you see. And I decided, then and there, that if I couldn't trust the lads I'd fought with, then I couldn't trust anybody. So I've not got close to another human being for ... how long is it now, did you say?'

'Over twenty years.'

'But then, because of you, I got close to Brunel.'

'To who?'

'Not that he called himself Brunel any longer. He told me that, for years, he's been going by the name of Brian.'

'I still don't...'

'I'd finally persuaded him to move away from the pipe, and he was sleeping in the black-lead factory tonight. It's his body you found.'

'I'm sorry,' Paniatowski said. 'Had you become very good friends?'

'Not in the normal way you think of friendship, no,' Pogo said. 'Brian had no time for that. He had no *space* for it. He was in Whitebridge on a mission – and that was all that mattered.'

'What kind of mission?'

'There were questions he wanted answering. He'd forgotten what they were, but he was convinced that being in this particular town would remind him of them, even if, half the time, he couldn't even remember what the bloody place was called.'

'I'm not sure I quite understand what you're getting at,' Paniatowski said.

'Why would you?' Pogo asked. 'I'm not even sure I understand it myself. We spent our days scouring the town, looking for clues. He thought a pub called the Engineers' Arms might have been the clue he needed, but it wasn't. We saw this big black shiny Bentley once, and he was quite excited about that for a while, but then he said it wasn't quite the right shape.'

'What did he mean by that?'

'God knows!' Pogo took another slug of vodka. 'Oh, and he told me he'd known a killer – a very bad man – but that it had all been a long time ago.'

'Did he say any more about this killer?' Paniatowski asked.

Pogo shook his head. 'He only mentioned him the once, and even then, I didn't take him seriously. To be perfectly honest with you, he wasn't right in the head. But none of that matters, you see, because despite it all, he still had a *purpose*! He still knew that the answer he was looking for was out there somewhere, floating in the darkness, and that if he grabbed out often enough, he might catch hold of it. He became an inspiration to me. And in return for that inspiration, I protected him.'

But not tonight, Paniatowski thought.

'But not tonight,' Pogo agreed, almost as if she'd said the words out loud. 'Tonight, when I should have been there with him, I was lying in an alley, thinking I was dying.'

'Who beat you up?' Paniatowski asked.

Pogo shrugged, as if it didn't really matter. 'Some lads.'

'What did they look like?'

'They all had short hair and wore big boots.'

'Did you do anything to provoke them? Anything at all they might have taken the wrong way?'

'Nothing,' Pogo said. 'I'd been to get some cigarettes, and I was just walking down this alley. They were waiting there for me. One of them said, "That's him!", and then they attacked me.'

Barry Thornley's gang, Paniatowski thought. It just *had to be* them.

Pogo took another slug of the vodka. 'And now Brian's dead, and the quest is over,' he said. 'I failed him – just like I failed that little girl in Germany.'

'You ... you mustn't blame yourself,' Paniatowski told him, close to tears.

'It's not about blame, it's about purpose,' Pogo told her. 'I've no purpose any more, and without purpose, there's no point in staying here.'

'So you'll be moving on?'

'Yes.'

'Where will you go?'

'Don't know. Doesn't really matter.'

'It matters to *me*,' Paniatowski said, as she felt a tear run down her cheek.

Pogo opened the car door and stepped out into the night. 'You can't look after me, you know,' he said.

'I could try,' Paniatowski said.

Pogo shook his head. 'We've not spent much time together, but we've spent enough for me to know that you can't even take care of yourself.'

Then he turned, and started to walk away.

And Paniatowski – with tears streaming down her face in earnest now – let him.

Because she didn't know what else she *could* do.

Twenty-Three

Scuddie had always thought that getting in real trouble with the police would be both glamorous and exciting.

In his daydreams, he would be taken straight to an interrogation room after his arrest, where at least three big buggers would be waiting for him. They'd ask him questions at first, but when he refused to talk, they would start to beat the shit out of him. Then, when that didn't work either, they would shake their heads wonderingly, and one of them would probably say, 'We've had some hard cases in here before, Scuddie, but none of them have been anything like as hard as you.'

After that, of course, they would let him go, and once out on the streets again he could bear his scars with pride and bask in the total admiration of the other hard mods.

It hadn't worked out like that. Since he'd been arrested, he'd been locked in a holding cell and virtually ignored.

As if he didn't matter!

As if they'd decided he was small fry, who they'd get round to when they had the time!

Even when they did eventually take him to be interrogated – on Friday morning, a full *twelve hours* after his arrest – there was only one man waiting for him. And while it was true that he was big enough to match the bobbies in Scuddie's daydream, he wasn't going to do much damage with those bandaged hands.

'When are the others comin'?' Scuddie asked.

'What others?' Woodend asked.

Scuddie lolled back in his chair. 'The ones who'll do the dirty work for you,' he said.

'Sit up straight!' Woodend snapped.

'You what?'

'Sit up straight, you bastard.'

Scuddie tried to think of a smart, funny reply he could tell the boys about later, but all he could come up with was, 'You'll get nothin' out of me, copper!'

And then he realized, with surprise, that while he'd been speaking he'd also been straightening his posture, just as Woodend had ordered him to.

'Why did you attack Detective Constable Beresford?' Woodend demanded.

'Who's he?' Scuddie asked.

Woodend sighed. 'So it's goin' to be like that, is it? All right, you sack of shit, why did you attack *Col*?'

This was getting better, Scuddie thought. This was how it was *supposed* to be.

'Didn't know he was a bobby,' he said. 'An' anyway, he was the one who started it. I was only defendin' myself.'

'So it was just you against him, was it?'

'That's right.'

'Well, your mates will certainly be relieved to learn you've said that,' Woodend told him.

'What are you talkin' about?'

'I should have thought that was obvious. Constable Beresford died last night, and since you were the only one actually *involved* in his murder, you're the only one who'll hang.'

'Hang!' Scuddie gasped. 'What do you mean?'

'It's when they place a noose around your neck, make you stand on a trapdoor an'...'

'They've got rid of hangin',' Scuddie said, with terror in his voice. 'I heard it on the telly.'

'What you heard on the telly, you ignorant sod, is that they're *goin' to* get rid of it. But if we rush through your trial – an' we will, because it's a bobby you murdered – there'll still be time, before the law changes, for you to have your neck stretched.'

'It wasn't just me. We all did it,' Scuddie said hysterically.

'I thought that might be the case, from the amount of bruisin' on his body,' Woodend said.

'So does that make a difference?' Scuddie moaned.

'It certainly does. Now it won't be just you that hangs – it'll be the rest of the gang as well.'

'It wasn't our idea,' Scuddie sobbed. 'None of it was our idea!'

'Then whose idea was it?'

'Bazza's.'

'I need details!' Woodend barked.

'Will ... will that make a difference to what happens to me?'

'It's possible.'

'Bazza said we should beat Col up at exactly nine o'clock.'

'An' then wait for the police to arrive?'

'No, he ... he said we should get away as fast as we could.'

'Then why didn't you?'

'Once we'd started, we couldn't stop. It was so...'

'Excitin'?'

'I don't know.'

'Tell me about the tramp you beat up.'

'Is he dead as well?'

'No.'

'Bazza told us to beat him an' all.'

'Him? Or any old tramp?'

'Him. Bazza pointed him out to us. He said we should make sure he was out of action for a few hours.'

'Right, that's it. They'll take you back to your cell now,' Woodend said.

'Don't ... don't you want to know anythin' else?'

'Nothin' that scum like *you* can tell me.'

For a moment, Woodend considered informing Scuddie of the fact that Beresford had come out of his coma, but he quickly rejected the idea. It would do the little bastard good to stew in his own juice for a few hours, he thought.

Woodend didn't like being driven by anyone else, but his hands were in such a state that there was no way he could hold the steering wheel, and so it was a police driver who took him to the morgue.

Dr Shastri met him at the door.

'So what's this important new information

you've got for me?' Woodend asked immediately.

'Good morning, Dr Shastri. I apologize for destroying your beauty sleep by sending you two cadavers in a single night,' the doctor said.

Woodend grinned. 'Good morning, Dr Shastri. I apologize for destroying your beauty sleep by sending you two cadavers in a single night,' he dutifully repeated. 'Now what's this important new information?'

'It concerns the second victim, Barry Thornley. How do you think he came to be on fire?'

'I should have thought it was *obvious* how he came to be on fire. He accidentally spilled some of the petrol on himself, an' when he was burning the poor bloody tramp, he set himself alight, too. Isn't that right?'

'I will answer that question in a moment, but let me ask you another one first,' Dr Shastri said. 'I found traces of fibre on Thornley's head. Did they, perhaps, come from one of your stylish sports coats?'

Woodend grinned again. No one else, in the whole of Whitebridge, would ever have described any of his sports coats as *stylish*.

'Probably,' he said. 'I wrapped it around him when I was tryin' to put out the fire.'

'And were burned yourself, as a result. I do not think there are many men who would run such personal risk in an attempt to save the life of a particularly nasty murderer.'

'To tell you the truth, I didn't even think about what he'd done. I saw he was on fire, an' I did my best to put that fire out.'

279

'So like you,' Dr Shastri said. 'And, in this case, at least, virtue has been its own reward.'

'I beg your pardon?'

'If you had stood by and done nothing, the damage to Thornley's head would have been much more extensive.'

'Yes, that's obvious enough.'

'And then, even a brilliant physician, such as I am myself, would have been unable to detect the fact that shortly before he was set on fire, he received a blow to the head.'

'Are you sayin' that somebody knocked him unconscious?'

'Possibly, but I suspect not,' Dr Shastri said. She smiled. 'You are always trying to persuade me to do your detective work for you, you lazy man, and this time I think I will indulge you.'

'Go right ahead,' Woodend said.

'If the person who struck Thornley on the head simply wanted him dead, why not hit him as hard as he possibly could? It would be much safer, because Thornley was what I believe you would call "a big strapping lad".'

'He was, an' I would,' Woodend agreed.

'Even if his murderer intended to burn him, his task would have been made much easier if Thornley had been unable to resist.'

'Agreed.'

'But his killer does not hit him with the maximum force he can summon. Instead, he delivers a blow calculated only to stun him, and when he pours the petrol over him, he restricts himself to pouring it over the trunk and legs. Now why was that?'

'So that Bazza could do just what he did do!' Woodend said.

'Just so,' Dr Shastri replied. 'You did not believe that Thornley had set fire to himself because you are stupid – you believed it because that is exactly what the killer *wanted* you to believe.'

There may, at some time in the dim and distant past, have been gloomier lunchtimes spent around the table in the Drum and Monkey, Woodend thought – but he was finding himself hard pressed to remember one.

The Dr Shastri Effect – the magical spell she wove, which seemed to imbue even the most dismal situation with a little light – had worn off, and black depression had followed.

They had been given their opportunity to find the killer, he told himself – and they had failed.

It could be argued, of course, that it was not their fault – that the killer had seen his opportunity and had grasped it with both hands. Yes, it could be argued that way, but it didn't alter the fact that two men had died, and that one of them – at least – had been completely blameless.

To make matters worse, he was in charge of a team of the walking wounded, and, with his bandaged hands, was one of them himself.

The doctors were predicting that Beresford would make a full recovery, but it would be quite a while before he was fit for duty again.

In Monika's case, it was her mind, rather than her body, that he was worrying about. She had endured so much – the horrors of war-torn

Europe, the sexual abuse from her stepfather, the feeling of alienation as the only Polish kid in an English school – and having to associate with Ron Scranton, a man who embodied most of the things she hated, was putting a terrible strain on her.

And then there was Bob Rutter.

What the bloody hell was he even *doing* there at the table? It was true that his resignation from the police was still pending, but his de facto resignation from the team was now entering its second week.

'I want to help if I can, especially after what happened to Colin Beresford,' Rutter said, reading his thoughts. 'I want to see if, this last time, we can work the old magic together.'

Woodend sighed. Well, why not? he wondered. What possible harm could it do?

'The reason that the killer murdered Barry Thornley in the way he did was because he hoped it would fool us into believin' that Bazza alone was responsible for the deaths of the tramps,' he said. 'But the reason he had to murder him *at all* was that he knew we were closin' in, and he saw Bazza as the weak link in the chain. Are we agreed on that?'

Rutter nodded. 'If Bazza knew that Colin Beresford was a policeman, then we can be almost certain that the killer – the man who was pulling Bazza's strings – knew as well.'

Woodend turned to his sergeant. 'Is that how you see it, an' all, Monika?' he asked.

'Why do you keep calling him "the killer"?' Paniatowski demanded angrily. 'It'd be much

282

easier – and quicker – to call him *Scranton*!'

'We can't be sure that Scranton is our man,' Woodend said gently. 'An' until we are, I'd be happier if we all just called him *the killer*.'

But the problem was that Monika *was* sure, he thought.

No, that wasn't strictly true, he corrected himself. It wasn't so much that she was sure, as that, since she'd read the British Patriotic Party's pamphlet, she *wanted* it to be Scranton – *needed* it to be Scranton.

'So the next question is, will the killin' stop now?' Woodend continued. 'An' if it *does* stop, will that be because he's no longer got anybody to do his dirty work for him? Or because he's achieved what he set out to achieve?'

'Given what happened to Bazza, I think it's clear enough that he's prepared to do his own dirty work, if he has to,' Rutter said.

'Unless he's already recruited someone else to take Bazza's place – and it was that new recruit who killed Thornley,' Paniatowski said.

'Now that *is* a depressin' possibility,' Woodend said.

'It's more than a *possibility*, if you ask me,' Paniatowski retorted. 'Scranton's got any number of thugs who'll do his bidding.'

'By fixatin' on Scranton like that, you're closin' too many other doors,' Woodend warned her.

'Why do we need to even *consider* any other doors, when we're already standing in front of the *right* one?' Paniatowski shot back, aggressively.

'Monika, please, if you'll just try to be objective for a minute—' Woodend began.

'Why don't we move on to something else?' Rutter interrupted. 'Something that there's a remote possibility we *can* all agree on?'

'Good idea,' Woodend said gratefully.

'Monika?' Rutter asked.

'If there *is* such a thing as an aspect we can agree on,' Paniatowski replied.

Rutter cleared his throat. 'Are we all willing to accept that last night's murder was not a random act?' he asked.

'Yes, I think we are,' Woodend said, glancing at Paniatowski for confirmation. 'By yesterday afternoon – at the latest – Big Bazza already knew who the victim was going to be. That's why he sent out his gang to beat up Pogo, who'd been acting as the victim's unofficial bodyguard.'

'So what we have to ask ourselves is whether the other two victims were *also* so carefully targeted,' Rutter continued. 'And *if* they were, *why* were they? Was it because they had something in common with the third victim?'

I've missed your contributions to these meetings, Bob, Woodend thought. And not just your contributions – I've missed *you*.

'We already have some background on the first two victims, but not enough to tie them together in any way,' he said. 'If we could identify the third, we'd have widened the field an' it might just be possible to start makin' connections.'

'Do we have any information at all on the third victim?' Rutter asked.

'Nothin' solid,' Woodend admitted. 'Remind us what your mate Pogo had to say about him, Monika.'

At the mention of Pogo's name, Paniatowski felt a slight stabbing pain in her chest. She wondered where he was now, and prayed that somewhere – somehow – he would find another purpose.

'Still with us, Monika?' Woodend asked gently.

'Yes, I was just collecting my thoughts,' Paniatowski replied.

She told Woodend and Rutter about Brian's fuzzy-minded mission, and how, half the time, he couldn't even remember the name of the town he was convinced held the answers. She mentioned his interest in the Engineers' Arms, and his enthusiasm for the shiny black Bentley, which had turned out to be 'not quite the right shape'.

'Not quite the right shape,' Rutter repeated thoughtfully.

And Woodend saw a gleam and intelligence in his eyes which had been missing for quite a while.

'He told Pogo he'd known a killer, but that had been a long time ago,' Paniatowski continued. 'Oh, and he also said that Brian wasn't his real name – that he'd actually been christened Brunel.'

'*Brunel!*' Rutter exclaimed.

'Does that mean anythin' to you?' Woodend asked, with a hint of hope in his voice.

'He must have been named after Isambard

285

Kingdom Brunel, the great nineteenth-century engineer,' Rutter said.

'So what?' Woodend asked, disappointedly. 'Folk are always namin' their children after famous people. One of Joan's cousins even called her kid Elvis – the poor little bugger!'

'Are you saying that his real name might be why Brian was so interested in the Engineers' Arms, Bob?' Paniatowski asked.

Rutter shook his head. 'No, I think there could be more to it than that.'

'Let's hear it, then,' Woodend suggested.

Rutter shook his head for a second time. 'I've got a vague idea in my head, but it's not ready to come out yet. Can you give me a couple of hours to chew it over, to see if I can make any sense of it?'

'Aye, there's no rush,' Woodend said.

And there really *wasn't*, he thought. Rutter's idea – like most of the ideas they'd managed to come up with on this bloody, bloody case – would probably do no more than lead them up a blind alley.

There was one more point which needed to be raised, he reminded himself – and he wasn't looking forward to it at all.

'When are you seein' Ron Scranton again?' he asked Paniatowski.

'Tonight, for dinner and dancing,' Monika told him, with the disgust more than evident in her voice.

'You don't have to do it, you know,' Woodend said, remembering he'd used almost exactly the same words to Colin Beresford.

'I *want* to do it,' Paniatowski replied.

And that was what Beresford had said, too.

Woodend automatically lifted his arm to check his watch, and found himself staring at thick surgical bandages.

'When I saw the police doctor this mornin', he told me that I needed to take an afternoon rest,' he informed Rutter and Paniatowski. 'So *I* told *him* that there was no time for afternoon rests durin' a murder inquiry. He wasn't impressed.'

Paniatowski smiled. 'I'm not surprised,' she said.

'In fact, he was so *unimpressed* that he said that if the only way to make sure I rested was to certify me as unfit for active duty, then that was a course of action he was quite prepared to take. All of which means that – as you've both probably already guessed – I shall be reluctantly followin' his advice, an' getting' my head down for a couple of hours.'

'I think it's for the best, sir,' Paniatowski said.

'Maybe you're right,' Woodend agreed. He stood up. 'Would you like a lift back to headquarters, in my chauffeur-driven vehicle, Monika?'

'I'll take her,' Rutter said.

'No need to put yourself out, lad,' Woodend told him. 'Like I said, I've got this chauffeur-driven car, an'...'

'I'll take her,' Rutter repeated firmly.

'Is that all right with you, Monika?' Woodend asked, disconcerted by the urgency that he'd detected in Rutter's tone.

Paniatowski just nodded.

'We've ... er ... got a little business together that we need to tidy up,' Rutter said, as if he felt compelled to explain. 'Nothing important, but it has to be done.'

'I'll see you both later, then,' Woodend said.

And he was thinking, They hardly ever see each other any more. What kind of business could they *possibly* have?

Twenty-Four

Stanton Hall was a Gothic pile, situated halfway between Whitebridge and Preston. It had originally been the county seat of the de Stanton family, but crippling death duties – allied with the personal excesses of some of the Lords de Stanton – had meant that, some fifty years earlier, the family had had to sell it.

It had been converted into what was then known as a private lunatic asylum, and half a century later it was still basically in the same line of business, although, since 'lunatic' was now a dirty word, it had been reborn as the Stanton Hall Mental Healthcare Centre.

Elizabeth Driver arrived at the place at just after three o'clock, and by half-past three was sitting in the director's office, looking out on to lush lawns and tennis courts.

The director himself was sitting opposite her. His face was slightly flushed, and he looked, thought Driver, like a man who felt that his small and cosy empire had suddenly come under attack – and who was prepared to do whatever it took to defend it.

She wasn't unduly worried by either his attitude *or* his determination, because while he might be considered a heavyweight around the corridors of Stanton Hall, she regularly ate men like him for breakfast.

'I don't think I really want to talk to any member of the press about our work here, Miss Driver,' the director said, trying to sound both firm and authoritative.

'Is that right?' Driver asked, interestedly.

'Yes, I'm afraid it is.'

'Then why I am here – in your office – at all?'

'Because I am well aware that reporters such as yourself often find it difficult to take "no" for an answer, and I thought it would save time if, instead of allowing you to badger my under-lings, you should hear of my decision directly from the horse's mouth.'

Elizabeth Driver smiled sweetly. 'How kind of you to spare me the time,' she said.

'I considered it only polite.'

'And what a load of old bollocks you can come out with, when you really put your mind to it.'

'I beg your pardon!'

'You agreed to this meeting for one reason, and one reason alone – you wanted to see if you could find out just how damaging the story I was planning to run could possibly be.'

'That's ... er ... not quite how I would have put it, Miss Driver,' the director said.

This was easy, Driver thought. Almost *too* easy.

'It's not how you would have put it, but it's the truth nonetheless,' she said airily. 'Well, you can relax. I'm not running a story at all. The only reason I'm here is as a favour to a friend.'

'What kind of favour?' the director asked suspiciously.

'He needs information on a patient,' Driver said. 'Or perhaps the man in question is an *ex-patient* by now. That's one of the things you can clear up for me.'

An appropriate look of outrage came to the director's face. 'That is quite out of the question.'

'Is it?' Driver asked. She held up her right hand for him to inspect. 'Look at these sweet little fingers of mine,' she said. 'You wouldn't think they had the power to destroy people, would you? But show them a typewriter, and that's *exactly* what they have.'

'You're threatening me!' the director said accusingly.

'What a clever man you are to have noticed that,' Driver replied.

'It won't work,' the director told her. 'This is one of the finest institutions of its kind in the country. You couldn't possibly uncover anything that would embarrass us.'

'Who said anything about *uncovering* anything?' Driver wondered. 'Have you ever read my column in the *Gazette*?'

'I may have glanced at it once or twice,' the director admitted. 'I can't say that I particularly—'

'And didn't it occur to you, clever man that you are, that some of the accusations I made were totally outrageous?' Driver interrupted him.

'Well, yes, as a matter of fact, it did.'

'There you are, then. No need for me to *un-cover* anything at all, is there? I'll just make it up.'

'If you do that, I'll sue!'

'Of course you will. And, in the end, the *Gazette* will no doubt have to print an apology and pay you compensation. But by then, the damage to your reputation – and to the reputation of this institution – will have been done.'

'And you'd lose your job,' the director blustered.

Driver laughed again. 'For all your cleverness, you really have no idea of how popular journalism works, do you?' she asked. 'What my boss wants to do is to sell newspapers – and selling newspapers is just what my stuff does. He wouldn't sack me just because he had to pay out a few thousand pounds. The revenue from the increased sales would make that seem like a mere drop in the ocean.'

'You're a monster!' the director said.

'Yes, I am,' Driver agreed. 'That's the other reason that my boss likes me so much.'

'Who is this patient who you want the information on?' the director asked, knowing when he'd been beaten.

Elizabeth Driver opened her handbag. 'His second name escapes me for the moment, but that's all right, because I've got it written on a slip of paper, somewhere in here.' She began to rummage through the contents of the bag. 'But I do remember the first name, because it's so unusual. He's called Brunel.'

The director's already sagging jowls sagged even more. 'Oh, him!' he said.

Bob Rutter, sitting in Elizabeth Driver's Jaguar outside the main entrance to Stanton Hall, was reviewing in his mind everything he'd done since he'd left the Drum and Monkey.

The first thing, of course, had been his 'little bit of business' with Monika Paniatowski. It had been harder work to get her to agree to it than he'd expected – so much so that, for a moment, he'd even contemplated telling her the truth. But, in the end, the truth had not been necessary, and Monika had signed on the dotted line.

He'd gone to the library next, where he'd immersed himself in the *Whitebridge Telegraph*'s births, marriages and deaths columns of a much earlier era.

And it was in those columns that he'd found *exactly* what he was looking for! Because despite Pogo's belief that Brunel had probably chosen the wrong town for his search, there was the proof positive – in the birth announcements for May 1921 – that he hadn't.

After this breakthrough, the rest had been easy, and it had taken no more than a couple of phone calls to point him in the direction of Stanton Hall.

He looked up from his musings and saw that Elizabeth had emerged from the main entrance, and was walking towards him.

Her hair was growing lighter in colour by the day, he noted. She must have decided to let the dye grow out, and in a couple of months she would be back to being the natural blonde she'd been when he'd first met her.

There'd been a time when that would have bothered him – because, as a blonde, she would have reminded him too much of his lost love, Monika Paniatowski. And there'd been a time, too, when he'd drawn comfort from the fact that her hair was so dark, because *that* had reminded him of his other lost love, Maria.

How petty such thoughts and feelings seemed, now that his whole life was about to change so dramatically, he told himself.

Elizabeth had reached the car, and climbed into the passenger seat.

'Well?' Rutter asked.

'Cast your mind back an hour or so,' Driver said. 'We were debating, were we not, who would be best at finding the information you needed? You thought it was you, and, naturally, I thought it was me.'

Rutter smiled. 'And who was right?' he asked.

'Perhaps we were both right. Perhaps you'd have done *just as well* as I did. But we'll never know for certain, will we?'

'You got it all!' Rutter said delightedly.

'I got it all,' Driver confirmed. 'You worked out where we needed to look for the information, and I teased the relevant facts out. We're a good team.'

'We are,' Rutter agreed. 'We're a *very* good team.'

Paniatowski had been expecting the call, but when the phone rang, she still felt her stomach lurch.

'It's me!' said the voice at the other end of the line. 'Ronnie!'

That was what Scranton had been calling himself for the previous couple of days, though she'd never asked him to.

Ronnie!

As if adding a few letters to his name would miraculously make him younger or more attractive!

'How nice to hear your voice,' she said.

'Are we still on for tonight? Dinner and dancing?'

'Yes, of course.'

There was a slight pause, then Scranton said, 'The thing is, I thought we might kick things off a little earlier than we planned.'

'Oh?'

'I've got this bottle of rather fine champagne, you see – it was given to me by one of my admirers in the movement – and I thought we could crack that open before we set off.'

'Sounds like a nice idea.'

'So shall I come round to your flat at, say, around six.'

Paniatowski gasped with horror.

'No!' she said, before she could stop herself.

'No?' Scranton repeated, puzzled. 'Are you all right?'

'I'm fine.'

'You don't *sound* fine.'

'Got something caught in my throat, that's all.'

'Lucky *something*,' Scranton said, and chuckled.

She should have agreed to Scranton's suggestion, Paniatowski told herself. But she simply couldn't – simply *wouldn't* – have the vile man in her flat.

'I've got an old friend staying with me,' she lied. 'A woman I met at police college. It wouldn't be the same with her there, so why don't we go to your place instead?'

'Ah, there's a problem with that, too,' Scranton said awkwardly.

'Have you got a friend staying as well?'

'No, but my flat's ... well, I spend so little time there, as a result of my work with the movement, that I'm afraid it's rather a mess.'

She was losing him, she told herself. What she should do – what the operation *demanded* she do – was to backtrack, and say she'd find some way to get her fictitious friend out of the house.

But she couldn't do it!

'I'm sure your place can't be much more of a mess than mine,' she said. 'And even if it is, it won't really matter, will it. There'll be us, and the champagne, and I doubt if we'll notice anything else.'

'I suppose you're right,' Scranton agreed reluctantly. 'Shall I give you the address?'

'If you wouldn't mind.'

Paniatowski took down the address and said her goodbyes. Then she rushed to the toilet and was violently sick.

As Bob Rutter walked along the corridors of police headquarters he heard someone whistling, and realized that that someone was him.

And why shouldn't he whistle? he asked himself. What he'd discovered at Stanton Hall alone had been enough to whistle about, and, since then, discoveries and revelations had been almost *falling* into his lap. The case wasn't over – it wouldn't be over until, as the Americans said, the fat lady sang – but it was as near to over as made no difference.

He knocked on Woodend's door, opened it without waiting to be asked, and found himself looking around an empty office.

It was then that he remembered that the doctor had ordered Charlie to rest, and that for once Charlie had taken the doctor's advice.

He was a *little* disappointed that Woodend was not there to take delivery of the large buff envelope he held in his hand, but not unduly so. After all, he argued, what the envelope contained was not so much his contribution to the case as a member of the team as it was his parting gift *to* the team.

The idea had not occurred to him in quite that form before, but now that it had, he rather liked it, and picking up a pen from the desk he wrote 'A Parting Gift' across the front of the envelope. He paused for a second, then added several exclamation marks, and placed the envelope on the corner of the desk, where Woodend couldn't miss it.

Rutter drove straight from police headquarters to the Royal Victoria, where he had every intention of dazzling Liz with his brilliance. But it was not to be. The porter on the reception desk told him that she had gone out for a while – and, unlike earlier, he really *was* disappointed this time.

'Would you like to wait for her in her suite, Inspector Rutter?' the porter asked.

'Would that be all right, do you think?'

'Well, I'm sure Miss Driver wouldn't mind,' the porter told him, 'and as far as the hotel's concerned,' he winked heavily, 'you're practically a full-time guest as it is.'

There was a time when Rutter would have been offended or embarrassed – or *something* – by the comment, but those days were long gone. And thinking about it, he decided that, after his afternoon's work, he had *earned* a little luxury.

He took the lift up to the top floor, and let himself into Driver's suite with the key the porter had given him. Once inside, he kicked off his shoes and sat down in one of the armchairs which were covered with leather as smooth and soft as a newborn baby's skin.

He wondered how he should fill in the time until Liz got back.

He could watch television, but there was never anything interesting on it at that time of day.

He could run a king-sized bath, and still be soaking in it when Driver returned.

Or he could...

And suddenly, he knew *exactly* what he wanted to do.

'You told me you wouldn't notice the way the place looked,' Ron Scranton said with a touch of rebuke in his voice, as he stood in his kitchenette with the bottle of champagne in his hands.

Paniatowski, who was sitting in one of the flat's two shabby armchairs, glanced around her and decided it was not really a *flat* at all, but a glorified bed-sit with its own bathroom.

'I know what I told you,' she agreed, 'but this place is still not quite what I expected. I somehow thought that a man who was so important to the movement would live somewhere a little less ... well, basic.'

The surprise she was showing was good from a tactical point of view, she realized – it fitted in very well with the plan of action she had mapped out earlier – but it was a *genuine* surprise, too.

'I'm not a man who notices material things,' Scranton said defensively. 'All my attention is focused on the cause that I would willingly give up my life for. Besides, I much prefer it that the movement puts the money it could have spent on me into the fighting fund.'

'Of course,' Paniatowski said, as if she should have thought of that herself. 'And it has the additional advantage of fooling our enemies into believing that you're much less important than you actually are.'

'Well, exactly!' Scranton said, embracing the idea with an almost desperate enthusiasm. 'They would look at this place, and think, "He can't be up to much." But they couldn't be more wrong, could they?'

He waited for Paniatowski to agree with him, and when she said nothing he quickly popped the cork, filled two glasses, and took the drinks over to the armchair corner of the room.

'To us!' he said, handing Paniatowski her glass and holding out his own for the toast.

'To the movement,' Paniatowski replied.

Scranton looked disappointed. 'I thought we could put the movement behind us for a couple of hours.'

Paniatowski laughed. 'As if the movement could ever be completely out of the thoughts of a man like you,' she scoffed.

'A man like me is still a *man*, if you know what I mean,' Scranton said.

Paniatowski nodded her head. 'Yes, I think I do.'

'And you led me to believe that, as unlikely as it seemed to me at first, you found me attractive.'

'I *do* find you attractive.'

'Then prove it!'

'How?'

Scranton gulped. 'We're all alone here, and there are clean sheets on the bed,' he said.

Paniatowski put down her glass, walked across the room to the bed, sat down and began slowly unbuttoning her blouse.

Oh please, don't make me take *all* my clothes off, she prayed to a god she had long ago ceased to believe in. I'll do it if I have to. But please don't make me!

Scranton's eyes were bulging with excitement.

'I've been waiting for this moment since the first time I saw you,' he moaned softly, as Paniatowski popped open buttons until there were none left to pop, and the blouse fell open. 'I've been *dreaming* about it.'

Paniatowski sighed regretfully, closed the blouse again, and began to button it up.

'What's the matter?' Scranton asked, in a voice which was almost a sob.

'I'm sorry, I can't,' Paniatowski said.

'You ... you can't?'

'I think it must be this room. I know you've given me all kinds of reasons why it should be so mean and scruffy, and I accept them. Really I do. But there's still a part of me that says, "Maybe he's not that important after all, Monika. Maybe he's just a pathetic little nobody who's *lying* about his importance because he desperately wants to sleep with you."'

'A nobody?' Scranton repeated.

'I'm sorry if I hurt your feelings,' Paniatowski said contritely. 'I didn't mean to. But you *must* see how I could get that impression.'

Scranton gulped, then, with a great show of reluctance, he said, 'Would a *nobody* have been authorized, by the very top people in the party, to purge society in the most extreme way possible?'

'Do you mean...?' Paniatowski began.

'I ... I ... might as well tell you, since you've already guessed,' Scranton said. 'Those two tramps who were killed...'

'Yes?'

'It was done on my direct orders.'

Paniatowski had finished buttoning her blouse, and now she stood up. 'How very interesting,' she said. 'Ronald Arthur Scranton, I am arresting you for the murders of Philip Turner and another vagrant, as yet unidentified.'

'This is a joke!' Scranton said. 'It *has to be* a joke. You're on our side. When I mentioned that Hitler had had the gypsies beaten up, you said that somebody should do the same thing here.'

'You do not have to say anything, but anything you do say may be taken down and used in evidence against you,' Paniatowski continued, calmly.

'But ... but ... you hate tramps and Pakis – and all the other scum of the earth,' Scranton gasped, as if he knew he was in the middle of a nightmare, and desperately wanted to wake up. 'You have to. For God's sake, you're a White Russian!'

Paniatowski laughed. 'Wrong again,' she said. 'I'm a Pole.'

The confusion drained from Scranton's face and was replaced with an expression of loathing and contempt. 'A Pole!' he repeated. 'A filthy Polak! And to think, I nearly ... I almost...'

'You didn't nearly *anything*,' Paniatowski said. 'I'd rather sleep with all the tramps in Whitebridge than let you so much as *touch* me.'

It had been meant to provoke him, and it did. Scranton picked up a heavy ashtray, and rushed across the room at her, screaming, 'Polak bitch! Dirty, filthy Polak bitch!'

Paniatowski waited calmly until he was almost close enough to hit her with the ashtray, then struck out with her right leg and kicked him on the kneecap.

It was a hard kick – harder than was strictly necessary – and Scranton collapsed on the floor and began rolling around in agony.

'Thank you, *Ronnie*,' Paniatowski told him, though she was sure he was in far too much pain to ever appreciate what she was saying. 'Thank you for giving me a reason to do something I really *needed* to do.'

Twenty-Five

It was Bob Rutter who had come up with the idea of driving out into the countryside for dinner.

'I discovered this restaurant a few weeks ago, and I've been dying to take you there ever since,' he told Elizabeth.

'Where is it?'

'Just the other side of the tops of the moors road.'

'Seems like a bit of a long haul on a winter's night.'

'It'll be worth it,' Rutter promised. 'I think it's as good as anything you'll find in London, and I'm sure you'll agree.'

'I'm sure I will,' Elizabeth said.

And though she didn't believe that for a minute, she did find his provincial pride quite sweet – and rather touching.

Rutter said he would drive, and she agreed to let him – because it was sometimes important to allow the man to feel he was in charge, and this might turn out to be one of those occasions.

Bob was going to propose, Elizabeth told herself, as he drove along the twisty, windy road of the high moors. He had been plucking up the nerve to ask her for some time, and had finally judged the moment was right.

She wondered how she would feel about it when he popped the question, and discovered that the truth was, she wasn't sure.

People got married either because they needed the sense of security or because they wanted children, she thought. But security was not an issue in this case – Bob was hers for as long as she wanted him. And as for children, there was certainly no room in *her* life for mewling, puking brats.

So why bother to tie the knot at all?

Yet she had a sneaking suspicion that the whole thing wasn't quite as clear-cut as she liked to pretend it was. Because if she was going to reject him, why had she agreed to go for the meal with him in the first place? If she was going to make him feel small by turning him down, why had she already gone to such great efforts to boost his ego?

They had reached the very top of the high moors, and just ahead of them was a small car park, built on the edge of the drop, where motorists could stop and admire the view. Rutter slowed down, and though there were no other cars on the road, he signalled before pulling in.

'Why have we stopped?' Elizabeth asked.

'You can see for miles from here,' Rutter said.

Elizabeth laughed. 'Not on a dark winter's night, you can't.'

'I used to bring Maria to this place,' Rutter told her. 'She could see no more in the daylight than we can see now, in the dark. But she liked the smells. She liked the peace and quiet.'

Bloody Maria! Elizabeth thought.

'I've never been much of a one for peace and quiet myself,' she said. 'And you still haven't told me why we've stopped.'

'I need a few minutes to think,' Rutter told her. 'You don't mind, do you, Liz?'

It would be a shame to destroy the atmosphere she had worked so hard to create by being difficult now, Driver thought. Besides, maybe this had been the plan all along. Maybe he'd never intended to propose inside the restaurant. Maybe the meal was to be a celebration of an agreement already reached.

'No, I don't mind,' she said.

Rutter fell silent.

He was probably thinking about their future life together, Driver told herself, and hoped he didn't imagine that that future life included Louisa, because looking after the daughter of the blind saintly Maria would be even worse than having kids of her own.

But Rutter wasn't thinking about the future.

He wasn't even *thinking* about the past.

Instead, he was watching a mental slide show of what had been his life – a slide show that he himself seemed to have no control over.

Click!

Young Bobbie Rutter, living above his father's greengrocer's shop, weighed down by the knowledge that his mother hated her life as a shopkeeper's wife, and thought that fate should have dealt her a much better hand.

306

Click!

His first day in grammar school – standing alone in the playground, a small, short-trousered boy, wishing that he had failed the eleven-plus as all his friends had, so that now he would be in the local secondary modern with people he knew, instead of surrounded by strangers.

Click!

A taller, more confident Rutter, being awarded the Headmaster's Prize for Excellence.

Click!

Euston Station. A big ambling man in a hairy sports jacket, looking around him with interest and then turning to Rutter and saying, 'Dear God, they're gettin' younger every day. Ever worked on a murder case before?'

'No, sir, I've only just been made up to sergeant.'

'They've given me another virgin. Typical. Absolutely bloody typical!'

Click!

His wedding day. Charlie Woodend, now very firmly his mentor, watching affectionately from the front pew as Maria walked down the aisle with such practised confidence that no one would ever have guessed she was blind.

Click!

Holding the newly born Louisa in his arms, and feeling a joy he would have never thought possible.

Click!

Lying in Monika*'s arms, and feeling a different kind of a joy – a joy which was already coated in guilt.*

307

Click!

Burying Maria. Watching her coffin being lowered into the ground. Praying that she had not died hating him, but knowing that if she had, the hatred was well deserved.

'This thinking of yours is certainly taking a long time,' Elizabeth Driver said, and though she was trying to keep her tone light, there was an underlying level of her natural impatience in it. 'What *is* on your mind?'

'I was thinking about your book on Maria,' Rutter said.

'Oh that!'

'I kept asking you how it was going, and you said it was going fine. But you wouldn't let me see it.'

Elizabeth Driver sighed. 'I've explained to you a thousand times, Bob, that I never show anybody my work until I'm completely satisfied with it.'

'But I couldn't *wait*, you see,' Rutter said. 'I had to know how it was going, before it was too late.'

'Too late,' Elizabeth Driver repeated, mystified. 'Too late for what?'

'I don't want to talk about that, right now,' Rutter said.

'Well, I do,' Driver said firmly. 'You can't go being all enigmatic on me, and then say you don't want to talk about it. I want to know what it will be too late *for*.'

'So I did something I'd never thought I would do,' Rutter continued, ignoring her. 'I searched

308

through your things at the Royal Victoria, and I found the book – only it wasn't about Maria at all.'

Elizabeth Driver was silent for a while, then she said, 'Ah well, I suppose you had to find out eventually.'

'It's full of lies!' Rutter said.

'I know it is,' Elizabeth Driver agreed. 'But the truth simply doesn't sell books.'

'But even though it is all lies, it will completely destroy Charlie Woodend. Monika, too.'

'You come out of it all right. You weren't going to, but I re-wrote whole sections of it to make sure you did. It took me for ever.'

'And am I supposed to be grateful for that?' Rutter asked.

'Yes, you bloody well are,' Elizabeth Driver replied. 'Anyway, why are you so worried about what happens to Cloggin'-it Charlie? He's been riding on your coat-tails for years. You've done the work, and he's taken all the credit.'

It was the perfect excuse she was presenting him with, and most of the people she knew would have grasped it with both hands.

Yes, they would have agreed, he's treated me badly in the past, so it's perfectly all right to stab him in the back now.

'What you've just said about Charlie is as much of a lie as the rest of your vile book,' Rutter said. 'I owe most of what I am to him.'

But *what* am I? he asked himself.

I'm a man who's made a mess of his life – who's made two women desperately unhappy.

If I was going to follow Charlie's example,

why didn't I follow it in *all* things? Why couldn't I have resisted Monika like Charlie resisted Liz Poole back in Salton, on that first case we ever worked together? He wanted her. God, he wanted her. But he thought of Joan, and he backed away. Why don't I have his *strength*?

Elizabeth Driver sighed with exasperation.

'You want to grow up, Bob,' she said. 'Your future's not in Whitebridge with Woodend – it's travelling around with me, living high on the hog and making passionate love every night.'

'Love?' Rutter repeated. 'Don't you mean *sex*?'

Elizabeth Driver shrugged. 'Isn't it the same thing?'

'How many copies of your manuscript are there?' Rutter asked. 'Three? One original and two carbons?'

'That's right.'

'I thought so. I've destroyed them all.'

'I really wish you hadn't done that. But it doesn't matter in the long run, because it's all still in my head.'

'And that's where I want it to stay,' Rutter said.

'No chance,' Driver scoffed.

'We don't need the book,' Rutter told her. 'We can have the life together that you've just described *without* the book.'

And silently, he added, At least, we can for a *little* while.

'I'm very fond of you, Bob,' Driver said. 'Really I am. In fact, I think I love you.'

'Well, then?'

'But if it comes down to a choice between you

and fame and fortune, fame and fortune win out every time.'

'I see,' Rutter said. He started up the engine again. 'The table's still booked at the restaurant, but I don't suppose either of us fancies the meal now.'

'No,' Driver agreed, feeling strangely dispirited. 'I don't suppose either of us does.'

'Of course, there is one way I *could* stop you writing the book,' Rutter said.

'And what way might that be?'

'I could kill you.'

What started as a gurgle in the pit of Driver's stomach soon developed into a full-blown laugh.

'Why do you find that funny?' Rutter asked.

'It's not funny in itself – it's funny because it comes from *you*.'

'What do you mean?'

'You couldn't kill me, Bob. You couldn't kill *anybody*.'

'Are you so sure of that?'

'Of course I'm sure. I know you better than you know yourself. And there's one big reason why you couldn't kill me – even if you hated me.'

'And what is it?'

'You couldn't do it because you'd never be able to live with yourself afterwards.'

Rutter looked out into the darkness, and though he could not see the sheer drop they were parked in front of, he knew it was there.

'You're quite right,' he agreed. 'I *couldn't* live with myself afterwards.'

Twenty-Six

'Why don't you save us all a lot of time an' bother, an' make a statement straight away?' Woodend suggested.

Ron Scranton, at the other side of the interview-room table, shot a look of pure hatred at Paniatowski, then turned to face Woodend and said, 'That Polak bitch nearly crippled me, and I want her prosecuted.'

'You were tryin' to brain her with an ashtray at the time,' Woodend pointed out. 'An' though, given the state my hands are in, it'll probably hurt me as much as it'll hurt you, I think you should know that if I hear you refer to Detective Sergeant Paniatowski in that way again, I'll have to take drastic action.'

'What do you mean? Drastic action?'

'I mean that I'll knock your teeth so far down your throat that you'll have to stick your fingers up your arse to bite your nails.'

'You can't threaten me!' Scranton said.

'Really?' Woodend replied, interestedly. 'That's funny, because I thought I just did.'

'Whatever I may have said to that Po— to Detective Sergeant Paniatowski, I was *tricked* into saying,' Scranton said.

'Tricked?' Woodend repeated. 'Ah, now I

understand. When you made your confession, you didn't know she was a police officer.' He turned to Paniatowski. 'That was a big mistake you made there, Monika. Although it's not strictly necessary, in the *legal* sense, to identify yourself when you're on an undercover operation, I think it would have been only fair to have let Mr Scranton know who you were right from the start.'

'Does showing him my warrant card in front of witnesses count as letting him know who I was?' Paniatowski asked.

'Yes, I think that would just about cover it,' Woodend agreed.

'So I knew she was a policewoman,' Scranton conceded. 'But that's not the point.'

'Then what is?'

'I thought she was one of us.'

'You appear to have been wrong about that.'

'And she offered me sex, but only if I'd tell her that I'd ordered those tramps' murders.'

'Is that right, Monika?' Woodend asked disapprovingly.

'He asked me if I'd sleep with him, and I said I might,' Paniatowski told him. 'I never mentioned the murders.'

'She's a liar!' Scranton said.

'Is she, now?' Woodend asked mildly. 'So she was the one who brought up the subject of the murders?'

'That's what I've just said, isn't it?'

Woodend reached into the pocket of his jacket, produced a small black box, and placed it on the table.

313

'This is the latest Japanese miniature tape recorder,' he announced. 'Now I know that, given your political an' racial views, you might not like the Japs much, but I think they're pretty bloody clever.'

He pressed the switch.

'I might as well tell you, since you've already guessed,' said a voice which was clearly Scranton's. *'Those two tramps who were killed...'*

'Yes?'

'It was done on my direct orders.'

'Seems to me that *you* were the first one to mention the tramps,' Woodend said.

'That's taken out of – what do you call it? – context,' Scranton blustered.

'So you're sayin' that when we play the whole of the tape, we'll hear Sergeant Paniatowski mention the tramps first?'

'No, but when I said that thing about killing them, it was because it was what she wanted me to say – what she was egging me on to say.'

'Difficult to prove, that, I would have thought,' Woodend said. 'But let's move on to motive, shall we?'

'I have no motive, because I didn't *do* it!'

'Of course, given that you're a right-wing nutter, you don't really need any motive at all,' Woodend said reflectively. 'But I'm inclined to believe there was at least *some* method in your madness. You were showin' the morons who hang on your every word that you really mean business. An' then, of course, there were the council elections to consider. You must have thought that even the *rumour* that you were behind the murders would have been enough to bring out the caveman vote.'

'This is ludicrous!' Scranton said.

'An' that would have been especially important since you were plannin' to stand against an incumbent – an' not just any incumbent.' Woodend paused. 'Why *did* you decide to stand against Councillor Lowry? Why, of all the wards to choose from, did you pick his?'

'None of your business.'

'Could there have been something personal in it? I think so. You've hated him for a long time, haven't you – ever since he beat the crap out of you in the primary-school playground?'

'How ... how do you know about that?' Scranton asked.

'An' then fate seemed to *keep* throwin' you together, didn't it?' Woodend asked. 'You ended up servin' at the same RAF camp, in Abingdon. That was where you started the fire in the Indian restaurant, wasn't it?'

'They never proved that was me.'

'No, but the RAF was convinced enough to give you a dishonourable discharge.' He turned to Paniatowski. 'Are you startin' to see any pattern here, Monika?' he asked.

'Indian restaurant in Abingdon burned down when our Ron was based there? Tramps set on fire in Whitebridge, which happens to be where our Ron lives now?' Paniatowski said. 'Yes, sir, I think I *do* see a pattern.'

'You must have hated serving on the same base as Lowry,' Woodend continued, 'because that really showed up the difference between the

315

two of you, didn't it? There was him, an officer an' a decorated war hero, and there was you, a mere aircraftman who, as we've just mentioned, was dishonourably discharged.'

'At least, unlike Lowry, I was discharged for doing something I believed in,' Scranton said.

'Lowry wasn't discharged *at all*,' Woodend pointed out.

'No, he wasn't,' Scranton agreed. 'But he would have been, if he hadn't resigned when he did.'

'This is all bollocks,' Woodend said.

'Soon after he got his medal, he started drinking heavily,' Scranton said. 'It was no secret. Everybody in the camp knew about it. And one day, he went too far – one day he took a chopper up when he was drunk, and crashed it.'

'I think you've got it round your neck,' Woodend said. 'He did crash a helicopter, but that was in Malaya, as a result of comin' under enemy fire.'

'And he crashed a second one in Abingdon,' Scranton insisted. 'And *that* was as a result of being pissed as a rat.'

'I don't believe you,' Woodend said.

'Then ask yourself this,' Scranton countered. 'Throughout all our political battles, why has Lowry never used the fact that I've got a dishonourable discharge against me?'

'I don't know,' Woodend admitted.

'It's because he's afraid of what I'd say in return. It's in both our interests to keep quiet about what we did in the RAF.'

It had been a mistake to talk about Lowry,

Woodend decided. It had done no more than to distract them from the main point.

'When did you first decide to use Barry Thornley to do your killings for you?' he asked.

'I didn't. *Because I had nothing to do with the murders!*'

'You're not denying you knew him, are you? That he was a supporter of yours?'

'He may have attended a few of my meetings,' Scranton said vaguely.

'An' at what point did you decide he had to die, too?' Woodend wondered.

'At what point did I do *what*?'

'At what point did you decide he had to die?'

'I read in the papers that his death was an accident – that he set *himself* on fire.'

'You shouldn't believe *everythin'* you read in the papers – especially when you already know better,' Woodend said. 'Bazza's death was *meant* to look like an accident, but the fire didn't do quite enough damage to him to disguise the fact that just before he died, you'd hit him over the head.'

'Somebody hit him over the head?' Scranton gasped.

'No, *you* hit him over the head,' Woodend corrected him.

'Last night?'

'Yes, that's when he died.'

'At what time?'

'You *know* what time.'

'What *time*?' Scranton insisted urgently.

'It was round about nine o'clock.'

Scranton exhaled a huge sigh of relief. 'Last
317

night, I was addressing a meeting of the BPP in the back room of the Woodcutters' Arms in Burnley,' he said. 'I got there at eight, and I didn't leave the place until after eleven.'

Over the phone, the barman at the Woodcutters' confirmed that Scranton had indeed been there the night before, and said he could produce at least twenty witnesses to back his claim up.

He could still be guilty, Woodend thought. Though he couldn't have killed Big Bazza himself, he could still have *ordered* it to be done. But the way he'd acted in the interview room – his amazement when he'd been told that Thornley had been murdered – argued otherwise. Scranton was either one of the world's great actors or had nothing at all to do with the killings, and the chief inspector had no doubt that it was the latter.

Now, as he and Paniatowski walked wearily back to their office, Monika turned to him and said, 'I'm sorry, sir, this was all my fault. You kept saying we didn't know for certain that it was Scranton, and I kept insisting it was. And why? Because I let my hatred of him – and everything he stands for – blind me.'

'I went along with you in the end,' Woodend pointed out. 'By the time you pulled him in, I was convinced we'd got our murderer. An' I went *on* believin' that until nearly the last minute.'

But Paniatowski herself hadn't believed it. Though she'd played her assigned role in the interrogation to perfection, she had known in her gut, almost from the start, that Scranton was not their man.

It was his flat which had convinced her, she thought, analysing where the conviction had come from. She had used the state of it as an excuse for calling Scranton an insignificant little nobody, without fully realizing that she didn't need an excuse at all, because the flat was positive *proof* of her assertion.

The big boys in the BPP in London might use Scranton for their purposes, but only as a foot soldier sent out to do the tedious work for them. They had no respect for him, because they knew – as she had found out – that he was no more than weak-willed cannon fodder.

And so where were they now? she asked herself, as they reached the office door. In one hell of a mess, she thought, answering her own question.

It wasn't just that they had to start again, they would be starting with a distinct disadvantage – because by concentrating their efforts on Scranton, they'd allowed the real killer's trail to go cold.

'I'll just get my coat, an' then we're out of here,' Woodend said dispiritedly. 'Drum and Monkey?'

'Might as well,' Paniatowski agreed, although she knew that, in their present state, drink would not help – that it would only serve to make them even more depressed.

The moment he opened his door, Woodend noticed the buff envelope on the corner of his desk.

'It's from Bob,' he said, recognizing the hand-writing. 'He calls it a parting gift.'

'I wonder what it is,' Paniatowski said. 'It's too big for a cheque, and too small for a pair of carpet slippers.'

It was not much of a joke, but given the circumstances, Woodend was grateful that she'd even *attempted* to be funny.

'It's probably just paperwork, tyin' up a few loose ends,' he said. 'Only Bob would ever think of callin' paperwork a "gift".'

'Aye, he was a bugger for his reports,' Pania-towski said, in conscious imitation of her boss.

And instantly, the atmosphere of gloom thick-ened.

Was a bugger, they both thought.

Bob Rutter was gone and never coming back, and despite the difficulties, the disagreements – the outright bloody rows – they would miss him.

'Shall I look at it now, or should I leave it until mornin'?' Woodend asked.

Paniatowski shrugged. 'Whatever you want.'

'I'll look at it now,' Woodend said, because he knew, just as Paniatowski did, that though they *would* eventually go to the pub, it was never going to be a good idea and the less time they spent there the better.

He sat down in his chair, and slit open the envelope. 'There's some documents an' a letter,' he told Paniatowski. 'If he's got anythin' nice to say about you, I'll read it out to you.'

Paniatowski grinned. 'And if he hasn't, you'll make something up?' she suggested.

'Well, exactly,' Woodend agreed.

Then, as he started to read the letter, the tiredness disappeared from his face, and was replaced by a look which combined amazement and concentration.

'Bloody hell fire!' he exclaimed.

'What does Bob say?' Paniatowski asked.

'Just give me a minute,' Woodend told her. 'I want to see if this all hangs together.'

But it was much more than a minute he needed. He took *five* minutes to read the entire package, and another three to check through it again.

And it was only after he had done that that he looked up at Paniatowski and said, 'We got it all wrong, Monika. We got the whole bloody thing backwards.'

Twenty-Seven

Tel Lowry and his mother lived on the outskirts of Whitebridge, in what had once been the rectory of a very rich parish, and now went by the name of the Old House.

'Very nice,' Woodend said, as Paniatowski parked his Wolseley in front of the house at eight o'clock on Saturday morning. 'It somehow manages to be impressive without fallin' into the trap of becomin' unduly ostentatious. If I had a lot of money to splash out on a house – not that that's ever likely to happen – this is just the kind of house I'd splash out on.'

'Are you really as relaxed about this whole thing as you sound, sir?' Paniatowski asked.

Woodend opened his door and stepped on to the driveway. 'Course I'm bloody not,' he said.

A uniformed maid showed them to the conservatory, where Lowry and his mother were having their breakfast.

Having never seen her before, Woodend studied Mrs Lowry with interest. She was getting old and she was fat, but he still thought he could detect, beneath the flabbiness, the woman who – according to Bob Rutter's notes – had left a smile on the faces of at least two wing commanders in RAF Abingdon.

Mrs Lowry was not looking at Woodend at all. Instead, she was glaring daggers at Paniatowski.

'I thought I made it plain, the last time we met, that I neither wanted to see you nor hear of you again, Sergeant,' she said.

'DS Paniatowski isn't here because she wants to be,' Woodend said. 'She's here because she's my bagman, an' where I go, she goes.'

'And why are *you* here?' Mrs Lowry demanded aggressively.

'I'll handle this, Mother,' Tel Lowry said. He turned to Woodend. 'What can I do for you, Chief Inspector?'

'Last night, we arrested Ron Scranton for the murder of two tramps an' the attempted murder of a third,' Woodend told him.

'Then I must congratulate you,' Lowry replied. 'But whilst it was kind of you to drive out all this way to inform me, I'm not sure it was quite appropriate. I'm the chairman of the Police Authority, not the chief constable, and it could be said that by reporting to me, rather than him, you're undermining Miles Hobson's authority.'

'You'd probably be right, if we'd been able to make the charges stick,' Woodend said. 'But we couldn't. We had to let him go.'

'In which case, I can see even less reason for this visit.'

'But *before* we let him go, he made some accusations about you that I think you should be informed of. He said, for example, that if you hadn't left the RAF when you did, you'd have been cashiered. So it was quite a stroke of luck, wasn't it?'

'What was?'

'That just when you were practically forced to resign, you had a job to go to?'

'A stroke of luck?' Lowry repeated, outraged. 'There was a tragic accident in which my father was killed and my brother was incapacitated – and you dare to call it *a stroke of luck*!'

'It's funny the words we use, isn't it?' Woodend mused. 'You say your brother was incapacitated, the newspapers said he needed to be permanently hospitalized. Everybody shies away from sayin' that his problems were more mental than physical – because there's still such a stigma attached to mental illness. We didn't even know ourselves what his real problem was, until my clever inspector thought to check up on it yesterday.'

'I fail to see—' Lowry began.

'An' it's funny you should use the word "accident" when talkin' about what happened to your father an' brother,' Woodend interrupted.

'It *was* an accident,' Lowry said. 'Just read the coroner's report.'

'I have,' Woodend told him. 'An' you're right, it was ruled an accident. But there were a number of questions which were never satisfactorily answered, not the least of which was why your father lost control of his Rolls-Royce on a clear road, in near-perfect drivin' conditions.'

'What's your point?' Lowry asked.

'No real point at all,' Woodend admitted. 'I just think it's curious.'

'You can leave now,' Lowry said.

'Of course,' Woodend agreed. 'Come on,

Sergeant.'

He was almost at the door when he turned and said, 'Oh, by the way, we identified the second victim. It was your brother, Brunel.'

'Oh God!' Mrs Lowry moaned.

'The reason it took us so long to get that identification was that Brunel was a name he very rarely used. In his later years, he was known as Brian, and when he worked at the factory, he went by the name of Barclay.'

'His father called him Brunel after Isambard Kingdom Brunel, but he hated the name,' Mrs Lowry said, in a dry, flat voice which showed she was in a state of shock.

'Whereas you, sir, stuck to the name you'd been given,' Woodend said to Lowry. 'All the other Tels I've ever known were christened Terence. But not you. You're named after Thomas *Telford*, another great engineer. It was my clever inspector who worked that out, too.'

'Get out!' Lowry said. 'Leave us alone with our grief.'

'I suppose it's time I stopped playin' games,' Woodend said. 'I must inform you that orderin' me to leave isn't an option that's available to you. In fact, there *are* only two options open, an' the first is that you agree to answer my questions.'

He said no more, but began a silent count ... one elephant, two elephants, three elephants...

He had reached fifteen elephants when Lowry said, 'And what, according to you, is my other option?'

'Your other option is to stand up, so I can put

the handcuffs on you,' Woodend said.

'You're threatening to *arrest* me?'

'It's not a threat, it's a promise.'

'I'll have your job for this!' Lowry snarled.

'Possibly you will,' Woodend agreed. 'But that's in the long term. What's your decision about what happens *now*?'

'To avoid the indignity of wearing handcuffs, I'll answer your questions,' Lowry said, 'but I'm warning you—'

'Yes, I know, you'll have my job,' Woodend interrupted him. 'Why did your father treat you so badly, Mr Lowry? Why did he send your brother to a private school, while you had to settle for bein' educated locally? Why wouldn't he let you join the family firm? Because that's the way it happened, wasn't it? It was not a case of you wantin' to strike out on your own – it was a case of you *havin' to*, because there was no place for you at Lowry Engineerin'.'

Something had happened to Lowry while Woodend had been talking. It was not just that his air of authority had disappeared – though it had. He had actually regressed, and though his body was still that of a grown man, his face belonged to a small, puzzled boy.

'All I ever wanted to be was an engineer,' he said. 'And the irony is that my brother had no interest at all in engineering. I kept the name I'd been christened with, but he changed his. Yet I was the one excluded from the firm, and he went into it only because he was pressured to do so.'

'But why join the RAF?' Woodend wondered. 'And why become a helicopter pilot? That's

326

surely got to be one of the most dangerous jobs you can have in a combat zone.'

'I wanted to do something that would finally make my father proud of me,' Lowry said.

Woodend nodded. 'But even that didn't work, did it?' he asked. 'You went into battle. You won a medal. An' when that medal was presented, your father didn't even bother to turn up for the ceremony.'

'No,' Lowry agreed dully. 'No, he didn't.'

'So you became a drunk, an' crashed your helicopter as a result. The career you'd worked so hard to build up was over, an' you saw it as all your father's fault. It must have been at that point that you stopped tryin' to please him – an' started to hate him.'

'This has nothing to do with my brother's murder, if indeed, it *was* my brother who was murdered,' said Lowry, regaining a little of his old strength.

'It *was* your brother, an' it has *everythin'* to do with his murder,' Woodend said. 'But let's get back to your father. Do you know *why* he was so cold with you?'

'No.'

'Your mother does. Tell him, Mrs Lowry.'

'No,' the old woman gasped. 'No, I won't.'

'Then I will,' Woodend said. 'When you were four years old, Mr Lowry, your father tried to have your birth certificate amended. The amendment was never actually made, but all the paperwork connected with it is still there, an' that's another thing that Inspector Rutter found.'

'I don't understand,' Lowry said.

'He wanted to have one of the columns chang-ed. Where is said "Father's name", he wanted it to say Alfred Granger.'

'Uncle Alf?' Lowry said. He turned to his mother. 'Is this true? Is *he* my real father?'

'That's what your father – that's what Joseph – thought.'

'But *how* could he have thought it? Were you having an affair with Uncle Alf?'

'You've no idea what it was like being married to Joseph,' Mrs Lowry said. 'I was a young woman, full of passion and the joy of life, and he was a cold, cold man, practically a machine.'

'And my father – your husband – found out?'

'We got careless. He caught us in bed to-gether,' Mrs Lowry said simply.

'You should have told me this a long time ago,' Lowry said anguishedly. 'It would have explained a great deal. It would have made life so much *easier*.'

'So there you were, your career in ruins, an' all because of the man you still thought of as your father,' Woodend said. 'It was at that point, wasn't it, that you decided to claim your rightful inheritance? Your difficulty was that you knew your father would never allow it – so he had to go.'

'Are you saying I *killed* him?' Lowry demand-ed.

'Well, of course I am,' Woodend replied.

'Based on one inconclusive accident report?'

'Based on what had happened before the acci-dent, which we've already discussed, an' what happened later, which we'll get to eventually.'

328

'You'll never be able to prove any of these wild accusations,' Lowry said.

'You're probably right,' Woodend agreed. 'But I'd still like to speculate on what happened, if you don't mind. It's possible you never intended to kill your brother. That's something only you will ever know. But the fact is that he was in the car, and he survived the crash. Now *why* was that a problem for you?'

'It's your fantasy,' Lowry said. 'You tell me.'

'I'm guessin' again,' Woodend admitted, 'but once more, it's a guess based on what happened later. My theory is that Brunel saw you tinkerin' with his dad's car. It didn't mean much to him at the time – maybe you were able to explain it away – but as the Rolls veered out of control, he must have realized why it was happenin'. But fortunately for you, he'd lost his mind, an' – as a consequence – had forgotten what it was that he'd seen.'

'With every wild accusation you make, you're digging yourself deeper and deeper into a big hole,' Lowry said.

'So Brunel was locked away in Stanton Hall,' Woodend continued. 'You must have thought you were safe enough with him in there, because, after all, he was a nutter. But all the time Brunel was in that place, he was tormented by the fact that he knew there was somethin' he needed to do, but he couldn't quite bring it to mind. Then, two years ago, he escaped – an' he was never recaptured. Now why didn't we read about that in the papers?'

'Go to hell!' Lowry said.

'I'll tell you why,' Woodend said, unperturbed. 'Since Brunel was a *voluntary* patient, there was no legal requirement to report him missin', an' it was neither in your interest, nor in Stanton Hall's interest, for it to become public knowledge.' He paused for a second. 'But you must have lain in bed at night worryin' about it, Mr Lowry.'

'I was naturally concerned about what had happened to my brother.'

'But as worried as you must have been by the disappearance, you must have been literally terrified when he turned up again in Whitebridge.'

'I didn't *know* he'd turned up in Whitebridge.'

'Oh yes you did. One of the tramps we interviewed reported seein' a man in a blue suit, goin' round checkin' on the tramps. DC Beresford thought it must have been a council official. But it wasn't, was it? It was you. You'd caught sight of Brunel earlier – maybe as you were drivin' through town – an' you wanted to find where he'd got to.'

'More lies,' Lowry said.

'Brunel had come back to Whitebridge to see if anythin' about the place would jog his memory. And there were things that did just that. He recognized the Engineers' Arms, for example. And then there was a big expensive Bentley which, accordin' to his mate Pogo, he seemed particularly fascinated by. That particular car didn't give him the answer he was lookin' for. But what if it had been a Rolls-Royce, instead? Then the floodgates might really have opened. And you couldn't risk that – so Brunel had

330

to die.'

'Is this true?' Mrs Lowry asked. 'Did you kill your own brother?'

'Of course not,' Lowry told her.

Mrs Lowry rose shakily to her feet. 'I need ... I need to lie down,' she croaked.

'Help her, Monika,' Woodend said.

Paniatowski put an arm around Mrs Lowry's shoulder and ushered her gently towards the door.

'Well, there's one person at least who thinks you're guilty as sin,' Woodend said, when the two women had gone.

'She's a confused old woman,' Lowry said dismissively.

'It's true she's old,' Woodend agreed, 'though I'd also have to say she seems to me to be far from confused. But to get back to Brunel – the problem was *how* to kill him, wasn't it? You could simply have bashed his head in, but then there was a strong chance we'd identify the body, an' the trail would lead back to you. You could have disposed of the body somewhere it wouldn't have been found. But it's a dicey business movin' bodies around. Lots of things can go wrong, an' you'd be surprised at the number of killers who've been caught while tryin' to dispose of their victims.' Woodend paused again, as if a new thought had just struck him. 'Or maybe you wouldn't be surprised at all,' he continued. 'Maybe you did your research before you finally formulated your plan.'

'I don't have to sit here and listen to this nonsense,' Lowry said.

'As a matter of fact, you do. Unless, of course, you'd rather hear it down at police headquarters.'

'Get on with it,' Lowry said.

'Even if you had managed to dump the body somewhere without gettin' caught, your problems weren't over. Because unless you cut it up into tiny little pieces – an' you don't strike me as the kind of man who'd have the stomach for that – there was always a chance it would be found eventually, an' could still be traced back to you. An' that's when you hit on the idea of makin' the body unidentifiable – that's when you decided to burn him.'

'He wasn't the only tramp to die in that way,' Lowry pointed out.

'Of course he wasn't,' Woodend agreed. 'He couldn't be. You had to find a way of establishing the idea that Brunel hadn't died because he was Brunel, with all that damaging information in his head – he'd died because he was a *tramp*. Hence the need for more deaths. An' that's when you hit on the idea of using Bazza.'

'Who?'

'Barry Thornley.'

'Ah, now I see what you're building this flimsy case of yours on!' Lowry said. 'Barry Thornley worked for me – as I discovered when I read about it in the papers.'

'So you're sayin' you didn't know him personally?'

'Of course I didn't. I have hundreds of people working for me. I may have seen him. I may even have spoken to him – I like to have a few words with *all* my men from time to time – but I can't even put a face to the name.'

'Bollocks!' Woodend said. 'Scranton liked to address meetings right outside your factory – probably with the specific intention of annoying you – and Bazza liked to attend those meetings. All you had to do was look out of your office window, and you'd have seen straight away that he was the right man for the job you had in mind.'

'The more you say, the more insane you sound,' Lowry told him.

'So what did you tell Bazza at your first meetin' with him?' Woodend mused. 'That Scranton was only the *public* face of the BPP, a distraction to hide the fact that the *real* work was being done by the *real* leaders, like you, behind the scenes?'

'I hate everything the BPP stands for!' Lowry said.

'Aye, you probably do,' Woodend conceded. 'But we're not talkin' about your principles here – we're talkin' about your survival instinct. An' you knew that if you were to survive, you'd have to do whatever was necessary – includin' pretendin' to be a rabid racist.'

'I would never...'

'Of course you did, Mr Lowry. All you had to do was say the sort of things that Scranton has been sayin' outside your factory an' in the council chamber, an' Bazza would have been convinced you were the genuine article. An' once he *was* convinced, he'd do anythin' you wanted him to do. He carried out the first attack for you,

333

an' was all geared up to commit the second an' third murders when I came along with my insistence on night patrols. You knew that would make the job harder for Bazza, so you tried to talk me out of it. But when I wouldn't budge, you realized that if you pushed any further, I'd start getting' suspicious. That's why findin' out about DC Beresford must have seemed like a godsend.'

'Who?'

'You didn't so much as blink when I mention-ed his name earlier, so don't pretend you don't know who he is now.'

'I really have no idea...'

'You knew that if Beresford was beaten up, all the bobbies out on the street would rush to his rescue, leavin' Bazza free to kill Brunel, an' you free to kill Bazza. An' please don't try an' pre-tend that the attack on Beresford was all Bazza's idea, because he didn't have the brain for it.'

'I wouldn't know whether he has the brain or not. As I said...'

'I know – you can't even put a name to the face.' Woodend paused to light a cigarette. 'Of course, Bazza's really big mistake wasn't made because he was stupid – it was made because he didn't really know what was goin' on.'

'I still have no idea what you're talking about.'

'The whole scheme only worked as long as the police saw the killings as random. But Bazza didn't know that was how we were supposed to see it. As far as he was concerned, you an' he were simply riddin' the town of vermin. He might have wondered why, when you didn't care

334

who the first two victims were, you were very specific about the third. But I doubt that, since, as I've already said, Bazza wasn't much of a thinker. Anyway, it was *because* you kept him in ignorance of the full plan that he set his lads on a tramp called Pogo, who'd been actin' as Brunel's unofficial bodyguard. That was what told us that Brunel's murder wasn't random at all – an' that's when your scheme started to unravel.'

'You can't prove any of this,' Lowry said.

'Of course we can. You'll have made mistakes, because murderers always do. There'll be some physical evidence to tie you into Bazza's murder – a footprint at the scene that we can match to shoes in your wardrobe, a splash of petrol on the clothes you were wearin' at the time. An' then there's the money that Bazza spent on his Spanish trip. Our forensic accountants could trace Judas Iscariot's thirty pieces of silver back to the source – so they'll have absolutely no problem provin' that Bazza's money came from you.'

For the first time since the interview had started, Lowry smiled. It was a strange smile, one which said that though he knew his career in politics was probably over, and though he accepted that his mother now believed he had killed both his father and his brother, there was still one small victory he could take comfort in.

'To do all you've just described, you'll need search warrants,' he said.

'Yes, I will,' Woodend agreed.

'You can't *get* a search warrant without at least

some evidence. And you have no evidence at all.'

'If I can connect you to Barry Thornley...'

'Ah, but that's just the point! You can't! Perhaps it's true, as you say, that I paid for his holiday, but without a search warrant, you'll never know.'

'When Bazza went to Spain, what we should have asked ourselves was not where he got the money from, but where he got the *time* from,' Woodend said.

'The time?'

'He'd already used up all his holiday time for this year. So who gave him permission to take an extra, *unscheduled* holiday? Well, we both know the answer to that, don't we? It was his boss! You!'

'He ... he told me his mother was sick, and he wanted to look after her,' Lowry said.

'His mother *wasn't* sick, an' even if she had been, he wouldn't have asked *you* for time off, he'd have put in a request to his supervisor.'

'That's just what he did do, and—'

'No, he didn't,' Woodend interrupted. He took Rutter's letter out of his pocket. 'The supervisor said, an' I quote, "You could have knocked me over with a feather when Mr Lowry told me he'd personally decided to give Thornley the time off, because he's normally such a stickler for goin' through the proper channels".'

'He's mistaken,' Lowry said weakly.

'An' he goes on to say, "Mr Lowry was really shaken by Thornley's death. He told me the lad had him completely fooled with that story about his mother's illness, an' if it ever got out, he'd not only be a laughin' stock, but his kindness might even get him in trouble with the police. So he asked me to keep quiet about it, an' I agreed".'

'Lies, all lies,' Lowry moaned.

'He seems a decent enough feller, an' out of loyalty to you I doubt he'd *ever* have said a word about it, unless he was given a good reason why he should,' Woodend continued. 'An' that's just what Inspector Rutter gave him – a good reason.'

'I ... I...' Tel Lowry gasped.

'A couple of minutes ago, you denied even ever havin' met the lad, but the truth is that you singled him out – despite the fact that he was only a lowly shop-floor worker – for special treatment. Now if you can produce a satisfactory explanation as to *why* you did that, then you're right in what you say – we *will* never get the warrant. But if you can't – an' you *know* you can't – then your goose is well an' truly cooked.'

Woodend was standing in front of the Old House. One police car, taking Tel Lowry into custody, was just disappearing down the driveway. Several others – containing forensics experts and the officers who would conduct the search – were just arriving.

It was all over bar the shouting, the chief inspector thought. By nightfall they would have all the evidence they needed.

If they needed any evidence at all.

If Tel Lowry – clearly now a broken man –

hadn't spilled his guts and confessed everything by then.

He saw Paniatowski approaching him, and was shocked by how dreadful she looked.

'What's happened?' he asked.

'I've just been on the radio to headquarters,' she said, as tears streamed down her face. 'They have found Bob's car.'

'What do you mean, they've found *Bob's car*?' Woodend asked.

'It ... it was at the bottom of a steep drop – and there were two bodies in it,' Paniatowski sobbed.

A uniformed constable was standing in the middle of the high moorland road, and when he saw the Wolseley approaching, he signalled it to stop.

Woodend grasped the gear lever as gingerly as he could, but it still hurt like hell. He knew he'd been a fool to insist on driving himself, but Monika had been in no state to do it – no state even to come with him – and on this particular journey, she was the only one he'd have wanted to have by his side.

He came to a halt, and the constable walked over to the car.

'I'm afraid you can't go beyond this point, sir,' he said, when Woodend had wound down his window. 'There's been a major accident ahead, and the road's closed.'

The chief inspector flashed his warrant card, held clumsily in his bandaged hand. 'I know there's been an accident,' he said. 'An' one of my lads is in it.'

'Sorry, sir, didn't realize,' the constable said. 'It's about another half-mile further up the road.'

I know that an' all, Woodend thought, as he pulled away. We've picnicked at that spot – me, Joan an' Annie – an' it's one hell of a drop.

Yet even now, he had not quite given up hope. Maybe the people in the car were not dead, but just badly injured. And even if they *were* dead, that didn't necessarily mean that one of them *had to be* Bob. Why would he drive around in his own cheap little car, when he could be behind the wheel of Elizabeth Driver's beautiful Jag? Wasn't it more than likely that he'd simply lent his car to somebody else?

He turned the bend, and the whole scene was laid out in front of him. There were five vehicles there – two police cars, one Land Rover, a heavy lorry with a crane on its back, and an ambulance.

The lorry was parked close to the edge of the drop, and was working hard at pulling the car back up the steep slope down which it had plunged. The ambulance men were loading two stretchers into the ambulance. The people lying on them had their faces covered.

Woodend slammed on his brakes and opened the door, but before he could get out, he found his way blocked by Dr Shastri.

'Don't, Charlie,' the doctor said.

'Is it...?' Woodend began, then found himself completely unable to finish the sentence.

Dr Shastri nodded. 'Yes, I'm afraid it is Inspector Rutter on that stretcher, and yes, I'm afraid he's dead.'

'I want to see him,' Woodend said.

'You can't,' Dr Shastri said firmly. 'Not now. You may view him at the undertaker's.'

'Damn it, woman, he was my lad!' Woodend exploded.

'And now he is in *my* care, and I will not permit you to see him,' Dr Shastri replied.

'Why?' Woodend asked. 'Is he horribly disfigured or somethin'?'

'No. His chest was crushed and his neck was broken, but there was very little damage to his face. Nonetheless, I have decided that you will not see him yet, and that is that.'

Aye, Woodend thought, if Shastri said so, that *was* that.

Epilogue

They buried Bob Rutter the following Wednesday, in the same grave as his wife.

There was an official wake, held in the Crown and Anchor – a pub which specialized in catering for policemen out on the razzle – and it was attended by most of the members of the Force not actually on duty, as well as a fair smattering of those who were.

Woodend, Paniatowski and a wheelchair-bound Beresford made a brief appearance at the Crown for form's sake, but, as far as they were concerned, there was only one place to properly drink to Rutter's memory – and that was where they went.

Once they were established at their usual table in the Drum and Monkey they talked their way through Rutter's career – his many triumphs and his occasional failures.

'He was a bloody good bobby,' Woodend said, summing it all up. 'One of the best. He was maybe a bit patchy in the last few weeks of his life, but he came up trumps in the end.'

Yes, Paniatowski and Beresford agreed, he had definitely come up trumps in the end.

'Did I ever tell you the story about how he had to fly to Germany, in connection with the Dark

341

Lady case?' Woodend asked.

No, the other two said, he hadn't.

'Well, you see, what I didn't know at the time was that—'

'How did it happen?' Paniatowski interrupted. 'He was a good driver, so how the *bloody hell* did it happen?'

It was a question they'd all been secretly wondering about, Woodend thought, and it was typical of Monika that she'd been the one with the balls to bring it out into the open.

'That moors road is a treacherous one to drive, especially at night,' Woodend said.

'But he *wasn't* driving along it, was he?' Paniatowski countered. 'He was parked at the viewpoint.'

'Then he made a mistake,' Woodend said. 'Two mistakes, I suppose. The first was he thought he was in reverse, when he wasn't. An' the second is that he hit the accelerator too hard.'

'Those are simply not mistakes that Bob would have made,' Paniatowski said firmly.

'Be careful what you say, Monika,' Woodend cautioned. 'Because if it wasn't an accident, it was suicide. An' if it was suicide, it was also murder.'

'And what if it was?' Paniatowski argued. 'What can anybody do about it now? Are they going to dig up his body, and put it on trial?'

'No,' Woodend said. 'But if Elizabeth Driver's relatives thought murder was a possibility, they could well decide to sue the estate for unlawful killin'. An' where would that leave little Louisa?'

'You're right,' Paniatowski agreed.

Woodend drained his pint, and signalled to the waiter to bring across another round of drinks.

'Besides,' he continued, 'do you really think Bob would have killed himself when he had his little daughter to consider? Oh, I know he made you her guardian – an' I know you'll do a wonderful job of bringin' her up – but would he have ever been so irresponsible as to willingly deprive Louisa of her own father?'

'No, he wouldn't,' Paniatowski said. 'He did a few shitty things in his time, but he'd never have done anything like that.'

'Well, there you are then,' Woodend said. 'Can I go back to my story about Bob's flight to Munich now?'

Paniatowski smiled weakly. 'Of course, sir,' she said.

But it seemed as if the story would never be told, because even as he re-launched himself into it, the bar door opened, and Dr Shastri walked in.

Her arrival caused quite a stir among the other drinkers. They were not used to exotically beautiful women in saris and sheepskin coats wafting across their line of vision, and they gaped at her as if they did not quite believe that she was real.

If Dr Shastri noticed the sensation she was causing, she gave no sign of it. Instead, she walked over to the team's table and said, 'I know this is a private party, but might I join you for a few minutes?'

'Of course you can, lass,' Woodend said. 'Can I order you a drink, or don't you...?'

'I do drink in private, as Sergeant Paniatowski knows, but I can't ever recall doing it in public,' Dr Shastri said. 'My family would not approve.'

'Well, then...'

'However, since my family are all in India, I would not say no to a double vodka, which I have only recently – and as a result of Monika's dedicated tutelage – learned to appreciate.'

Woodend grinned, and ordered the drink. When it came, Dr Shastri knocked it back in a single gulp, which left even Monika Paniatowski impressed.

'My official post-mortem report on Inspector Rutter will not be published until tomorrow,' Shastri said, placing the glass back on the table and running her index finger briefly across her lips, 'but I thought that the three of you might like to hear my findings in advance.'

'It's very kind of you, lass, but I don't think that will be necessary,' Woodend said awkwardly.

'I, on the other hand, think it is *very* necessary,' the doctor countered. 'Bob Rutter was dying long before his car went over that edge. He had been dying for some time.'

'What?' Woodend said.

'It might not have shown much on the outside, but inside he was riddled with cancer. It was inoperable, and he would have been dead within a few months.'

'And do you think that he knew?' Monika Paniatowski asked.

'He knew,' Dr Shastri confirmed. 'On the first day of your investigation, he asked me to recom-

344

mend a doctor who would give him a complete medical check-up.'

'So did he already suspect that something was wrong?' Woodend asked.

'No, I am fairly sure that he didn't.'

'So why did he want a medical *at all*?'

'I have no idea,' Dr Shastri lied. 'At any rate, I rang the doctor after I had completed my autopsy, and he told me that he had made Bob aware of his condition as soon as he possibly could, which, as it happened, was when he returned from Oxford, last Wednesday morning.'

'So there was no wonder he looked so bloody rough when I saw him Wednesday lunchtime,' Woodend said. 'I thought he was just feelin' guilty about not pullin' his weight on the case. But it wasn't that at all. He was lookin' rough because he'd just been given a death sentence.'

'And on Wednesday *evening*, he asked me if I'd be willing to be Louisa's guardian, if anything should happen to him,' Paniatowski said.

'But ... er ... despite his illness, there's no doubt his death was an accident, is there?' Woodend asked.

'Do you think there's a possibility that he committed suicide?' Dr Shastri replied.

'No, I ... er ... don't think that at all,' Woodend said.

'And neither do I,' Dr Shastri told him. 'The way his hands were gripping the steering wheel would indicate that he was attempting to regain control of the vehicle until the very last second.'

'That's a relief,' Woodend said. 'I mean...'

345

'You mean it merely confirms the suspicions of your own, professionally trained, eye?' Dr Shastri suggested.

'That's exactly what I mean,' Woodend agreed gratefully.

Dr Shastri stood up. 'I am afraid that in my attempts to demonstrate to you my drinking prowess, I drank rather too much, rather too quickly,' she said. 'Now I am feeling rather squiffy, and if you'll excuse me, I think I'll go home and lie down for a while.'

She was not the least bit drunk, Woodend thought admiringly. It was just that she had done the job she'd set out to do, and now she was gracefully withdrawing.

Paniatowski stayed for another ten minutes, then she, too, stood up and said, 'I have to get back to my ... to my ... I have to get back to Louisa.'

'Try that again,' Woodend ordered her.

'I ... I have to get back to my ward,' she said sheepishly.

'And again!' Woodend said.

'I have to get back to my *daughter*,' Paniatowski said.

'Aye, you do,' Woodend agreed. 'An' me an' young Beresford have to stay here an' keep knockin' back the ale until the pair of us are pissy-arsed drunk.'

Dr Shastri was sitting on her living-room sofa, slowly and elegantly smoking a cigarette – which was another unseemly habit that her family back in India would have disapproved of.

She was not alone. Curled up against her was Scheherazade, her fluffy white Persian cat.

Shastri was running through in her mind, for one last time, an account of the last moments of Bob Rutter's life. But not an official account – nor yet the one she had given Woodend. This was an account of what had *actually* happened.

'I shall be frank and open with you,' she said to the cat, 'because I know that I can rely on your discretion.'

Now that she was taking notice of it, the cat began to purr softly.

'Inspector Rutter was a nice man – a thoroughly decent man,' Shastri said. 'And an honourable one – which, to a poor misguided Indian like myself, still counts for something. Elizabeth Driver, on the other hand, appears to have been a thoroughly nasty piece of work, who was more than willing, when it was to her own advantage, to use her power as a journalist to destroy other people's lives. Perhaps she'd been planning to destroy Bob Rutter's life. Do you think that is likely, Scheherazade?'

The cat gave her a questioning look.

'You are quite right to doubt that,' Shastri agreed. 'It is not at all likely, since his life was already almost over. But what if she had been planning to destroy the lives of people he felt close to? How would he have felt about that, my furry princess?'

The cat cocked its head, and placed a demanding paw on her arm.

'I lied when I said that Inspector Rutter's hands had been clutching tightly at the steering wheel,' Shastri continued, gently brushing the cat's ears. 'The truth is that they were not on the wheel *at all*. And there was one other thing, which I did not so much lie about as omit to mention. There were recent scratch marks all down Mr Rutter's right cheek. And you know all about scratching, don't you, my little destroyer of furniture?'

Scheherazade emitted a low meow, to indicate that while the stroking was pleasant, it was still not vigorous enough.

'Of course, I knew immediately what had caused the scratches, because I am, after all, a trained doctor. And I knew that Charlie Woodend would know, too, because *he* is a trained detective. Which is why I did not allow him to see his old colleague until the undertaker had worked his magic.'

The cat's purring grew louder, as Shastri worked some magic of her own.

'Why did I not want him to know the truth, my slayer of mice? It is perhaps a little complicated for your furry brain to understand, but it is a question of life assurance. If Charlie had known the truth, he might have done something which would have cost baby Louisa a great deal of money. He would not have *wanted* to do it, you understand, but he would have felt *compelled* to. That is the English way. I, on the other hand, come from a culture which understands that whilst doing what is right and doing what is legal can sometimes be the same thing, it is not always *necessarily* the case.'

Scheherazade meowed again, and Shastri

realized that in telling her story, she had been neglecting her duties.

'And what happened to the skin which had been ripped from Mr Rutter's face, you ask?' she said, increasing her stroke rate again. 'Why, I found it under Miss Driver's nails – and immediately destroyed it before it could do any more damage. What a single-minded person Miss Driver must have been, Scheherazade. In her situation, you or I would have panicked. But she was made of sterner stuff, and in the final few seconds of her life, her one thought – her only remaining desire – was to inflict as much damage as she could on the man who was deliberately plunging her to her death.'